SHRAPNEL

ISSUE #11   THE OFFICIAL BATTLETECH MAGAZINE

SHRAPNEL

THE OFFICIAL BATTLETECH MAGAZINE

Loren L. Coleman, Publisher
John Helfers, Executive Editor
Philip A. Lee, Managing Editor
David A. Kerber, Layout and Graphic Design

Cover art by Ken Coleman
Interior art by Jared Blando, Brent Chumley, Jordan Cuffie, Liam Curtner, Mark Hayden, Harri Kallio, Chris Lewis, Natán Meléndez, Florian Mellies, Benjamin Parker, Matt Plog, Klaus Scherwinski, Tan Ho Sim

Published by Pulse Publishing, under licensing by Catalyst Game Labs
5003 Main St. #110 ▪ Tacoma, WA 98407

Shrapnel: The Official BattleTech Magazine is published four times a year, in Spring, Summer, Fall, and Winter.

Available through your favorite online store (Amazon.com, BN.com, Kobo, iBooks, GooglePlay, etc.).

ISBN: 978-1-63861-116-5

COMMANDER'S CALL: FROM THE EDITOR'S DESK 4
Philip A. Lee

SHORT STORIES

THE PLOWSHARE 6
D. G. P. Rector

SIGNING DAY 27
Chris G. Lane

GHOSTBIRD 44
Bryan Young

UP CLOSE 81
W. T. Brown

HELL'S HIGHWAY 106
James Hauser

THE SPACE COWBOYS FROM QUATRE BELLE 164
R. J. Thomas

SEAL THE DEAL 191
Russell Zimmerman

SERIAL NOVEL

THREE WAYS HOME, PART 3 OF 4 134
Tom Leveen

POETRY

SOLAHMA DEATH SONG 127
Phillip Johnston

MERRYMAKERS 162
Alayna M. Weathers

ARTICLES

VOICES OF THE SPHERE: THE NEW MERCENARY MARKET 24
Stephen Toropov

COCKPIT AMENITIES IN MODERN BATTLEMECHS
[OR WHEN YOU GOTTA GO, YOU GOTTA GO] 70
Wunji Lau

INNER SPHERE INGENUITY 94
Matthew Cross

INFORMATION SOFTWARE AT WAR:
THE AUTOMATED BATTLEMECH RECOGNITION FRAMEWORK 128
James Bixby

THE FEW AND THE MANY:
THE CANOPIAN MEDICAL INDUSTRY'S CULTURAL ISOLATION 156
Wunji Lau

AFTER-ACTION REPORT: LONGBOW MOUNTAIN 181
Eric Salzman

GAME FEATURES

TECHNICAL READOUT: BTL-C-20 BATTLE COBRA 38
Étienne Charron-Willard

UNIT DIGEST: FIRST KEARNY HIGHLANDERS 77
Étienne Charron-Willard

COMIN' TO TOWNE: A ROLE-PLAYING ADVENTURE 100
Eric Salzman

BATTLEFORCE SCENARIO: OUR TWO WEEKS' NOTICE 186
Tom Stanley

COMMANDER'S CALL
FROM THE EDITOR'S DESK

Greetings, MechWarriors! It's the end of the year again, and that means year-end holidays and presents.

The first present in this issue is a nice bit of kismet I couldn't really have planned even if I tried. Over the years, there's been a nice bit of overlap between *BattleTech* and *Shadowrun*, in that several authors have written short stories, novellas, and novels for both lines (myself being one of them!), so it's always fun to see authors make the leap from one to the other. The *BattleTech*-to-*Shadowrun* crossover seems to happen quite often—for example, the novella *Mercy Street*, the *Shadowrun* debut of Bryan Young, whose much-acclaimed Fox Patrol series sprang to life in these very pages, will be arriving very soon—but what's really exciting to me is when *Shadowrun* authors hop the fence from *Shadowrun*'s "magic, cyberpunk, noir" into *BattleTech*'s "stompy war robots" territory, because not only have these authors often been secret *BattleTech* fans all along, they also bring new perspectives to the universe. So join me in welcoming not one, but *two* such authors in this issue: R. J. Thomas and Russell Zimmerman! R. J. and Russell join the esteemed ranks of crossover authors such as William H. Keith, Michael A. Stackpole, Robert N. Charrette, Jason Hardy, Ilsa Bick, Jennifer Brozek, Stephen Kenson, Jean Rabe, Phaedra Weldon, and many others, and I hope you dig their stories as much as I did.

The second present is a Unit Digest for the First Kearny Highlanders, a modern, ilClan-era unit of the fan-favorite Northwind Highlanders mercenary unit. This Unit Digest will be a great way to use the 'Mech miniatures in the forthcoming Northwind Highlanders Force Pack (which should be available in Q1 2023)!

The third present has its genesis in "Chaos Campaign Scenario: The Mad Stampede," from issue #9. James Hauser, the author of that scenario, makes his *BattleTech* fiction debut in this issue with "Hell's Highway," a short story about one particular Mad Stampede, which puts us in the driver's seat of a Hell's Horses combat-vehicle convoy competing in a risky race for glory on a Jade Falcon-occupied planet. If you enjoyed playing that scenario, or if you like Clan-centric tales, you're going to love this story! As an added bonus, this story contains an exciting new piece of art by Jared Blando.

In this issue, we also have two stories from returning authors. Tom Leveen brings us the penultimate part of his four-part serial, *Three Ways Home*, and things are really heating up in it—quite literally, in fact! Then Bryan Young takes a break from his Fox Patrol series to offer "Ghostbird," which is unique in that it serves as both a prologue *and* a sequel to his novel *A Question of Survival*. (The novel isn't essential to enjoying this story, but it's definitely worth the read. And speaking of the Fox Patrol: if you're interested in either catching up on some Fox Patrol stories you've missed in earlier issues, or if you want to check out an all-new Fox Patrol story, Bryan's *Fox Tales* collection is also available.)

We're also featuring quite a few new authors in this issue. The aforementioned stories by R. J. and Russell follow an Outworlds Alliance aerofighter pilot and the son of a struggling 'Mech manufacturer, respectively. Our opening story, "The Plowshare," by D. G. P. Rector, is immortalized in the wonderful cover art by Ken Coleman. Chris G. Lane's "Signing Day" takes us through a brand-new mercenary's recruit's first day on the job, and "Up Close," by W. T. Brown, wrestles with the demons of a former Com Guard MechWarrior who survived the Battle of Tukayyid.

For game content, we have a Technical Readout for the *Battle Cobra* that ComStar and the Word of Blake reverse-engineered; a report on Longbow Mountain, which closes the case on an assassination mystery; a technology article about unique Inner Sphere tech advances, and another article detailing the history of 'Mech-recognition software (what MechWarriors call the "warbook"); an exploration of the surprising efficacy of Canopian medical services; a catalog of cockpit amenities for MechWarriors; a holiday-themed RPG adventure called "Comin' to Towne" (see if you can spot all of the hidden holiday references in it!); and our first playable *BattleForce* scenario.

I hope you enjoy your gifts from all of us here at *Shrapnel*, and may your holidays and year-end celebrations be safe, fun, and filled with memorable moments.

—**Philip A. Lee, Managing Editor**

THE PLOWSHARE

D. G. P. RECTOR

**CORDOBA CITY
ROSKAN
COREWARD DEEP PERIPHERY
20 MAY 3049**

With a hand so covered in burn scars the flesh looked melted, Gorton held his bottle of stale beer. He'd worked 1,500 hectares today, more than twice as much as any other farmer. But then, he had *Tomoe*, and they didn't.

Through the open doors of the bar, he could hear raucous laughter, cheers, and jeers at whatever idiot program was being rebroadcast. Roskan was so deep in the Periphery they only got a merchant ship perhaps once a year, sometimes less. This year it had come even later than usual, but the colonists hadn't noticed. Every JumpShip captain worth their salt knew a good collection of holovids was worth a fat stack of C-bills to the Roskanni. These people didn't know what the Inner Sphere was really like, but they could tell you exactly who won the Solaris Heavyweights in '36. They had no idea how lucky they were to be this far out.

Gorton liked it here. Roskan was as quiet as quiet could get. Nobody knew who he really was, just that he'd made his money with *Tomoe* in the past, and now they'd come here for retirement. They didn't know valuable she was, how you could probably buy half the colony for her price tag.

Well, no, that was a lie. They knew she could do the work of a score of threshers, clear hundreds of hectares of forest in a day, and they were glad of it. She was one of the most sophisticated pieces of machinery on the planet. Go figure she'd first been made for killing.

Memories were coming back harder these days. Most people Gorton's age started to get fuzzy, see the past in rose hues. For him it was the opposite. He heard voices, saw sights, sometimes beautiful, sometimes terrible, all as if they were happening in front of him. He remembered the Diamond Mountains of Novo Canton lit by laser fire, and the waters of Zhang's Ocean, churning beneath steel feet. He could see it all clearly, with his BattleMech's HUD laid over it.

Even now, looking into the darkness where *Tomoe* stood sentry at the edge of the field, he could place a perfect reticle over her. The same with the whole damn town. Sometimes Gorton felt his arms tense, as if he had a fistful of lasers just waiting to be released, to burn everything in sight. A colonist would smile at him, remark on the weather, and Gorton would bite his tongue. Secretly, he wanted to scream at them: *DON'T YOU KNOW WHO I AM?! DON'T YOU KNOW WHAT I AM?!*

Of course they did. They'd seen it all in perfect holovision. He was a MechWarrior, a gallant knight-errant from a bygone era. Who else would have come all this way to protect them from pirates lurking in the Periphery? People didn't run as far from civilization as Gorton had just to find a quiet place to die.

His beer was almost empty when Gorton realized something was wrong. There was no more laughter coming from the bar. A muffled voice came on the holovid-set. Everything else was silent, save the scuffle of boots against the unvarnished floor. For a moment, Gorton had the paranoid fantasy that somehow these people had heard him. He'd done it before, started talking to himself when he'd believed he was just thinking.

Then he realized why the vid's sound was so muted: it was a live broadcast.

Quietly, Gorton got up from where he sat on the porch and stepped into the bar. From the back of the crowd he watched the screen. The images were grainy: something falling from the sky, fires burning among the trees. Then, a flight of helicopters, what passed for the colony' defense force. The lead chopper fired a salvo of missiles. Lasers streaked through the darkness in response, and one by one, the choppers exploded in flames. The last image, a tracking-error-riddled freeze frame, was of a BattleMech emerging from the forest.

"—at this time encouraging all residents to take shelter. Do not continue agricultural work. Militia units are to report to supply depots—"

The voice of the Colonial Authority Broadcast System was droning on, but no one in the bar was listening.

"*Pirates*" was the word whispered among the crowd. It had been years since Roskan was last hit, but it was always possible. Gorton shook his head. He'd never seen a 'Mech like that before, but even in that grainy image there were details he could make out. It was pristine, and it had some kind of insignia emblazoned on the chassis. Not the crude kill-markers and snarling fright masks of a bandit crew, no. It was a military unit.

They weren't being raided. This was an invasion.

As all eyes in the bar fell on him, he knew what they were going to ask. He had to go back to work. *Real* work.

"Crap," was all Gorton could think to say.

"—that's when Hornet-Three went down. We're still light on details, but Protector Johannes thought it was essential that you all be up to speed."

The man speaking was Colonel Milovic. "Colonel" was a self-appointed title: he was little more than a bureaucrat, the same as "Protector" Johannes. Gorton didn't have a high opinion of either of them, but as they'd let him live on their world, he couldn't exactly speak against them either. Still, something rankled him about people who could find desk jobs on a colony that needed so much manual labor.

Milovic didn't look like the sort of man who spent his life behind a desk. He was trim and fit beneath his gaudy blue-and-gold uniform. No one else in the Roskanni militia had a dress uniform like his, just earthy brown fatigues and second-generation flak jackets.

Gorton was again reminded that he was surrounded by amateurs. In the years he'd spent among the Roskanni, they'd only chased away two pirate raids, and to call them "raids" was generous. More like aborted landings: a quick exchange of missiles and long-range laser fire, then the pirates had scuttled right back into their DropShips and hightailed it to whatever rathole they'd crawled out of. With opponents like that, it was no wonder a preening buffoon like Milovic was the best this planet could do, as far as soldiers went.

They were at Cordoba City's supply depot, a place mostly for storing thresher machines, spare parts, and their arms stockpile. While Gorton sat with Milovic and the others in a back room, the rest of the militia was busily cleaning and preparing their weapons. They'd ride out in a convoy together, with every volunteer from the surrounding farms. There were maybe 200 people among Cordoba's Defense Reserve, less than half of them fighting fit. As for the convoy, it would be made up of trucks meant for grain and lumber. A single autocannon round would light one up like a Landing Day bonfire.

Gorton was crowded into the impromptu command center with Milovic, his grease monkey Bien, and a few militia officers. The militia's captain was a woman called Janice Tsung, owner of the biggest farm in the area.

"So they're around Joramun Heights?" Janice asked.

"That's the last location we spotted them," Milovic replied. "They haven't made any moves for Limonov City yet, which is unusual. The Limonov Guards unit is digging in, and we're trying to get as many of the reserve choppers flight-worthy as we can."

"Well, I guess we should head out, shouldn't we? Is there anything else we need to know?" Janice asked.

Milovic looked at Gorton. Gorton shrugged. He'd stayed silent during the briefing. He didn't want Colonel Milovic to think he was questioning orders. Or worse, plant the idea that he should be in command. The militia might just take him up on that, and that was the last thing he wanted.

Milovic cleared his throat.

"There is one more bit of business," he said. "We discovered the enemy had tried to contact us several times during planetfall. Apparently they thought we had better comms than we currently possess. After that initial engagement, they sent us a message on our standards comm bands."

"Asking for surrender?" Janice asked.

"No. They transmitted...well, the language is a little bit difficult to decipher. It sounded something like an apology."

"An apology?" Gorton blurted.

Milovic nodded. "We think they want to enter some kind of negotiation. Protector Johannes wants all militia forces present, in case things go wrong. We're hoping they're as good as their word, and maybe this can be resolved peacefully."

"I doubt that," Gorton said.

"So far they haven't fired on anyone else. Our scanners have had a hard time picking them up, but they don't seem to have moved beyond the Heights since they arrived. At present, there is no reason to doubt them."

"Nobody who drops a full lance of BattleMechs just wants to chat," Gorton said.

Janice nodded solemnly. "If we've got to fight, my people are ready," she said, sounding more certain than she looked.

"Good," Milovic replied. "Well, if there's nothing else, we'd best head out. I assume you and your vehicle are ready, Mr. Gorton?"

They still didn't know Gorton's last name, which was fine with him. Bien spoke up, always eager. He was young but the closest thing the Roskanni could muster to a real mechanic. The kid was a genius. He'd adapted *Tomoe* to Gorton's requested specifications, and kept her running smoothly.

"She's ready," Bien said proudly. "Purring like a kitten, even after all that forestry work last week."

Milovic nodded. "Glad to hear it. All right everyone, see you in Limonov. Dismissed."

Janice threw a half-hearted salute that Colonel Milovic crisply returned. No one else in the room bothered.

LIMONOV CITY
ROSKAN
COREWARD DEEP PERIPHERY
21 MAY 3049

They arrived a few hours before dawn, while the world was still shrouded in blue light. Limonov was as close to a capital as the colony had, a small outcropping of rectangular metal buildings nestled in among massive grain silos and sprawling lumber yards.

Gorton halted *Tomoe* between a pair of silos, not far from the main boulevard. He dismounted while Bien ran her through a few final checks, before they both snatched a scant hour or two of sleep at the local barracks. The militia were not so lucky. Bleary-eyed, they'd been improving the entrenchments around the city's outer perimeter.

Dawn came, and with it a gentle prodding from Bien. He explained Milovic's plan in hushed tones, something the colonel had cooked up during the long ride over in his staff car.

"Sounds like theater," Gorton grunted.

Bien shrugged. "That's exactly what the colonel said. 'My grandsire was a Lyran diplomat, and he said theater is half of diplomacy' and blah-de-blah-blah. Orders are orders though, right?" he said with a smile.

The kid had never been in an actual military outfit a day in his life. For him, this was an adventure. Hell, he'd probably been praying something like this would happen.

"All right," Gorton said. "Scrounge me up a bottle of that local vodka, yeah? Then we'll get situated."

"Vodka? You really think you should be drinking on the job, old man?"

"When you get your own 'Mech, you decide who drinks in her and who doesn't, all right? Now hurry it up."

Bien hustled off. Gorton sat on the cot he'd commandeered, running his hands over his scalp. His hair had gone thin a long time ago. He could still feel the burn scars in some places.

As he rose, Gorton caught a look at himself in a shaving mirror someone had set up. He had old, tanned skin the texture of leather. His remaining hair was white and long, and he had a drooping mustache the same color. The stubble on his weak jaw was still iron gray for some reason. He reached a hand up to the neck of his shirt and pulled it down slightly. There it was: an expanse of smooth scar tissue, just barely peeking out beneath his collarbone. His whole chest looked like that, and down one of his legs too.

Tomoe had been cross with him that day. He hadn't treated her right, and she'd taught him a lesson he would never forget. Now he and the old girl were headed for battle once again.

He hoped she didn't have any new lessons in store.

"I've sent the signal, sir," the comms operator said.

"Good," Milovic replied. "Now we just wait. Remember, no sudden moves. You're all to stay at attention, am I clear? This is theater, remember that. Half of diplomacy is theater. We make an impression on them, let them know we're not afraid. Understood?"

Gorton was watching from *Tomoe*'s cockpit, hidden and running near zero. Just her comms and scanners were up, as was a screen-link with the cams in Milovic's entourage. The colonel had taken his people and their gear a good forty meters beyond the perimeter, standing foolishly far from cover.

The camera swept the open field beyond Limonov, up to the forested hills of the Joramun Heights. Then it froze. Even this far away, Gorton could hear the telltale *thump-thump-thump* of a BattleMech's tread.

Like monsters in a fairy tale, they seemed to materialize out of the misty woods. There were five of them, war machines of a make he had never seen before. The lead was the largest, easily an assault class, strange and menacing.

It had a human shape, one arm ending in a heavy cannon, the other in a clenched fist. Its head resembled a scowling face, with ethereal green eyes. The 'Mech reminded Gorton of the stone gods of old Terra. The kind people used to offer the hearts of their enemies to.

The giant surveyed the field with the cold imperiousness of a conqueror. Then it did something Gorton had not expected. It charged.

The giant's speed was incredible. Each stride tore up the earth; plumes of mud shot upward in its wake, as if artillery shells were raining down behind it.

"Steady," Milovic murmured over the comm, voice quavering. "Steady. It's all theater. Just theater."

Gorton took a slug from his bottle of vodka, hands ready to switch *Tomoe* to combat mode.

The giant bore down, eyes fixed on the colonel's small party, heedless of the world around it. When it was less than a dozen meters away, it came to a sudden and graceful halt. A spray of mud and clods of earth landed at Milovic's feet. Gorton could tell the colonel was silently fuming.

The giant was still. Faint vapor trails wafted up from its chassis, the dead sprint heating it in Roskan's cool morning air. Now that it was so close, Gorton could finally get a good look at what was painted on the BattleMech's torso. It was a simple, striking sigil: a scorpion clutching the sun.

Another vehicle came to a stop beside the giant, a hovercraft that had sped along behind it. These invaders were more clever than Gorton had given them credit for. The giant's charge had been a distraction as much as anything else. The militia's missile pods could barely damage an assault 'Mech if they were lucky, but the hovercraft would have been a different matter entirely. He hadn't even noticed the damn thing's heat signature.

The doors on the craft slid open, and an assortment of strange figures stepped out. There were armed guards in gray-and-black combat fatigues, and people who must have been technicians, judging by the equipment they carried. Most curious among them was a woman leading a dog-sized lizard on a leash. It flicked out its tongue, tasting the air.

The motley assortment stood to attention, and then with what sounded like a groan, the giant slowly lowered to one knee. A hatch opened, and the 'Mech's pilot descended a short chain ladder with a measured, dignified pace. Upon reaching the ground, he glanced briefly at his assembled troops, then strode toward Colonel Milovic.

He looked like something out of legend. Tall and broad, he wore a gray breastplate with that scorpion insignia proudly emblazoned on it. His face was concealed behind a black litham, exposing only a pair of deep-green eyes. Atop his head he wore a spiked helm trimmed with fur, like the steppe warriors of ancient Terra. A black cape billowed behind him in the morning breeze.

He came to a halt less than an arm's length from Colonel Milovic. Compared to this strange warrior, Milovic looked like a child playing dress-up. His uniform seemed even more gaudy and ridiculous.

As if on cue, the leashed reptile let out a long, throaty growl. It whipped its tail back and forth and scuffed the ground, but provoked no reaction from the outsiders. Milovic visibly flinched.

"You are the leader, I presume?" he asked, regaining some of his composure.

"I am Star Captain Rao, of Clan Goliath Scorpion," the outsider replied.

"I'm Colonel Milovic, of the Roskan Colony Defense Force. Sir, you have made an illegal landing on our planet. I request that you withdraw your forces immediately, or we will be forced to fire on you."

"We attempted to issue *batchall*," Rao replied, "but it seems your communication systems suffered interference. We have expressed our regret at the first contact between your forces and our MechWarriors. I trust your warriors responsible for this provocation have been punished?"

"I share your regret that we came to blows before proper diplomacy could be conducted," Milovic said, brushing over the question. "But on behalf of Lorena Johanssen, Protector of Roskan Colony, I must again ask that you withdraw your troops. You've come here armed for war, Captain—"

"Star Captain," Rao corrected.

"S-Star Captain, quite right. You've come armed for war. We are a peaceful people, but we are prepared to defend ourselves."

Rao fixed him with a cold look.

"By the ancient rites of the Clans, I claim this world and its people," Rao said slowly. "I issue challenge to your warriors, that this be settled in honorable combat on a field of your choosing. You may choose your forces, and they shall be matched appropriately."

"I think you'll find our defenses are—"

Rao snorted. "The pile of earth and mud you have erected will not save you. Do you not understand, freebirth? I offer you mercy. Send your best MechWarriors, and the Goliath Scorpions shall match them. If they are defeated, my warriors and I shall take your colony into the protection of our Clan. If you triumph, we shall leave this world unharmed. Honor demands no less."

Milovic studied Rao for a moment.

"We may choose the grounds?" he asked.

"It is the way of the Clans," Rao said. "What forces do you bid?"

Milovic inclined his head, speaking into his collar. Gorton switched to their private comm channel.

"Do you think you can take one of them?" the colonel whispered.

"I'm not sure—"

"Yes or no? Do you think you can do it?"

"If I have to," Gorton admitted. "That assault 'Mech could be trouble."

"Good. Power up and get over here."

The private line went dead, and Milovic spoke aloud again. "Very well, Star Captain. The tradition of the honor duel is known among us. We shall meet you, and *this* will be our champion!"

Gorton had already put *Tomoe* on full power. He marched his BattleMech down the main boulevard and came to a halt behind the trenches. Just as the invaders wore their scorpion sigils openly, so too did Gorton's 'Mech have its own icon: a snarling warrior maiden clutching a naginata, standing atop a pile of severed heads. The image was emblazoned on the center of the 'Mech's chest, along with the hiragana lettering for "Tomoe." The 'Mech was a *Black Knight*, a model from the old Star League. Gorton's pride and joy. She was an old but formidable warrior, just like her pilot.

He watched the camera link, studying Star Captain Rao. Though his face remained hidden, the look in his eyes shone clear. He stared at Gorton's 'Mech with incredible intensity. There was no fear, only a mixture of recognition and something else: hatred. Gorton couldn't fathom what would provoke a reaction like that, but the Periphery was full of maniacs.

"The *Black Knight*, *Tomoe*, piloted by Gorton, our MechWarrior," Colonel Milovic said with relish. "I am sure it is more than a match for any of your 'Mechs. The battle...the battle shall be at Agrippa Lake. Twenty kilometers from here."

"We sighted it on our descent," Rao replied coolly. "Very well. Our great *ristar*, MechWarrior Ketelle, shall face your champion in her *Hellbringer*. Dawn tomorrow. Is that settled, freebirth?"

"Dawn tomorrow," Milovic agreed.

"Well bargained and done!"

"Quite so."

Rao barked an order to his troops, and they remounted their vehicle. At least Gorton wouldn't have to face the giant. He watched the hovercraft and the Goliath Scorpion 'Mechs return to the forest. All save a peculiar machine whose arms ended in a pair of massive particle projection cannons. It seemed to regard the field, and Gorton's *Black Knight* in particular. Ketelle and her *Hellbringer*, no doubt. He felt as though a pair of eyes, hard and hateful, stared at him from that 'Mech.

Then it turned and disappeared into the forest with the others.

AGRIPPA LAKE
ROSKAN
COREWARD DEEP PERIPHERY
22 MAY 3049

The walk to Agrippa Lake was eerily pleasant. Gorton's vodka bottle was strapped down in the holster of his pilot's chair, where most MechWarriors kept a pistol for emergencies. A quick pull was enough to steady his hands. *Tomoe* had seen him through worse. He kept the 'Mech at a light jog, one eye on his scanners, the other watching the forest he moved through.

The mist had come in again during the night, one of the most pleasant things about Roskan. Hot days, cold nights. Like the world itself was trying to cool down from the day's work.

At last, he reached Agrippa Lake, a vast silver disc stretching off into the mist. There was a clearing along its shores, and up into the hills huge swaths of forest had been cut down into a logging trail. He and *Tomoe* had done a fair amount of the logging themselves. The 'Mech's giant saw could do the work of a hundred lesser machines, and her dexterous hand could carry a whole load by itself.

It was dull work, but it was better than what Gorton had been doing for most of his life. None of the trees ever begged him for mercy.

As before, the Clan 'Mechs emerged one by one from the tree line at the far side of the clearing. Dawn's light had begun to pierce the morning mist. The leader, the BattleMech with a face like a scowling god, stood at the forefront again. A message came through on the open band.

"Freebirth," said Star Captain Rao, "do you understand the nature of this Trial of Possession?"

"Me an' your champ fight it out. Winner takes the colony, that right?" Gorton replied, trying to sound casual. There was no need to let the invaders know how scared he was.

"*Aff*. The victor may also claim the defeated warrior and their 'Mech as *isorla*. The honor of representing Clan Goliath Scorpion goes to MechWarrior Ketelle, pilot of our Star's *Hellbringer*. In this solemn matter, let none interfere."

With that, the comms went dead. The *Hellbringer* stepped forth, a square-shouldered, heavily armed machine. It stood and faced him across the clearing, totally still.

For a moment, Gorton thought the damn thing was going to bow to him, like they were in a dojo. Then *Tomoe*'s scanners blared that they'd detected a 'Mech's engine going hot. Ketelle wasn't waiting. She was charging up.

Gorton wasted no time pushing *Tomoe* back into action. He ran her in a wide arc, keeping his left side to the *Hellbringer*. Its first volley, a pair of brilliant blue PPC bolts, went wide. Then the Clan 'Mech was on the move. A streak of missiles followed close on, boxing Gorton in. He threw *Tomoe* into quick reverse, skidding her to a halt, and spun to face the *Hellbringer* head-on.

Warning lights flared. An impact had struck *Tomoe*'s shoulder, and Gorton hadn't even noticed. She had armor enough to keep soldiering on, though. With practiced ease, Gorton sighted in on the *Hellbringer* and powered up his weapons.

Alpha strike, that was the way. End this quickly. He had ten tons on the *Hellbringer* at a guess. It couldn't have armor on par with *Tomoe*, even if its firepower was impressive.

He raced toward the *Hellbringer* as the Clan pilot stood her ground, firing repeatedly at him. One shot took *Tomoe* in the torso, another in her left arm. Sparks flew, warning lights triggered, but Gorton waited, thumb braced against his firing stud.

Then it came. *Tomoe*'s voice, clear, crisp, and feminine, recorded centuries ago. First it spoke in Japanese, then repeated the words in English, a design quirk no one had ever bothered to fix. He understood both, of course, but it was on the English that he slammed the firing stud down on.

"Taageto rokku," *Tomoe* said. "*Target locked.*"

Every laser and PPC on *Tomoe*'s chassis burned into life. A brilliant volley of blue and green ripped into the *Hellbringer*'s frame. He followed it quickly with a series of laser bursts from *Tomoe*'s chassis, then another shot from the PPC in her arm.

"Netsu joutai keihou," *Tomoe* said, the heat gauge dangerously near red. "*Heat level warning.*"

"Yeah, I feel it old girl," Gorton whispered back.

He'd done damage, but not enough. The *Hellbringer* was still standing. It strafed to the side, firing. The pilot's precision was incredible: she was running at full speed and still landing hits on a moving target. If Gorton hadn't been that target, he would've almost admired her.

"Freebirth," a voice crackled over his comm unit.

Ketelle, Gorton realized. She sounded young.

"You lack discipline," she chided. "I have the blood of Kerensky's greatest warriors in my veins. You have no hope of victory."

Gorton darted *Tomoe* through another volley of shots. Water. He had to head for water. His heat gauge still wavered painfully close to critical. Returning fire now would be disastrous.

"I got killers in my line going back ten generations," Gorton grunted. "Nothin' to brag about, kid."

"Know this, freebirth: I shall give you no quarter. A bondsman like you would only shame my Clan."

Gorton switched his comms off. He couldn't understand a word the woman was saying. She was clearly as nuts as the rest of her people.

He slowed *Tomoe* down and rotated her right side to face the *Hellbringer* as he reached the water's edge. A fall wouldn't help him in this fight, and he knew there was plenty of muck beneath the lake's surface that could trip up his old 'Mech.

Another volley of missiles impacted all around him, short-range projectiles. A few found their mark, and suddenly his heat gauge spiked again.

Fried a heat sink! Damn!

Crazy she might be, but stupid she wasn't. She was picking his 'Mech apart with incredible precision. He switched his comm back on, hearing Ketelle's gloating voice.

"—There is nowhere you can hide from me, freebirth," she hissed. "Face your death like a warrior, and I will make it swift. It is more than you deserve for defiling that machine."

"Defiling what?" Gorton asked, completely perplexed.

He spun *Tomoe* around. He had to keep her moving until he could fire his weapons again without roasting himself. Another shot struck *Tomoe*'s torso, tearing off one of her lasers.

Just my luck, Gorton thought. *Well, at least it'll help with the heat problem. Can't overheat if I can't fire the damn gun.*

He forced *Tomoe* up out of the water and moved across the clearing. The *Hellbringer* kept pace with him, but luckily its next salvo went wide. Ketelle was getting too eager. Like most young pilots, one good hit made her think she'd won the battle already.

"You know what you have done," Ketelle continued. "That *Black Knight* is a sacred weapon! It belonged to the ancient Star League. It belongs to *us*!"

Gorton increased speed, trying to outpace the *Hellbringer* despite his 'Mech's protesting heat gauge. He headed up the ridge, onto the logging trail, the *Hellbringer* in hot pursuit. Lasers and missiles streaked by, but with *Tomoe* going close to her top speed, it was difficult for Ketelle to acquire a lock.

"My people fought for the Star League," Gorton shot back. "*Tomoe*'s mine! You can have her when you pry my charred corpse out of her cockpit!"

"I intend to," Ketelle said. "The Goliath Scorpions will redeem that BattleMech. The damage you have done to it will be repaired."

A PPC shot took *Tomoe* in the rear. Gorton's scanners flickered and died, electronics sent into a cascading failure by the sudden burst of energy.

"Don't do this to me girl, come on, don't do this," Gorton pleaded as he worked the controls.

He could still move, but his sensors were blind. He flicked reboot switches frantically, running *Tomoe* in a zigzag up the logging trail. It was a dangerous game he was playing; there were plenty of old growth stumps here that could trip her up. Of course, the *Hellbringer* would have to contend with that too. Gorton hoped a little distance could buy him time to think, to plan—

He felt the whole 'Mech shake as another wave of missiles struck her leg. Dizziness washed over him, feedback from his neurohelmet. The 'Mech tumbled forward. Gorton jerked back on the throttle, willing her not to fall. She teetered drunkenly, and he tilted the foot pedals, sending her into a crouch.

Teeth chattering, Gorton grabbed the vodka, pressed it to his lips and drank a fiery shot. The liquor's burn made him angry, fearless. He embraced the old rage he used to feel as a young man, the bloodlust.

Another shot hit *Tomoe*'s shoulder.

The scanners surged back to life. *Tomoe*'s armor was nearly gone in a dozen places, the firing control for her PPC was fried, multiple heat sinks were burned out. She was wounded, but she could still fight.

With an animal yell, Gorton forced *Tomoe* back to her feet, and he rounded on the *Hellbringer*. Ketelle was closing on him fast, firing everything she had. Missiles and lasers impacted all around his 'Mech, but Gorton returned in kind. He triggered another volley, linking all of *Tomoe*'s remaining lasers and firing them in a brilliant burst of light at the oncoming 'Mech.

He was rewarded with the sound of an explosion. The *Hellbringer*'s missile pod was sheared clean off. Its left arm was pitted and blackened, sparks and coolant leaking from it like the blood of a dying man. He fired again, holding his ground as the *Hellbringer* came on, his lasers tearing up tree stumps and mud with wild abandon.

"Your defiance is useless, freebirth!" Ketelle roared. "You shame yourself and your legacy with what you have done to that *Black Knight*! You disgrace a warrior's weapon! You turn it into nothing but a beast of burden for the laborers beneath you! You shall pay for that transgression with your life!"

The arm, Gorton realized. That's what this insane Clanner was ranting about. He had replaced *Tomoe*'s left arm with an agro-saw, a tool for threshing and cutting down trees. It was more useful for the peaceful life he'd wanted to live. Now, these Clanners wanted him dead for it.

He backed *Tomoe* up the hill, scanning his surroundings as he kept a stream of fire on the *Hellbringer*. Ketelle was brave, but the damage he'd done was enough to give her pause. If she was smart, she could have just backed off and let her PPCs do their work. Ketelle was young, though. She wanted the glory of watching his 'Mech burn up close, of watching him die not through a scanner screen, but with her own eyes.

There! A thrill ran through him as he sighted what he'd been looking for. He kept backing up, drawing Ketelle in.

Tomoe's calm voice informed him he was beyond the critical heat threshold, that she was engaging an automatic shutdown sequence. Gorton snatched the bottle of vodka, spilling it over his coolant vest, and gulped down another mouthful.

"Not yet, girl, not yet!" he shouted as he hit the manual override.

More warning lights came on. Sweat was pouring down his brow. Instruments around him were glowing red; sparks flew from one

console. He was pushing *Tomoe* to her limit, beyond it with each volley. Wouldn't be long before he caused another catastrophic failure or gave himself heatstroke.

Ketelle thundered toward him, weapons firing. He could practically feel the bloodlust emanating from her. The MechWarriors of House Kurita called it *sakki:* the killing urge so powerful that others could sense it. Gorton had felt that way many times before, and he was sure others had felt it coming from him, too.

When the *Hellbringer* was close enough, Gorton acted. *Tomoe* was near crippled, but her legs and feet still worked fine. Next to him was a stack of freshly cut timber, abandoned when the Clanners had made their landing. He worked one of his controls, and *Tomoe* kicked it with all the might the 75-ton machine could muster.

The logs flew toward the *Hellbringer*, impacted harmlessly against it, then fell beneath its feet. The 'Mech already at top speed, there was no way even a pilot as skilled as Ketelle could remain standing with a dozen tumbling logs beneath it. The *Hellbringer* stumbled and plunged backward, hitting the ground hard.

Gorton seized the opportunity. He was still too far beyond *Tomoe*'s heat threshold to safely trigger her lasers, but her fist and agro-saw were more than enough. *Tomoe* lunged at the fallen *Hellbringer* and pummeled it mercilessly. An armored foot stomped through its shoulder, severing its PPC, and the agro-saw sparked across the fallen 'Mech's chest.

Ketelle forced the *Hellbringer* to stand as blows rained down on it. Lasers pulsed, blasting into *Tomoe*'s chest, but Gorton felt no fear. He hacked and slashed and pounded, his vision gone blood red. At last the saw sheared clear through one of the *Hellbringer*'s knee actuators, and the machine fell to the ground once again.

The lasers stopped firing. Some still sparked uselessly, but it was obvious the *Hellbringer* had suffered a catastrophic failure. He'd ripped half the 'Mech's armor away, exposing its internal structure and circuitry like the bones and sinews of a corpse. His opponent was helpless.

Gorton placed one of *Tomoe*'s feet on the *Hellbringer*'s torso, just beneath the cockpit.

"Do it, you freeborn filth," Ketelle hissed.

Gorton could feel the heat in his veins, the shaking in his fingers. So many times he'd been here before, heard cries for mercy, oaths of defiance. He had never listened to any of them, just finished the job and moved on.

Today was different, though. He'd come to Roskan to get away from the screams of dying MechWarriors. He wasn't about to change that.

"Quarter," Gorton said.

"Never," Ketelle growled back.

"I'm not asking you, kid, I'm giving it to you. Fight's over. I win."

He switched his comms to a wide band and turned *Tomoe*'s ravaged chassis to face the other Clan Mechs.

"You hear that?" he called. "I win. Now, let's talk. Face-to-face."

Once he had dismounted from *Tomoe*, Gorton found Ketelle waiting for him beside the broken hulk of her 'Mech. Blood dripped from one of her eyebrows, and the bodysuit she wore was ripped and singed, but she stood with the same rigid, military bearing all the Clanners seemed to have.

He had been right. She was young as hell, barely over twenty if she was a day. At least a head taller than him, too.

Her lip curled when she saw him. "You are...old," she said, with a mixture of shock and disgust.

"Yeah, I am. Come on," Gorton grunted.

He had a survival rifle slung under his shoulder just in case, and the half-empty vodka bottle in one hand. He walked alongside Ketelle at a steady pace to the meeting spot. The rest of her kin had advanced to the halfway mark and dismounted from their own 'Mechs. All of them were dressed identically to Ketelle, save Star Captain Rao, who still wore his fearsome armor and war helm.

"It is finished, Freebirth," Rao said. "Ketelle is your bondswoman, sworn to serve you forevermore if you wish it. Her *Hellbringer* is yours as well. We will depart the field with all due haste."

Gorton shook his head. "Take 'em both. They're no use to me."

Rao's eyes narrowed. "That is not our way."

"I don't give a damn about your ways. If she's mine, I'm giving her to you. Understand?"

Rao glanced at Ketelle. She lowered her head.

"I believe," she said quietly, "the freeborn wishes to grant me *hegira*, the right to withdraw."

"Very well," Rao said. "We shall indulge you, and your curious whims."

"Be a waste, that's all," Gorton said, wiping the sweat from his brow. "Like I said, no use to me."

His skin was hot all over. He had nearly fried again. It was like *Tomoe* was angry with him, like she didn't want to be on the field any more than he did.

"You are not so different from us, freebirth," Star Captain Rao said. "We feared your profligacy, but despite the damage you inflicted on the *Hellbringer*, it can be repaired. It will be a valuable asset when the time comes for the Clans to retake the Inner Sphere. We...appreciate this. You are an honorable man."

"I wasn't talking about the damn 'Mech!"

Commander Rao was silent, and Gorton saw a look of confusion in the man's eyes. He didn't understand. He genuinely didn't understand.

"Ketelle's death would have brought her honor against a valorous foe such as you," Rao said. "Is it not so among the warriors of the Inner Sphere as well?"

"Oh, it is. Sure as hell is. I can't sleep at night for all the 'honor' I've given out over the years."

Gorton looked past Rao's broad shoulders. The other MechWarriors with him were all young, like Ketelle. They had the same intensity, the same hardness Gorton himself had when he was young.

Children, all of them. Children hungry for war.

Gorton looked back at Rao, the impassive giant. Older than them, their commander and surrogate father. A scorpion proudly worn on his chest. Who in their right mind took a scorpion for a sigil?

"You know, when your people get to the Inner Sphere, I think they're gonna feel right at home," Gorton said bitterly.

"That honor belongs to the other Clans. For now."

Gorton had no idea what that meant, and he didn't care.

"Get the hell off my world," he said.

Rao stared at him, eyes hard. Then, the edges of his eyes curled upwards slightly. He was smiling. The Clanner executed a stiff, formal bow, then turned on his heel and walked away. Ketelle bowed, as did the other Clanners, and then they followed their leader.

Soon, Gorton was alone on the battlefield. Alone, save the smoking hulk of the *Hellbringer*...and *Tomoe*.

CORDOBA CITY
ROSKAN
COREWARD DEEP PERIPHERY
7 JUNE 3049

Gorton sat at the edge of Cordoba City, drinking stale beer once again, and admiring *Tomoe* in the pale twilight. Bien had done a fine job getting her back in shape in the weeks since the Clanners had left. One thing still rattled around in Gorton's head, though.

"Should we put her old arm back on?" Bien had asked.

They had it stored away. It was perfectly functional, armed with a laser. It would be a simple job to remove the agro-saw. And the Clanners had hinted more of them would be coming, not just to Roskan, but to the Inner Sphere itself. Hard times were just starting. Gorton was sure of it.

In the end, he had said no. The harvest wasn't done, and there was still plenty of lumber work to do.

As he sat in the darkness, looking up at his old companion, he remembered a story he'd once heard. Long ago, the One God had demanded his people turn their spears into pruning hooks, their swords into plowshares. It wasn't until he got to Roskan that he'd really thought much on it. He didn't know if the legend had any basis in reality, but he hoped it was true.

Gorton hoped one day he could make *Tomoe* into a tool of peace, not a weapon of war.

And he prayed that someday, he could do the same for himself.

VOICES OF THE SPHERE:
THE NEW MERCENARY MARKET

STEPHEN TOROPOV

Across the war-wracked history of the Inner Sphere, nothing is as consistent yet ever-changing as the mercenary trade. Twenty years of intensifying warfare have once again cemented the hired gun as an indispensable fixture of BattleMech warfare, and the fall of the Republic of the Sphere and the ascent of the ilClan have only created more business opportunities for enterprising warriors with negotiable loyalties.

Business is booming at hiring halls across the Inner Sphere, but the dawn of this new era for mercenaries has brought fundamental changes to the way the industry works. New employers are rising from shattered realms; the once unassailable Mercenary Review and Bonding Commission is a shambling wreck of its former self, facing new competition from Clan Sea Fox; and the death of ComStar's C-bill combined with pervasive economic unrest raises the question of exactly how a sellsword's wage can even be paid. In light of these developments, we interviewed participants in the mercenary trade from across known space to see how they view the profession, now and in the future.

—INN REPORT, 26 APRIL 3152

Captain Dean Sohnle, CO, Reel's Roughriders, New Hope (Free Worlds League): There's still good business in the League, sure, but the jobs are changing. Time was a small unit could roll up to any podunk indie world and get a plum gig scaring off pirates as far from Clanners as anywhere in the Sphere. Then the indies all got annexed, and now the market is all dukes and presidents looking to take the Clans head on. Bigger money, much bigger risk, and still no way to know if unexpected 'Mechs with eagle insignias will shoot at the bad guys and not you. Bright side, payment's now in Sea Fox scrip that spends almost anywhere.

Major Morana Tichy, CO, Undead Battalion, Dustball (Malthus Confederation): The Hinterlands is a paradise. Even high-minded folks can't afford to be picky 'round here, and they all pay in OmniMechs that fell off the back of a DropShip. The boy scouts can sign on with the Kell Hounds or the Tamar Pact, and folks willing to take more...discreet employment—like us— can always find work with more iniquitous enterprises. Whenever we're done with this place, we'll have coin in our pocket, 'Mechs in our bays, and blood on our knives. That's enough to make me one happy sellsword.

Qīngtiān Isakov, employment broker, Herotitus (Fronc Reaches): The Herotitus Hiring Hall has a rep in the Sphere for being shady, but really, what's the alternative? Can't work with bonding agents who aren't here, and neither the old money MRBC or the upstart Sea Foxes deign to show up this far from moldy old Terra. House bills are all worthless out here, so you take wages in whatever you can use. The fact is there's jobs that need doing and mercs willing to do them. Being snooty isn't gonna fill bellies or fuel tanks, so y'all can keep your fancy paperwork and I'll keep hiring.

Clodagh Scullion, legal counsel, Bellemore Warfare Solutions, Galatea (Isle of Skye): These days, the MRBC is mostly in it to get its beak wet. Until we can pull together some new body to put the MRBC out of its misery, you gotta budget for a generous bribery fund. Still, I'd much rather that than subject me and my unit to extreme enforcement of Sea Fox honor based on a bond with more terms and conditions than a high-end noteputer. For the love of Terra, mercs and tankborn have a century-long tradition of shooting each other on sight. I'm not gonna roll over now and do business with them. Better a crooked Spheroid than a backstabbing Clanner.

Captain Langston Dean, CO, The Lost Dreamers, New Avalon (Federated Suns): I grew up on Marlette, then jumped to Republic space after Gray Monday to make my fortune. Got folks in the unit from all over, but deep down I've always thought of myself as a true son of the Suns. Now the First Prince offers me my own landed estate for a nest egg, and all I have to do to earn it is clear out the Dracs? Haven't said yes so enthusiastically since my wedding. I just worry that not everyone who takes a deal this good will be prodigal patriots who grew up on Marlette, if you catch my meaning.

Anika Ladefoged, logistical administrator, Crater Cobras, Avon (Draconis Combine): There's never been a more lucrative time to hire on with the Dragon, if you're smart about it. Just make sure you know who's really hiring you. The poor saps who ended up on *Kanrei* Toranaga's payroll got chewed up with the rest of his samurai when the Dragoons left and the Suns bit off the Dragon's Tongue. We made sure we hired on with someone loyal to the Coordinator, and we get paid handsomely to stay home and watch the Dominion border. Just enough raiding back and forth to keep up ammo shipments, but the intel wonks say the Dominion's too busy internally to worry about anything major, and Yori isn't eager to send us at them. A good deal for them Combine, and an even better one for us.

Lieutenant Kurt Tanner, XO, The Killer Penguins, Kandersteg (Lyran Commonwealth): I ran with Wolf's Dragoons back in the day. Good money at the time, but jumping ship was the best career move I ever made. Big names like that get caught up in grand, bloody vendettas way too often, and that's bad for business. "Tradition" and "honor" might mean something to the bigwigs, but rumor is the 'Goons got punked by the Wolves, and hard. When the job starts being about anything other than staying alive and getting paid, you've made a mistake. Running with smaller crews keeps you nimble, and staying nimble keeps you in the black.

Star Captain Mansa, Fox Khanate, CSF *Megalodon* (Clan Sea Fox): The Khanates have dealings in every corner of the Sphere, and wherever Sea Fox warriors and merchants go, we find mercenaries. Why should we look down upon them? They are warriors, they are merchants. Their loyalty is to money and not to a Clan, true. But if an honorable Clan is the fount through which the money flows? If Clan honor is seen to be the force which guarantees the profits of the lucrewarrior? Then Clan Sea Fox has conquered yet another market, and once again a combination of force of arms and shrewd negotiation has brought us honorable profit.

SIGNING DAY

CHRIS G. LANE

JOHANSSON'S STATION
BOLESLAV
SATALICE IV
2 SEPTEMBER 3029

"Well, what ya waiting for?" came the somewhat brusque inquiry from behind.

Jed turned to look up at his dad sitting on the porch. "I'm goin'."

Standing from his perch on the stairs, he leaned down and picked up his pack by the top strap, swiped off the pervasive chalky dust that had accumulated in the short time he'd been sitting, and slung it over his right shoulder.

Half turning, he glanced back at his dad one more time. His father, for his part, stared straight ahead from his rocking chair on the front porch of the dilapidated shack that served as the general store for Johansson's Station. Jed could see how hard this was for him, so he simply said, "I love you, Dad. I'll see ya later," turned back around, and began walking.

He heard a gruff throat-clearing. "Best git movin'. Yer burning daylight."

Jed kept walking, and didn't look back. He and his father had been alone since his mum passed from the fever in 3015, and this parting, while necessary, was hard for them both.

Satalice IV was a tough world, covered mostly by volcanic plains, and susceptible to extreme weather on a frequent basis. Consequently, except for a few refuges of wealth, most of the populace lived in poverty with the accompanying issues of famine and disease. This was the reason for Jed's sad parting this day. He was off to find a new life of adventure, and hopefully prosperity.

Two regiments of off-worlders, mercenaries in the employ of the Lyran Commonwealth, had recently landed on Satalice IV and were diligently attempting to evict the local Draconis Combine troops and reclaim the planet for the Commonwealth. The Lyrans had lost control of Satalice IV to the Combine just four years ago, so most of its citizens, especially the lower classes, still identified as Commonwealth citizens living under the oppressive occupation of the Combine military. This resentment toward the "Snakes," as the Draconis soldiers were derisively known, provided fertile recruiting grounds for the invading mercenary units.

Following their initial landings and successfully pushing back the local garrison forces, the mercenary units sent recruiters to rural and impoverished towns, seeking to expand their ranks with natives already inclined toward a robust dislike of the occupying Snakes. This presented a great opportunity for young people like Jed. Since service in the Draconis Combine Mustered Soldiery as a poor person with no political connections was a grim prospect at best, this chance to sign on with an off-world unit was too good to pass up.

After about twenty minutes of walking south down Main Street, the dirt road that ran through Johansson's Station, a gust of wind kicked up a curtain of dust, causing Jed to squint against the stinging spray. As he looked up to gauge the weather, he heard faint thunder coming from the hills to the south. Not wanting to get caught out in a flash storm, he pulled up his bandanna to cover his nose and mouth against the assault of flint-scented sand and picked up his pace toward the train stop at the end of the road. Being out on these plains in the heat of the day could quickly become unhealthy, and he silently admonished himself for his careless timing.

Jed hurried to the small train stop's enclosed bench and pushed open the plexiglass door before quickly shutting it against a small shower of sand that tried to slip in with him. Inside the small and stuffy enclosure, he lowered his bandanna and shook the sand from his jacket and hair.

The first thing he noticed was only one other person occupied the bench. The young man seated on the far end glanced hesitantly in his direction, almost as if afraid to make eye contact. Jed recognized the boy as Roderick Johnson, from the moisture and wind farm just east of Johansson's Station. He had fond memories of times spent with Roderick, back when they were small children pretending to save their farm from marauding pirates, or hunting cinder rats with improvised slingshots.

Striding forward, Jed extended his hand and said, "Hey there, Roderick. It's good to see a familiar face. What brings you out in this weather?"

Roderick flinched at Jed's approach, but offered a small smile along with a weak handshake before replying in a quiet voice, "Same as you, I reckon. Headed out to sign up with off-worlders."

Dropping onto the bench, Jed patted Roderick on the shoulder. "That's awesome! We can begin this adventure together. What'd they offer you?"

"They were mighty interested in my tech skills. Keeping my family's farm running got me a three-year contract with 'em. How 'bout you?"

"Well, I didn't do so great on that test they gave us, so it's just straight-up infantry duty for me, I'm afraid." Jed shrugged and smiled.

Roderick replied with a nod and a shrug that said *What can you do?*, and the conversation petered to a stop. Glancing out through the plexiglass sides of the train stop, Jed again heard, and then felt, more thunder off to the south, followed by more flashes of light over the distant hills. He was about to ask Roderick if he thought they'd get caught out in a flash storm, but the arrival of the maglev train gliding almost soundlessly into the stop interrupted him.

"This is us." Jed stood and once again shouldered his pack. After pulling his bandanna back over his face, he opened the door and held it as Roderick lowered his head and rushed out ahead of him. Letting the door close behind him, he jogged after Roderick and followed him up the stairs of the closest car.

The inside of the train was comfortably cool after the heat of the day, and blessedly dust free except for what Jed and Roderick had tracked in. Jed was pleasantly surprised to find the train mostly empty, allowing him and Roderick to grab two seats next to the large window running down the left side of the passenger car. Jed stowed his pack in the rack above his chosen seat, then plopped down and took a moment to survey his new surroundings and the expansive view.

Leaning forward in his seat, he peered out the window toward the front of the train as best he could, and once again caught sight of some brief flashes of light in the hills to the south, just visible through the persistent blowing dust. *Must be storming some out toward the off-worlders camp.* He hoped the mercenary recruiter would be on time to pick them up, and have some covered transport.

The outside hatch in the rear passenger car thumped and hissed as it closed, and then Jed felt a brief lurch as the train began its silent journey south. Lying back against the soft seat cushion, he smiled at the feeling of the cool air on his face from the vents by the window and closed his eyes as he dozed off into sleep...

A persistent pulling on Jed's right arm began to annoy him, as he was just fine and content to continue lying right there. *Wait...lying? Why am I lying down? Wasn't I on the train with Roderick, on our way to join up with the off-worlders?* This series of thoughts acted as a lifeline he climbed back toward awareness. His first conscious sensation after the persistent tugging was of a loud hissing and screeching sound, followed by an acrid burning smell that made his nose itch.

Opening his eyes, Jed quickly oriented himself and realized he was somehow out of his seat and lying on the *wall* of the passenger car. Looking to his right, he saw Roderick pulling on his arm while shouting something he couldn't make out over the continuous noise.

Jed allowed Roderick to pull him into a standing position on the wall—now floor—and was immediately rewarded with a headache for his efforts. He gingerly felt along the right side of his head until he found the lump causing him pain.

Roderick was once again tugging on his arm and shouting. "We have to go, Jed! Come on! They may come back!"

Allowing himself to be pulled and led by Roderick, Jed stumbled toward the back of the passenger car as he struggled with the awkward footing caused by the train car's wall being repurposed into a floor. In addition to the car being on its side, it was now missing the entire rear bulkhead, which had somehow been ripped off, and the rear car where they had boarded was nowhere to be seen.

As they moved toward the rear to exit the car, Jed finally registered what Roderick had been yelling at him. "Wait, *who* may come back? What happened? Why are you in such a hurry?"

Roderick turned to reply, but a loud roar and a deafening ripping sound drowned out whatever he had planned to say. Several explosions rocked the train car as Jed stumbled out the ripped-open back and onto the hard, dusty ground outside.

Hitting the ground on his stomach caused Jed to suck in a sudden mouthful of flinty-tasting dust while gasping to recover from the wind being knocked from his lungs. He spit out dust and lifted his head to take in his surroundings just in time to spy the source of the aforementioned roar as a low-flying dark-gray aerospace fighter shot past the train. Jed had just enough time to spot the red-and-black dragon symbols under each wing.

Snakes must've gotten word this train was carrying new recruits for the off-worlders. He stood and brushed himself off, then glanced around for Roderick, and hopefully some cover in case the enterprising pilot should return.

Jed stepped over the mag rails the train used to be perched on, and moved to the far side of the train to get some idea of where they were. Stepping around the capsized passenger car, he tripped over a thin piece of sheet metal and cursed at the pain in his shin. When he kicked the piece of metal clear of his path, he noticed the burnt and bent piece of detritus had the word TANNERSVILLE printed on the other side in big, white block lettering.

Well, I guess we made it to the station after all.

Coughing from the thick smoke in the area, Jed headed toward the station terminal to seek cover and hopefully find his ride, until he realized the terminal building was the main source of all the smoke in the air. Bits of the foundation, along with a smoking hole in the ground, was all that remained of the Tannersville Station terminal.

"Jed! Jed! Over here!" came Roderick's excited call.

Toward the end of the train, Jed spotted Roderick standing in the back of a small hovertruck and waving his arms frantically. The driver of the vehicle, a man wearing khaki fatigues and a broad-brimmed hat of the same color, looked in Jed's direction. The truck rose from the ground and, in a quick spurt of dust, rapidly approached Jed as he stood.

The truck slowed to a stop next to him, the fans slowing to idle. The driver looked out and called, "Jedidiah Johansson?"

"Yeah, that's me."

"Outstanding! I'm Sergeant Reynolds, and you are my last pickup before I head back to the forward operating base. Climb in. We need to haul ass outta here before that air jockey comes back to finish what they started!"

"Shouldn't we see who we can help first?"

A quick look of irritation passed over the sergeant's face as he reached through the driver's-side window, grabbed Jed by his jacket, and yanked him up against the door of the truck. "Son, there is not a damn thing we can for these folks," the sergeant growled at him. "Now you git your narrow little ass in this vehicle *right now*, or I am gonna leave you here for the Snakes to finish. You get me?!"

Jed nodded, and ran around to the back of the truck. He climbed over the tailgate, which featured a red-and-blue star with a white *W* in the middle. In the truck bed, he settled on a bench next to Roderick just as the sergeant goosed the engine and took off to the south at alarming speed.

"Welcome to the Waco Rangers, boys!" the sergeant yelled back at them with mirth in his voice.

Jed glanced at Roderick as he began to wonder what he had walked into the middle of, and if he had made a big mistake.

As the truck bounded down the dirt road at a breakneck pace, both Jed and Roderick had to frequently grab the sides of the truck bed to avoid being tossed out. After a few moments, Jed pulled his bandanna back up to cover his nose and mouth because the bed of the truck had quickly filled with the flinty-tasting dust kicked up by their passage.

Following a nerve-racking and dust-filled ride of about twenty-five minutes, the sergeant took a sudden right turn, and Jed saw an open gate flash past them on either side. They had arrived at the Waco Rangers' FOB.

With a final sudden jolt, the sergeant slammed on the brakes, sending both Jed and Roderick sliding into the back of the truck's cab with a loud *thud*. A moment later the driver's door slammed shut with a loud *bang*, and the sergeant's broad hat and face peered into the bed.

"Well, what the living hell're you two waiting for, an engraved invitation? Move your asses! Let's go! Now!" He continued with a steady barrage of shouts as Jed and Roderick scrambled to their feet and jumped over the side of the truck bed to join the sergeant. "You two are only going to be my problem for a few more minutes, so try and keep up! You get me?!" he continued.

"*Yes, sir!*" Jed and Roderick both shouted while standing up a little straighter.

Another look of annoyance crossed the sergeant's face as he leaned into them both and replied with a shout, "God damn it! You don't' sir' me, I work for a living! *Do you get me?!*"

"*Yes, Sergeant!*" came the chorus reply.

"Outstanding!" the sergeant replied. "Now the colonel says the Snakes are on the move, so we don't have a lot of time. Follow me, double ti—"

The sergeant never finished his sentence as a sudden, deafening ripsaw sound tore through the sky, followed by a thunderclap explosion.

Out toward the FOB's southern perimeter, Jed spotted the Rangers 'Mech on guard duty, a *Griffin,* stagger back two steps as its left arm shed armor, then smoke and flame. The cause quickly became apparent as a *Victor*, sporting the insignia of the Ninth Rasalhague Regulars and the dragon emblem of the Draconis Combine, stepped out from the trees with its right-arm autocannon still raised, smoking and pointed at the *Griffin.*

"God dammit!" The sergeant turned and sprinted toward the nearest observation post about twenty meters away.

Jed stood still for a moment, stunned by the sudden precariousness of his situation. Following an uncertain glance shared by Roderick, he took off after the sergeant, Roderick hot on his heels.

As they ran, an announcement blared from the camp's PA system: "*ATTENTION! ATTENTION! SNAKES AT THE SOUTHERN PERIMETER! SNAKES AT THE SOUTHERN PERIMETER! ALL PERSONNEL REPORT TO ACTION STATIONS! ALL PERSONNEL REPORT TO ACTION STA—zzzzzttt.*"

The sergeant scrambled up the OP's ladder, Jed and Roderick right behind him. All three hurried across the shaky plywood floor and approached the stacked sandbags that formed the OP's walls. The height of the platform, easily close to ten meters, provided a good view over the surrounding structures, and allowed an unobstructed view of the FOB's southern perimeter.

The sergeant produced a pair of binoculars from his belt, leaned on the sandbags, and scanned the trees on the south side of the camp. "Dammit! I warned 'em they'd need to move that tree line back another two hundred meters. But does the captain listen? Nooo. Shit!"

Jed saw movement in the trees behind the enemy 'Mech. Another 'Mech in woodland camouflage stepped out next to the *Victor,* which was turning to track the staggered *Griffin.* As it cleared the trees, the Draconis Combine *Thunderbolt* raised its right arm and let loose a bright ruby bolt of energy from its large laser. The beam burned into the armor high on the *Griffin*'s torso, and further exacerbated its pilot's efforts to control the stagger from the *Victor*'s attack. Consequently, even though the *Griffin* managed to raise its particle projection cannon to retaliate, the shot went wide and over the head of the encroaching *Victor,* missing it entirely.

Squinting into the bright cerulean glare of the *Griffin*'s errant PPC shot, Jed stood mesmerized next to the continuously cursing sergeant as he watched the conflict unfold. He found himself silently urging the beleaguered and outnumbered *Griffin* pilot to escape.

Just then the whole OP shook. A loud crash and a pounding sound causing Jed to look behind them. A Rangers *Phoenix Hawk* was stomping through the camp to reach the southern perimeter and assist the struggling *Griffin.* Jed found having a 45-ton, ten-meter-tall 'Mech stepping just a few meters away from him to be a humbling experience, to say the least.

Just then, another loud roar spun his head back around to the south in time to see the *Griffin* ignite its jump jets and soar away from the attacking *Victor* and *Thunderbolt,* to get some time to recover from the damage that had scarred the 'Mech's torso and destroyed its left arm.

After the *Griffin* touched down, a Rangers *Valkyrie* flew overhead on its jump jets and landed with a ground-shaking *thud* near the wounded *Griffin.* The *Valkyrie*'s pilot loosed a fight of ten long-range missiles that peppered the *Thunderbolt*'s right side. The popping sounds and bright flashes pulled the attention of both attacking 'Mechs from the wounded *Griffin* to the newly arrived *Valkyrie.*

Another flash then drew Jed's focus back to the front, to see the Rangers *Phoenix Hawk* fire the large laser in its right hand and strike the *Victor* in the left leg.

"Yes!" exclaimed the sergeant. "Looks like the sentry 'Mechs're getting things under control. All right, rooks, follow me! I need to get your worthless asses to the training cadre so I can report to my action station at the perimeter. Let's move it!" He physically propelled Jed and Roderick to the ladder of the OP.

Jed half climbed, half fell down the ladder to stay ahead of the cussing sergeant, with Roderick so close on his heels he nearly stepped on him. Reaching the bottom of the ladder, Jed barely scrambled out of the way as the sergeant slid down the ladder at breakneck speed and sprinted across the compound. Jed took off in pursuit of him, Roderick trailing close behind.

As they ran through the ever-increasing crowd of Rangers infantry filling the compound, Jed could still hear distant explosions from what he assumed was the ongoing 'Mech battle on the southern perimeter, and he now thought he could also hear the popping sounds of small-arms fire joining the cacophony accompanied by an acrid, burning smell.

Rounding the corner of a Quonset hut, Jed ran headlong into the sergeant, who suddenly slowed and yelled "Grenade!" as he spun and grabbed Jed.

Jed only had time to spot a small dark object tumble along the ground before there was a flash, and what felt like a large truck knocked him off of his feet and bounced him into the Quonset hut.

The next thing he knew, he was flat on his back with the coppery taste of blood in his mouth. His ears were ringing so loud he thought his head was going to explode.

As his vision cleared, a dark figure stepped over him, a shape that slowly resolved itself into a Draconis Combine soldier pointing his rifle in his face as the soldier's boot on his chest pushed him flat on his back.

Jed's breath caught. His blood ran cold, and his stomach fell as he could see the soldier's finger tighten on the rifle trigger. As he stared up at what would be his last seconds of life, Jed thought of his dad, and hoped he would be all right without him.

He took a deep breath—and then the Combine's soldier's head suddenly disappeared in a red mist. His rifle, and then his body, landed on top of Jed.

Hands roughly grabbed Jed under the shoulders and pulled him out from under the soldier's corpse as he wiped blood from his eyes and spit it out of his mouth.

"Come on, rook!" the sergeant yelled. "We gotta move now! The Snakes are flanking us, and if we don't move like we have a purpose, we'll be cut off!! Now move your ass!"

"Yes, Sergeant!" came Jed's automatic reply. And then, "Wait, I've got to grab Roderick."

Stepping back around the Quonset hut, he spotted Roderick lying against the building and hurried over to him. "Hey, Roderick! Come on, we've got to get out of here!"

Crouching and grabbing Roderick by the shoulder, Jed turned him over to help him up. Looking down at his friend and neighbor, what he saw was no longer recognizable. Roderick's face and chest were just a wet red mess, not even human.

Letting go of his friend's body, Jed's knees suddenly gave out, and he fell down and vomited up everything in his stomach.

He was once again grabbed roughly from behind, pulled to his feet, and spun around to face the sergeant.

"God damn it, boy! We have no time for this shit! If you want to live to see another day, you stick to me like glue from now on. Either that, or you can stay here and join your friend. *Do you get me?!*"

"Yes, Sergeant," came Jed's muted reply as he trotted after the sergeant.

As he passed the headless corpse of the Combine soldier who had tried to kill him, he stooped down and picked up the soldier's rifle. A quick review of it revealed it was a standard semiautomatic rifle, similar to the one his dad kept for dealing with raiding varmints. As Jed continued running after the sergeant, he worked the bolt to ensure a round was chambered and began scanning ahead for more Combine soldiers.

The next period of time devolved into a blur of violence and fear. Jed managed to keep up with the sergeant, but he also vaguely remembered shooting two Combine soldiers, then scavenging ammunition from their corpses, and physically attacking another Combine soldier that had dropped down from a roof right behind the sergeant. The recollection of feeling his rifle butt sinking into that soldier's face as he struck over and over again made him feel nauseated all over again.

When events returned to a more normal pace, Jed found himself sitting in a trench next to the sergeant as they both panted for breath like two overworked dogs. He noticed the rifle he was holding was empty, as evidenced by the bolt being locked back, and he had several fresh cuts and scrapes on his arms and hands he did not remember acquiring.

Loud explosions, and what sounded like more 'Mech weapons fire, accompanied by the cheering of nearby Rangers, caused Jed and the sergeant to carefully rise and peer over the lip of the trench toward the southern perimeter of the FOB. A Rangers *BattleMaster* and *Marauder* had joined the 'Mech battle at the tree line and had the Draconis Combine 'Mechs in a full retreat.

"That would be the colonel and the XO come to save the day, it appears," the sergeant said dryly. He patted Jed roughly on the shoulder. "Looks like you survived, kid. You've seen the elephant and lived to tell the tale. Pretty good for a rook who doesn't know his ass from a hole in the ground."

The sergeant smiled to soften that last bit. "Come on. Let's get you checked out by a medic, and then I'll introduce to the training cadre."

"Yes, Sergeant!" was all Jed could think to say about his first day on the job.

BTL-C-20 BATTLE COBRA

Mass: 40 tons
Chassis: Alshain Type 69-40S
Power Plant: Nissan 200
Cruising Speed: 54 kph
Maximum Speed: 86 kph
Jump Jets: None
    Jump Capacity: None
Armor: Paulina Ferro-Fibrous
Armament:
    17.5 tons of pod space available
Manufacturer: Arc-Royal MechWorks, Com Guard Tukayyid Omega-Epsilon Facility X
    Primary Factory: Arc-Royal (discontinued 3090), Tukayyid (destroyed 3068)
Communications System: Blade 12
Targeting and Tracking System: Spanke 112-A

The recovery of tremendous amounts of Clan salvage from Wolcott and Luthien enabled the Draconis Combine to successfully pursue an OmniMech development program. Because of this success, analysts were astounded at ComStar's lack of similar results following their incredible victory on Tukayyid, which had given them unprecedented access to Clan salvage. Theoretically in possession of some of the smartest minds and largest technical databases in the Inner Sphere, ComStar should have brought forth legions of new OmniMech models from the reopened factories of Terra.

Ultimately, ComStar's take on the *Battle Cobra* was characteristic of their failures in the aftermath of Operation Scorpion. Many of ComStar's top minds rebelled to join the Word of Blake, leaving low-level engineers in charge of one of their most important projects in centuries. However, the Word of Blake's daring capture of Terra in 3058 sent ComStar back to square one. ComStar's leadership ordered their remaining technical teams to complete the simplest OmniMech project underway at any cost. The *Battle Cobra*, with its straightforward weapon pods, reached full production five years later.

Holding the keys to almost all of ComStar's initial OmniMech research, the Word of Blake chose to further refine the 'Mech's design instead of rushing it to completion. Eventually entrusted to the now-infamous Devon Cortland, the Blakist *Battle Cobra* project would gradually evolve into the first of the notorious Celestials: the *Preta*.

Capabilities

The adaptation of the *Battle Cobra* to Inner Sphere technology forced several compromises. First, the bulkier frame resulted in an astonishingly cramped chassis. To complicate matters, the late decision to make the OmniMech compatible with ComStar's cutting-edge C³i system necessitated a smaller engine. The resulting regenerative cooling system demanded the installation of bulky heat sinks in the *Battle Cobra*'s already crowded torso. Though these alterations proved nightmarish to ComStar techs, it resulted in a more durable platform when compared to its Clan progenitor: the tightly packed chassis would often block shots that would otherwise damage the fusion engine. The result was a 'Mech that struggled against other contemporary OmniMechs, but excelled in a conventional support role.

Battle History

After Terra's loss, the *Battle Cobra* became one of ComStar's last proprietary 'Mechs, making it an instant target for Blakist forces during the Jihad. Orbital bombardment of Tukayyid's ComStar facilities destroyed the *Battle Cobra*'s factory, leaving ComStar survivors with little more than its schematics, but a quickly negotiated partnership with Arc-Royal MechWorks netted a new manufacturer. However, the *Battle Cobra* still dropped out of production for several years, and its numbers dwindled as ARMW struggled to deliver the troublesome OmniMech.

One of the ComStar *Battle Cobra*'s greatest moments of glory occurred during the Fourth Army's attack on Chertan. What should have been an easy campaign, pitting skilled Com Guard soldiers against two Protectorate Militia divisions, turned into a slog. The Militia troops, hiding in the blasted ruins of Chertan's industrial sectors, rebuffed all attempts to eject them from their entrenched positions. Two Level IIs of *Battle Cobra*s, one of the largest concentrations of them in the Com Guards, were brought forward to spearhead further assaults. Working in concert with battle-armor suits in a facsimile of the Blakist Choir formation, the *Battle Cobra*s ably supported their allied infantry. Scouting battle armor, upon covertly spotting a Blakist position, would relay the information to the waiting *Battle Cobra*s. Depending on the situation, the OmniMech would either reconfigure to call in indirect missile support with TAG or iNarc systems or use more offensive weapon loadouts to isolate and destroy pinned ground forces.

Though *Battle Cobra*s proved essential in taking Chertan and other Protectorate planets, their front-line duty also significantly reduced their numbers. The dissolution of the Com Guards at the Jihad's end cost ARMW the *Battle Cobra*'s primary client, and the struggling manufacturer eventually shuttered the line to focus on its more popular products. With the original Clan *Battle Cobra* now marching off Arc-

Royal's lines, the days of its Spheroid counterpart are undoubtedly numbered. Even so, the few mercenaries that use them swear by their rugged, versatile nature.

Notable 'Mechs and MechWarriors

Adept II Connor Lughson: Heir to a minor noble house on Scudder, Connor's family had neither the funds nor the inclination to train him in the finer details of BattleMech combat. Believing his future might be richer in ComStar's influential hands, Connor joined the 244th Division shortly before the FedCom Civil War. Assigned to a newly produced *Battle Cobra*, Connor never expected his service with the Com Guards would tie him so closely to his heritage. The 244th followed Victor Steiner-Davion through the thick and thin of the Civil War. The adept and his *Battle Cobra* were one of the few of the unit to survive to the war's end, and he returned home a true hero of both his house and his nation

Type: Battle Cobra BTL-C-20
Technology Base: Inner Sphere
Tonnage: 40
Role: Brawler
Battle Value: 944

Equipment		Mass
Internal Structure:	Endo Steel	2
Engine:	200	8.5
Walking MP:	5	
Running MP:	8	
Jumping MP:	0	
Heat Sinks:	10 [20]	0
Gyro:		2
Cockpit:		3
Armor Factor (Ferro):	125	7

	Internal Structure	Armor Value
Head	3	9
Center Torso	12	17
Center Torso (rear)		5
R/L Torso	10	14
R/L Torso (rear)		5
R/L Arm	6	11
R/L Leg	10	17

Space Allocation

Location	Fixed	Spaces Remaining
Head	1 Ferro-Fibrous	0
Center Torso	None	2
Right Torso	Double Heat Sink	3
		3 Endo Steel
		3 Ferro-Fibrous
Left Torso	Double Heat Sink	0
		3 Endo Steel
		6 Ferro-Fibrous
Right Arm	2 Endo Steel	4
		2 Ferro-Fibrous
Left Arm	2 Endo Steel	4
		2 Ferro-Fibrous
Right Leg	2 Endo Steel	0
Left Leg	2 Endo Steel	0

Notes: Features the following Design Quirks: Extended Torso Twist.

Weapons and Ammo	Location	Critical	Tonnage
Primary Weapons Configuration			
Large Pulse Laser	RA	2	7
Double Heat Sink	RT	3	1
Improved C³ Computer	CT	2	2.5
Large Pulse Laser	LA	2	7
Alternate Configuration A			
3 Medium Lasers	RA	3	3
TAGRA	1	1	
Guardian ECM Suite	RA	2	1.5
Double Heat Sink	RT	3	1
Improved C³ Computer	CT	2	2.5
3 Medium Pulse Lasers	LA	3	6
Small Pulse Laser	LA	1	1
Beagle Active Probe	LA	2	1.5
Battle Value: 1,113	Role: Brawler		
Alternate Configuration B			
2 MRM 10	RA	4	6
Ammo (MRM) 72	RT	3	3
Improved C³ Computer	CT	2	2.5
2 MRM 10	LA	4	6
Battle Value: 895	Role: Brawler		
Alternate Configuration C			
iNarc	RA	3	5
Ammo (iNarc) 4	RA	1	1
Ammo (iNarc) 12	RT	3	3
Improved C³ Computer	CT	2	2.5
iNarc	LA	3	5
Ammo (iNarc) 4	LA	1	1
Battle Value: 726	Role: Scout		
Alternate Configuration D			
2 Light PPCs	RA	4	6
Targeting Computer	RT	3	3
Improved C³ Computer	CT	2	2.5
2 Light PPCs	LA	4	6
Battle Value: 1,221	Role: Sniper		
Alternate Configuration E			
MML 9	RA	5	6
Ammo (MML) 39/33	RT	3	3
Improved C³ Computer	CT	2	2.5
MML 9	LA	5	6
Battle Value: 840	Role: Missile Boat		

Weapons and Ammo	Location	Critical	Tonnage
Alternate Configuration F			
Plasma Rifle	RA	2	6
Ammo (Plasma) 30	RT	3	3
Improved C³ Computer	CT	2	2.5
Plasma Rifle	LA	2	6
Battle Value: 1,300	Role: Brawler		
Alternate Configuration G			
Snub-Nose PPC	RA	2	6
Machine Gun	RA	1	.5
Double Heat Sink	RA	3	1
Ammo (MG) 100	RT	1	.5
CASE II	RT	1	1
Plasma Rifle	LA	2	6
Machine Gun	LA	1	.5
Ammo (Plasma) 20	LA	2	2
Battle Value: 1,217	Role: Brawler		
Alternate Configuration H			
Thunderbolt 15	RA	3	11
Ammo (Thunderbolt) 4	RA	1	1
Ammo (Thunderbolt) 8	RT	2	2
CASE	RT	1	.5
3 ER Medium Lasers	LA	3	3
Battle Value: 1,305	Role: Missile Boat		
Alternate Configuration I			
iNarc	RA	3	5
Ammo (iNarc) 8	RA	2	2
Ammo (iNarc) 4	RT	1	1
Ammo (SRM) 25	RT	1	1
CASE II	RT	1	1
Laser Anti-Missile System	CT	1	1.5
2 Medium Lasers	LA	2	2
2 SRM 4	LA	2	4
Battle Value: 1,019	Role: Skirmisher		
Alternate Configuration J			
Large Re-engineered Laser	RA	5	8
Targeting Computer	RT	3	3
Supercharger	CT	1	1
Medium Re-engineered Laser	LA	2	2.5
ER Medium Laser	LA	1	1
M-Pod	LA	2	2
Battle Value: 1,269	Role: Skirmisher		

GHOSTBIRD

BRYAN YOUNG

JADE FALCON TRAINING FACILITY
HAMMARR
SUDETEN
JADE FALCON OCCUPATION ZONE
9 JANUARY 3152

It had only been a month since Alexis had been snatched from her Clan, her home, and her family on Quarell. No longer was she a Ghost Bear; she had been taken into the Jade Falcons by its new Khan, Jiyi Chistu. At first, she had resented being taken, but the promises of family in the Rasalhague Dominion had been hollow. If she wanted a family, she would have to build her own. But build it she had, and she was startled by how quickly she'd come to think of herself as a Jade Falcon.

She stood in the antechamber, watching on the monitors as her *sibmate*, Daniel, undertook his Trial of Position. He looked the part of a stereotypical Ghost Bear-turned-Falcon, young and fit like a warrior, but with a constant, waspish sneer on his face. In the simulation, he piloted a 75-ton *Savage Wolf* armed with two extended-range particle projection cannons and a suite of four short-range missile launchers, and for the first 'Mech in his trial, he faced a 55-ton *Gyrfalcon*—just like the one Khan Chistu piloted.

"He is never going to make it," Sophie said beside Alexis.

"I agree," said Thomasin.

Neither of them had taken their own Trial of Position yet, though they were part of the only *sibko* allowed the chance so far. Thomasin and Sophie were Alexis' closest friends, and had been almost from the moment she'd entered the Bearclaws Ghost Bear *sibko*. The three had been inseparable and were all so different. Thomasin was tall and well built, a smile etched constantly across his chiseled, still-teenage face. Sophie was short for a Trueborn cadet, with black hair she kept pulled into two tight buns and a stern look, always in thought. Alexis fit between them in height and build, and nestled between them to couple as often as their free time allowed.

"He can do it. They've given him every chance." Alexis folded her arms, noting the weight disparity between the 'Mechs in the trial. "He's got to."

Thomasin scoffed. "When has he *ever* done what he was supposed to?"

"When it counted." Alexis thought back to the Trial of Possession on Quarell, when Falcon Khan Jiyi Chistu had claimed her and the rest of her Ghost Bear *sibmates*. She thought back to when it really mattered, when she had asked him for help to interrupt the trial. Even though their gambit had failed, Daniel had accepted the consequences alongside everyone else, despite his bastard of an attitude and their long, long history of rivalry.

On the simulator screen, the *Savage Wolf* ran straight for the smaller *Gyrfalcon,* but the *Gyrfalcon* ignited its jump jets and flew right over Daniel.

"It is just like the last trial," Thomasin said, referring to Khan Chistu's domineering and aggressive fight against Star Colonel Emilio Hall of the Ghost Bears. The Star Colonel had lost the duel and, in turn, Alexis and all of her *sibmates*.

For the briefest moment, Alexis wondered what the Star Colonel was doing now, and what things were like back on Quarell. She doubted the Bears were in the same dire straits as the Jade Falcons of Sudeten, but she supposed anything was possible. Then she discarded all thoughts of her former home. She had to remind herself that home was where her family was, and that family consisted entirely of Jade Falcons now. All of them on Sudeten. And Khan Jiyi Chistu served as some sort of figurehead of the family, outside of the fact that he led the Clan. He truly had become a personal father figure to them all. Aloof, to be sure, and not always there, but he made the time when he could.

"You are the future of Clan Jade Falcon," he never hesitated to remind them. A new, stronger Jade Falcon, bringing the best of what the Ghost Bears had to its fore without all the decay Alexis had found herself excited to leave behind.

It was only natural.

The *Gyrfalcon*'s large lasers shimmered blue on the screen, consuming much of the ferro-lamellor across the *Savage Wolf*'s right arm. The armor soaked up as much of the damage as it could, but Alexis knew another hit like that and Daniel would be in real trouble.

Star Captain Dawn, their falconer and a wisp of a MechWarrior with freckles dappling her serious, fair face, stood at the front of the viewing room and addressed all assembled. "What would you do if you were in his position?"

Thomasin smirked. "Win."

Sophie laughed at his response, but Alexis didn't. "He is not reading the field or examining his opponent. He is shooting where his opponent was, not striking where they will be."

"How would you correct the situation, Cadet Alexis?" Dawn asked.

Alexis chewed on her bottom lip for a moment before coming up with the answer. "The *Savage Wolf* outmasses and outclasses the *Gyrfalcon*. Yes, the *Gyrfalcon* has greater maneuverability, but the *Savage Wolf* should dominate the field and get in close to leverage its short-range missiles, but not so close as to make itself a nice target. Seriously, Star Captain, by all rights, that *Savage Wolf* should be massacring its opponent."

"You are right, Cadet. Unequivocally." Star Captain Dawn smiled at her, approving of her, not just her answer. There was a kindness to the veteran MechWarrior Alexis had latched onto from her very first day as a Jade Falcon, a camaraderie she couldn't explain.

The Star Captain had been kind when she didn't have to be and had nothing to gain by it, and both had experienced being discarded and then finding a second chance.

They understood each other.

Accepting Dawn's approval, Alexis shifted her attention back to her *sibmate*'s Trial of Position, and considered the fight from the *Gyrfalcon*'s perspective. The 'Mech was piloted by a full Jade Falcon warrior who no doubt had more experience than Daniel. In either case, the size differential between the 'Mechs seemed like a hedge against the Khan's bets. The Clan needed MechWarriors badly. It was why Khan Chistu had come to Quarell looking to take Alexis and her *sibmates* away. She imagined it could have been intimidating to sit in a *Gyrfalcon*, look up at Daniel's looming *Savage Wolf*, and try to come up with a plan to take down the larger 'Mech. But Alexis knew how she would have approached that problem, too.

Before her life in the Clans, she'd spent her entire existence learning how to deal with bigger opponents. Because if she didn't do that, she didn't eat...

ANTIMONY
QUARELL
RASALHAGUE DOMINION
8 SEPTEMBER 3144

The sharp pain in Alexis' stomach reminded her it had been two full days since she'd eaten. Possibly three if she didn't count the crust of bread and moldy soup she'd found the day before that. It hadn't tasted good, but she choked it down.

"That one," Tova said to Alexis, pointing at the woman walking across the street. A thickly built Ghost Bear, swaggering and arrogant in her uniform.

Tova was the ringleader of this little cadre of street rats, starving as they all were. If they couldn't score something huge, they'd all starve sooner or later. That was the worst part about starving. It was a slow death no one should ever have to endure, let alone a group of eight- to twelve-year-olds, all running from a foster system they knew would be worse than the streets of Quarell. Alexis wasn't the youngest among them—that honor went to little Onika—but she had the lightest fingers in the group, and whatever other problems they had with her, they knew she'd get what they pointed her at.

In this case, it was the Ghost Bear's wallet, fat with bear-krona, bulging in the pockets on the side of her pants.

"That's a *Ghost Bear*," she whispered to Tova.

"And you know you can do it."

"What happens if I get caught?"

"Then we'll come back for you."

"Promise?" Alexis asked, making sure.

"Promise."

"Okay."

Alexis darted from the alleyway into the busy thoroughfare outside Antimony's main city center. There were shops everywhere and all manner of activity spilling out into the street. The numerous restaurants made a bouquet of incredible smells, all of it food she couldn't afford. It made her all the hungrier for that wallet.

She had to move quickly because she knew she didn't fit in here. She hadn't had a shower in weeks, and her clothes were crusted with dirt that could only come with sleeping on the street. Ducking behind a pillar, she watched the Ghost Bear stop and talk to someone on the street, laughing at something. Alexis wondered what it would be like to laugh like that, without a care in the world.

Keeping her eyes fixed on the wallet and her surroundings, she knew she needed to be fast. The Ghost Bear was larger than those Alexis would ordinarily choose for a target, impossibly tall and built like a true warrior. The woman's delicate features that reminded Alexis of a mother, but one who could snap her like a twig. Alexis needed to remember that, and either stay the course or reconsider and leave.

She couldn't leave though; she had to do this.

Alexis was small, thankfully, and went unnoticed. Sometimes that worked against her. A Ghost Bear would be trained to feel the absence of their possessions, so she'd need to be quick and use her size to her advantage.

As the Ghost Bear moved on, Alexis scurried forward, making her move. The wallet was there, just inside the pocket. The smell of the food would have been a distraction for any of the other kids, but she focused in on her goal and sharpened her will against everything else.

Bumping into the Ghost Bear provided two sensations simultaneously. The first was a need for haste as her fingers sought to slip the wallet from its pocket. The second was the unmistakable closeness to another human being, which she had not felt in a long time. After being touch starved for so long, even the collision felt as powerful as a hug.

Alexis drew the wallet from the pocket, and her eyes widened. It *was* thick. There was likely enough bear-krona in it to feed her for a month.

But her pick had been snagged by something. Panic filled her when she found her hand stuck.

The Ghost Bear was gripping it tightly.

Alexis struggled to get away before the wallet's owner even saw her. "Let me go."

But it didn't work. That big hand was clamped too tightly around her wrist.

Her mark turned around to regard her, never letting go.

Alexis brought a foot up and tried to kick her away, but the Ghost Bear still wouldn't let go. Alexis was stubborn, too. If this woman wasn't going to let go of her wrist, she wasn't going to let go of the wallet.

She expected the Ghost Bear would be angry, but her face was mute with no reaction. Alexis could typically read people pretty well for her age—she'd had to learn that skill to survive—but she had no idea how her mark would finally break.

But there was no anger from this woman. No reproach. As far as Alexis could tell, she didn't even seem to care.

When the Ghost Bear laughed, Alexis only tried harder to escape and ignore the kindness in her face.

"Hello there," the woman finally said.

Alexis twisted around, doing her best to get away. "Hello yourself."

This only caused the woman to laugh harder. When her laughter, absent any mocking or anger, subsided, she tilted her head curiously. "Where did you come from?"

Alexis groaned, trying to free her wrist, but still unwilling to let go of the wallet. "The street. Now let me go."

Twisting her head, she sought any sign of her street family across the way, barely glimpsing Tova in the alleyway beyond. Making eye contact with her de facto leader, Alexis pleaded for help. For them to come rescue her, just like they said they would.

But Tova merely faded into the alleyway. Never to be seen again.

Alexis wrenched her head back to the Ghost Bear, who only smiled. "I like your moxie, little bear. It amuses me."

"Let me go."

"Are you hungry?"

"I said let me go."

"Where do you live?"

"The street." Ignoring the sting of Tova's betrayal, Alexis gripped the Ghost Bear's wrist, hoping to free her other hand, but her grasp was too tight. The strength of a Clan warrior was no joke.

"Which street?"

"Just let me go, okay?"

"Are you hungry?"

"No, I just ate, now let me go."

"I will feed you, just stop struggling."

"Not on your life."

The Ghost Bear stood there like a stone statue, unmoving, but also unangered.

Alexis couldn't stand it. "Let me *go*!"

The woman's grip only tightened. Then, through that implacable smile, she said, "I do not think so. I know just where to take you."

The tall woman with dark black hair—Star Colonel Aoi Bekker—had kept Alexis locked up in the social worker's interview room for hours. Aoi and the social workers had asked her all manner of questions, some she couldn't answer and some she could but didn't. They wouldn't break her.

No matter how much food these Ghost Bears put in front of her.

At first, she tried to resist eating. Surely they must have poisoned it, or put something in it to make her calm down. Her stomach sounded like a growling dog, which wasn't far from the truth. That sharp pain just behind her belly button could no longer be ignored. Unable to resist, she reached out for the biscuit at the edge of the plate. They wouldn't notice if one biscuit was missing, even if she did dip it in the gravy.

The first bite filled her mouth with a crescendo of tastes unlike anything she'd ever experienced before. The biscuit and butter, smothered in creamy gravy, was the best food she'd ever tasted in her entire life. And it hadn't come out of the garbage.

One biscuit turned into two.

At that point, the damage was done, and the rest of the food just had to be eaten. Maybe she could hide the plate and let them think no one had offered her anything.

Ravenously, she ate.

HAMMARR
SUDETEN
JADE FALCON OCCUPATION ZONE
9 JANUARY 3152

Alexis blinked.

Her thoughts had carried her kilometers away and years ago, to a time before all this, before full bellies and MechWarrior training on a distant planet far from her former home.

She looked around to realize Daniel's Trial of Position had ended. He had scraped by as a MechWarrior in Clan Jade Falcon, but only barely. He had managed to take advantage of his *Savage Wolf*'s additional tonnage and armor, and smashed it against the *Gyrfalcon* until the other pilot had had no advantage at all. The two 'Mechs had blown so much armor off each other that they were both firing into internal systems toward the end. Daniel had shot wildly at his enemy, likely hoping he would get lucky and just end it once and for all. They had ground each other into nothing, but Daniel had made his kill. And a kill was a kill, no matter how sloppy.

As Daniel stepped out of the simulator pod, Star Captain Dawn shook her head. "I would like everyone to welcome MechWarrior Daniel to Clan Jade Falcon."

Polite applause broke out in all corners of the room.

"You are a MechWarrior now, but that was a sloppy kill. You have much to prove if you are to rise higher in this Clan."

Alexis saw in his face all the hallmarks of a complaint ready to spill out, but Daniel—*MechWarrior* Daniel, now—straightened his posture and managed to keep his tongue secure. He would not be starting any fights with Star Captain Dawn, who had shown him nothing but grace, patience, and understanding the entire time they'd known her. She had helped impress on Alexis, Daniel, and anyone else how dire a situation the Jade Falcons were in. And how she had only recently gained rank as a MechWarrior herself. And how Clan Jade Falcon had transformed into something new and better out of the ashes of former Khan Malvina Hazen's follies.

Star Captain Dawn made Alexis feel like she was in the family the Ghost Bears had always promised her.

She took a breath, wondering who would be next to take their Trial of Position, and she did not expect to see Star Captain Dawn lock eyes with her.

"Cadet Alexis. It is your turn. Get in."

Wide-eyed, Alexis nodded.

She knew this moment would come eventually, though she never thought it would be as a Jade Falcon, inside a simulator pod on a planet she'd never even heard of before arriving here. She had always thought she would take her trial in a *Kodiak* in the marshlands of Quarell as a Ghost Bear, a proud and free cadet of the Rasalhague Dominion.

Alexis knew from hard-won experience that you didn't always get what you want.

The darkened simulator pod reeked of sweat. It had a heater to simulate the rising heat of a real 'Mech. In the last trial, Daniel had pushed his *Savage Wolf* to its upper limit since he'd lost so many heat sinks in the fight—a dangerous gamble if he wasn't able to end his enemy.

The controls had been standardized for the trial, and they would all be fighting in a *Savage Wolf*, though the 'Mechs they faced could be randomized. Alexis hoped she got a 'Mech whose loadout she recognized. She'd spent her years in a *sibko* studying all kinds of 'Mechs, but only during the last month had she learned what models the Jade Falcons had to offer. Two weeks ago, she hadn't even known what a *Savage Wolf* was, let alone that it was something the Jade Falcons had developed with Clan Sea Fox. Regardless, it still felt like a solid 'Mech.

She put the neurohelmet on and plugged in the leads to her cooling vest, which would regulate her body temperature and monitor her vital signs. She imagined the *ursari*—no, that wasn't right... She was taught by a Falconer now. Alexis scolded herself and resumed her thought. She imagined the *falconers* would monitor their vital signs throughout the trial to ensure they were meeting the proper physical parameters for a Clan MechWarrior.

After she was strapped in and hooked up, the lights on the console brightened, and the cockpit simulator roared to life.

"Cadet Alexis," Star Captain Dawn said through the comm system. "For the first phase of your trial, you will be facing a *Rifleman*. For your second phase, a *Phoenix Hawk IIC*. And, if you make it to the third phase, a *Gyrfalcon* stands ready to prove your mettle."

Once her combatants were revealed, Alexis started doing the math in her head, and realized her trial was a little more lopsided than

Daniel's had been. But she was a smarter MechWarrior, and she would find her place in her new family. Her *Savage Wolf* outmassed two of her opponents, leaving the *Phoenix Hawk IIC* as the only 'Mech that truly worried her. It was bigger, and its Ultra-class autocannons could blast her to bits. There was every chance she would never have to face it, though. She had to contend with the *Rifleman* first.

If Alexis played her cards right, she could out-range it. Whoever was piloting the *Rifleman* would know that, too, so they wouldn't let her snipe at range for very long. She needed to play it smart, and if she did, she would leave this cockpit a MechWarrior, her head held high as a true, full member of the Jade Falcon *touman*.

Things moved so quickly it felt like she blinked once more and the fight was on.

Alexis angled her 'Mech backward. Keeping to the edge of the engagement zone, she climbed onto a ledge of rocky terrain to get a better vantage point and to hopefully find a sniper's nest. If the worst happened and this turned into a close fight, she'd pound her opponent with short-range missiles. The red carets on her head-up display danced in the distance, drawing her attention to the tiny dot of the *Rifleman* at the other end of the engagement zone.

The opposing 'Mech had found a perch at roughly the same elevation, but as soon as it got a bead on her—well out of range—it ducked back down into the valley, obscured by rock and trees.

"Damn it," she muttered.

She needed to enter the labyrinth of rock valleys to engage or find a higher vantage point. Scanning the topographical map on her HUD, she found just the spot, but it would be a hike to get there. If the *Rifleman* had found the right position, it would be able to get at least one shot on her, but it was a risk she would have to take. The mesa she'd chosen was high and wide enough to support her, but the path was narrow, and it would take every bit of her skill to get there and make the spot work.

That was the whole point of a Trial of Position, right? To test every skill each cadet had, and make sure they would be warriors who would not simply roll over and die in their first engagement.

They had to be the best.

Alexis didn't have a specific interest in being the best, but she *did* have a vested interest in surviving whatever they threw at her. Some—though not all—of her Trueborn *sibmates* were willing to put themselves in danger just to win victory and glory for the Clan. As a freeborn, Alexis had other priorities hardwired into her from a young age: namely, to continue living in the most efficient way possible.

She would do that by eliminating enemies and treating those around her she loved—another concept that seemed foreign to most

Trueborns—with the respect they deserved. For those like Daniel, she would begrudgingly treat them like distant family, who would still likely be there when it mattered.

Angling the *Savage Wolf* up the ledge to reach the mesa was no easy task. It would have been easier if Alexis had been piloting a 'Mech with hand actuators instead of massive PPC arms, but she made do with what she had.

From the high rise in the terrain, Alexis spotted the *Rifleman*. Knowing they would need to close the distance, they were traveling through the maze of ravines and slot canyons. But that gave Alexis the perfect vantage point to take potshots. Thanks to her simulated computer systems and the targeting reticle on her HUD, Alexis found an easy shot to take.

She fired.

Both PPCs blazed a hot white-blue, streaking across the field in two gashing lances toward the *Rifleman*. Like her *Savage Wolf*, the *Rifleman* boasted cannons for arms, too, but the *Rifleman*'s appendages were double barreled, sporting a pair of large lasers and devastating autocannons that would strip the armor from her *Savage Wolf* with relative ease if she allowed it to get too close. Since the *Rifleman* was largely in profile, one of her PPCs shot went wide and disintegrated the nearby rock, but the other hit and melted the *Rifleman*'s torso armor like candle wax.

"That's more like it," Alexis said to herself.

With any luck, she would expose the *Rifleman*'s internal structure with another shot or two. Looking down at the rangefinder, she saw her target was still outside its own range, so she'd be able to get at *least* one more shot in before it could start returning fire.

Lining up her PPCs again, Alexis led the target and fired. The *Rifleman* was moving quickly through the terrain, and getting her shots off was tricky. The pilot was no dummy, and she was going to have to earn her spot in the Clan.

But Alexis always knew that would be the case.

As before, she scored one miss and one hit, though not in the same place. The particle cannon blast ripped at the shoulder of the *Rifleman*, superheating it and tearing at the metal seams.

"Come on," Alexis said. "Why can't anything be easy?"

By that time, the *Rifleman* had gotten within autocannon range, and fired both of them at Alexis.

It was real now.

She was taking fire.

When the first autocannon shell hit, she felt it against the 'Mech, and the situation became dire. With the reality of its feeling and the rising heat, Alexis had to remind herself she was in a simulator.

According to the damage readouts, the blow was a glancing one. The projectile had lacerated a sliver of armor from her *Savage Wolf*'s leg, but nothing that would threaten her success. If the *Rifleman* closed range or its aim got any more accurate, however, she would be in real trouble.

Lining up her next shot, Alexis wondered what would happen if she failed her trial. Would they bust her down to a lower caste? Would they force her to patrol the 'Mech yards with a needler pistol? Would she just end back up on the streets of Sudeten?

She was not about to let that happen.

Reassessing her vantage point, Alexis saw another opening. The *Rifleman* had focused its attention on getting into a position on her right flank, so if she moved left and did her best to corner her opponent from the side, she might be able to find an advantage.

Alexis ran, hopped her *Savage Wolf* down the other side of the mesa, and headed to her left, keeping the *Rifleman* to the rightmost edge of her field of fire. With no jump jets to soften her landing, she hit the ground hard, and the cockpit rocked with the impact. The red caret in her HUD danced in her peripheral vision, keeping her constantly aware of where the *Rifleman* was in relation to her. She knew they were keeping tabs on her in just the same way, looking for any opening. Alexis was still at a higher level than the *Rifleman*, though, and unless her opponent found a path to scrabble up another ten meters of elevation, they would remain at a disadvantage.

Twisting her 'Mech's torso to take a shot, Alexis knew it was a long one. The trees and the change in elevation obscured the *Rifleman*, so really the only thing she had a shot of was its top half.

That was all she needed.

Her PPCs sent lances of lightning across the battlefield, but they obliterated nothing but the trees in the distance, transforming them into giant matchsticks.

Alexis turned again and jumped into the same ravine that— according to her map overlay—the *Rifleman* had wound its way through earlier. Maybe she could come around behind it and get a clear shot at its exposed back. That would be the best-case scenario, but after the life she'd had, she felt more likely to encounter the worst of anything.

She descended the slope to find herself in the same web of canyons as the *Rifleman*.

Though she lost visual on her target, her HUD's red-enemy caret tracked the 'Mech by other means, giving her a general direction to head.

She hated that the computer tagged her fellow Falcons as enemies. She understood it was a trial, and for intents and purposes they *were* the enemy, but they were supposed to be her family, too. The infighting among the Ghost Bears—thanks to the vote to join or refuse membership in the newly formed Star League—had driven a wedge in what it meant to be part of a family. There had always been elements of that family that had not accepted her, of course. The thought of her former Den Mother sent a shudder from the base of Alexis' neck right down her back. Until the vote began dividing folks, the Ghost Bears were, by and large, the welcoming family she had sought on the streets of Quarell.

But the Ghost Bears had lost her, and probably broke apart behind her, for all she knew. It didn't matter; she had the Jade Falcons now.

She turned another corner in the canyon, the red caret getting closer.

"Come on, just give me one good shot at your back..."

Alexis pushed the *Savage Wolf* as much as she could to make all the tight turns in the narrows. It slowed her considerably, but she knew the *Rifleman* faced the same problem.

One more tight turn, and Alexis found herself face-to-face with her foe.

"Shit."

The *Rifleman* had doubled back. She wasn't going to get that shot at its rear; her opponent had her in their sights, ready to blast her. It opened up with everything it had.

Alexis' screen flashed blue-green with the wash of its large and medium lasers, and she practically felt the kick of its autocannon as its rounds hammered into her 'Mech.

Her damage indicators flashed from green to yellow across the board as alarms screeched in her ear. Glancing across her readouts, she found she'd taken a significant amount of damage across her torso and legs. The right leg got the worst of it. If her *Savage Wolf* walked away from this engagement, it would be nothing short of a miracle.

The targeting system toned amid the bedlam, reminding her she had a target lock on the *Rifleman*. Tightening her grip around the triggers, Alexis fired back with everything at her disposal. The short-range missiles peppered the front of the *Rifleman*, exploding in a ragged line across its right arm, the cockpit and torso, and the left arm. Then the blue fury of her particle projection cannons lashed out and liquefied armor across the *Rifleman*'s front, revealing the precious insides of the 'Mech, a skeletal framework of inner workings and myomer muscles.

Alexis gasped at the sight. One or two more shots like that and she would be a MechWarrior, but she would need to stay alive long enough to make the kill.

The *Rifleman* backed up into the canyon.

They were both trapped. There was nowhere to go, so this is where it would end, savagely attacking each other until one was left standing.

Alexis would not go down like this.

With no chance of regaining her range advantage, Alexis charged, hoping her burst of speed might make her a harder target.

The *Rifleman* fired everything it had again—Alexis could only imagine the heat from all those lasers building up and causing problems—and braced herself for the inevitable. More than half of the shots missed, but the remainder obliterated the rest of the armor on her 'Mech's midsection, exposing her own internal structure.

She looked down at her damage indicators and found her center torso flashing a dangerous red. "Damn it."

Alexis took aim at the *Rifleman*'s center mass and fired again, hoping at least one of her shots would have enough of an impact to end this and make her a MechWarrior.

ANTIMONY
QUARELL
RASALHAGUE DOMINION
8 SEPTEMBER 3144

By the time the Ghost Bear Star Colonel came back into the room, Alexis hadn't had time to get rid of the evidence. She merely looked up, her face covered in food like a mangy mutt, and blinked.

"So, you were hungry?"

Alexis sheepishly nodded.

"They tell me you do not have a family," the Star Colonel said, sitting down across from her. "It is all right. Continue eating. Do not let me stop you."

Alexis narrowed her eyes, unsure if she should continue. "I have family."

"Who?" the Ghost Bear fired back.

"My friends," Alexis said matter-of-factly, taking another bite of the crispy breakfast protein.

The Ghost Bear smirked; the look told Alexis everything she needed to know about the Star Colonel. "You mean the friends who left you the second I grabbed you?"

Alexis stopped chewing.

In fact, she didn't feel all that hungry anymore. The hunger in her belly had been filled, but that fullness had been replaced by a sinking feeling. Where had her friends gone? If one of them had been captured instead of her, she would have done everything she could to rescue them. There was no telling if their next trip to the cold and sterile intake centers would be their last. Would they finally fold them into the broken foster-care system? Or just jettison them into space?

Alexis had no idea.

The only thing she felt was alone.

The Star Colonel grinned slyly, a bear that had just caught a salmon. "Would you like to have a real family?"

Confused, Alexis dropped her hands into her lap. "What's that supposed to mean?"

"It means you could become a Ghost Bear. We are a family."

Alexis' head tilted, unsure of what the Star Colonel was actually saying. Perhaps the too-bright lights of the sterile intake room were making her hallucinate.

"The Ghost Bears will take care of you, feed you three meals a day without you having to beg, borrow, or steal. We can be the family you have never had. But in return, you must learn to become a MechWarrior and leave your life on the street behind."

Alexis gulped. Unsure.

The Ghost Bear offered a welcoming hand out. "Is that something you might be interested in?"

Alexis didn't know much about MechWarriors. She'd seen the Ghost Bear BattleMechs doing drills and patrols on the outskirts of Antimony, and the only thing she knew about them was that she needed to stay away. A patrol officer or social worker was dangerous enough, let alone a full-blown BattleMech. They were scary, intimidating, and could end a life in a blink.

But there was power there.

And if all she had to do to find a family and never go hungry was learn to pilot one, it would be a small price to pay.

Alexis mumbled something through a mouthful of food.

"What was that, little one?"

"I said fine. I'll be a MechWarrior."

The Ghost Bear laughed, but there was a warmth to it, like a gentle fire. It held no reproach. "There is more to becoming a MechWarrior than just saying so. You will have to join a *sibko*, a sibling company. Essentially, you will go to school with other Ghost Bears, and if you train properly and study carefully, in eight or ten years, you will pilot a 'Mech and become a proud warrior in our Clan."

Alexis nodded, thinking about the safety and comfort she hoped to find. "If that's what I need to do to be a MechWarrior, I'll do it."

HAMMARR
SUDETEN
JADE FALCON OCCUPATION ZONE
9 JANUARY 3152

"I am a MechWarrior," Alexis said to herself, in complete disbelief.

The *Rifleman* lay in a smoking heap at the feet of her *Savage Wolf*. She'd made it.

But then realization dawned on her.

Looking down at her console, her alarms and damage indicators screamed and flashed. Her 'Mech had also been savaged in the conflict. The MechWarrior in the *Rifleman* had been good. Far better than she had hoped. But that had only been the first phase of her trial.

Red carets and more alarm bells rang in her ear as she realized the next 'Mech of the challenge had already been unleashed. An 80-ton *Phoenix Hawk IIC* stalked her. It was out there somewhere, waiting for her to show her face and blast her to smithereens.

She knew if she could somehow defeat this second 'Mech, she would be awarded the rank of Star Commander. Were she to take down the third 'Mech, she would become a Star Captain. None of those scenarios seemed likely. The *Phoenix Hawk IIC* not only outmassed her, but it hadn't taken a lick of damage, and she was one shot away from being completely out of commission.

Alexis was under no illusions. She would not become a Star Captain, but she would make a show of it by lasting as long as she could against the *Phoenix Hawk IIC*, as a point of personal pride. She would not go down quietly, even if her 'Mech was nothing more than a smoking wreck, armor slagged off and the inner structure exposed. That it could walk at all was a minor miracle, but she would put on a show for the rest of the trial. She would not quit or acquiesce. She was a MechWarrior now.

The *Phoenix Hawk IIC* would be barreling toward her from the far end of the engagement zone. She might have a minute or two before combat started in earnest. On the other hand, her opponent boasted jump jets, making them more agile and able to leap over the simulated terrain to find her all the more quickly. To maximize her advantage, Alexis knew she needed to play things unpredictably. No doubt, her opponent—she still hated thinking of a fellow Jade Falcon as an opponent—would assume she was injured enough to pull back to lick her wounds. Her *Savage Wolf* was a long-range 'Mech, for the most part, so her target would expect her to seek a distant, long-range vantage point and take potshots.

Instead, she did the opposite.

Alexis pushed her battered 'Mech as fast as it would go, right in the direction of the enemy.

Sometimes the most unpredictable course of action was the best. When outmatched and severely disadvantaged, the element of shock and surprise could still go a long way.

"I'm coming for you," she said to the *Phoenix Hawk IIC* pilot, as though they could hear her across the simulated battlefield. "And I'm not going to make it easy."

COPPERTON
QUARELL
RASALHAGUE DOMINION
10 SEPTEMBER 3144

"Where are we?" Alexis asked, staring out the window of the hovercar.

"This," Star Colonel Aoi Bekker said, "is the *sibko* training facility where you will learn to be a MechWarrior."

"Oh" was all Alexis said. More than anything, she hoped they had food as good as what she had had back in Antimony. She hated that her stomach did her thinking for her, but a full stomach felt *safe* somehow. She didn't know how else to describe it.

The facility looked like a cross between a warehouse and an elaborate school complex. The emblem of a screaming ghost bear, surrounded by six clawing paws pinwheeling in a circle around it, was writ large on the side of the building. Any who approached would have an easy time assuming what could be found inside.

Star Colonel Bekker led Alexis from the car and marched her up to the building's main entrance. The doors—made of thick, mirror-tinted glass—slid open on their approach.

Everything seemed so large to Alexis, so overwhelming. Buildings scared her. They were so big and imposing, and there were much fewer places to escape if she needed to.

"It is all right, little bear," the Star Colonel said in a matronly tone. Just enough to comfort her. "Once you walk through those doors, your life will be forever changed. You will leave behind your last name, your previous life, and everything you held dear. But in its place, you will find commitment to a cause and your *sibmates,* who all aim to be the best of the best. It will be dangerous at times. Sometimes it will be lonely. But if you make it through, you will never want for any of your basic needs again."

Alexis didn't quite know why the Star Colonel was saying all of this to her until she realized her feet had stopped right at the threshold of the door. Something, some invisible force, stopped her from taking one step further.

Alexis looked up to the Star Colonel, suspicious, trying to read her face. If there was one thing Star Colonel Bekker was, it was consistent. There was still no hint of disappointment or any feeling that this was all a trap. To Alexis, the Star Colonel felt nothing but genuine, and that was something she'd never been able to trust before.

"What happens to me if I don't make it?"

Bekker offered a wry smile. "If you wash out of training, you will still be in a higher caste than you are now. That will grant you more opportunities than the street will. And if you happen to die in training—"

"That happens?"

Bekker nodded. "It happens, yes. Being a MechWarrior is dangerous, but training to become one is equally so. And if you die, then you will be mourned as a Ghost Bear rather than left in the street. You have nowhere to go but up, little bear."

Alexis looked back into the building, a sprawling complex, bigger than she could have imagined.

The Star Colonel stood beside her. "Shall we?"

Finally, Alexis nodded, and the two of them stepped inside.

The Star Colonel led Alexis through hallways, up a staircase, and through more hallways. Alexis wasn't sure where they were going or why, but she knew she'd made her choice. She was going to be a Ghost Bear, and they would make her a MechWarrior, and she would never feel small or hungry ever again.

Finally, their path ended in a conference room. Facing the door was a trio of instructors.

Star Colonel Bekker pointed to each one as she spoke.

"Alexis, I would like you to meet the parents of your new family. These are *ursari*, the trainers that will instruct you in the ways of the MechWarrior. Your Den Mother is Star Captain Enrique Hawkins. For now, he is in charge of your *sibko's ursari*. To his left is Star Commander Nobu, and to the right is Star Commander Sasha. Listen to them, and you will do well."

Alexis didn't know if she was expected to say something, but the Den Mother smiled and broke the silence with a firm tone. "Thank you, Star Colonel Bekker. Alexis, I want to formally welcome you to the Bearclaws. From what the Star Colonel has told me, you are new to Clan life, so we will do everything we can to make sure you have the best possible chance to become a MechWarrior."

"Thank you," Alexis said, trying to stay polite. She knew being polite in situations with authority figures was an easy way to curry favor and make them underestimate her. She wanted them to underestimate her. She wanted them to think she couldn't take care of herself. It was easier to get what you wanted if no one expected you to be competent.

The Den Mother turned to Star Commander Sasha, a severe-looking woman with sharp lines all the way down her uniform. Alexis had underestimated Star Colonel Bekker's height: Star Commander Sasha was now the tallest woman she had ever seen. Her hair was a white-blond that matched the blue ice of her penetrating eyes.

"Star Commander Sasha," the Den Mother said, "please show Alexis to the barracks and welcome her to the family."

"*Aff*," the Star Commander said. But there was no love in her voice, and for the first time since Alexis had made her decision to become a MechWarrior, she wondered if she'd made a mistake.

HAMMARR
SUDETEN
JADE FALCON OCCUPATION ZONE
9 JANUARY 3152

Alexis had not yet made visual confirmation of the *Phoenix Hawk IIC* stalking her. If she could spot her opponent first, she would have the element of surprise, and that was her only chance to advance to the next phase of her trial. A slim chance, she knew, but she was going to give it everything she had.

If she could somehow pull off a miracle, she would eliminate any doubt in Daniel's mind that she was his better and he should have trusted her all those years. They had spent so much of their *sibko* training with a strange tension between them—her trying to prove herself and him seeming so entitled to everything. She had tried, over and over and over again, to prove herself to her entire *sibko*, and it never stuck with all of them. Maybe she could remove the doubts from their minds once and for all.

Her *Savage Wolf* might have been a simulation in a computer, but it creaked and groaned like a real 'Mech with that much damage would have done. The computer must have registered several heat sinks as damaged, because even through her cooling vest the heat grew more and more oppressive. Alexis wished she could wipe the sweat from her brow as it beaded above her eyes and threatened to interfere with her aim, but her neurohelmet got in the way. She didn't like running 'Mechs hot, but with as much damage as she'd taken, she had no choice.

Pressing on, Alexis scrabbled up another rise, hoping to get some visual on the enemy 'Mech. Then she cursed herself again for thinking of the *Phoenix Hawk IIC* as an enemy. The pilot was a Jade Falcon and part of her extended Clan family. She couldn't allow herself to think about her family as enemies, even in an exercise—she'd learned that lesson the hard way. They were a whetstone to sharpen the blade of her skills, working together, not as opposing forces.

No matter how she thought about it, she still had to fire on them.

But she had to *see* them first.

Her HUD offered no help, nor did any of the other imaging views she cycled through. Where had her opponent gone? It wasn't in her forward view anymore, and she'd lost track of the red caret. Had the terrain between her and her target confused her sensors somehow?

"Show yourself," she whispered at the screen.

But no 'Mech appeared.

So she kept moving.

Cat and mouse.

Falcon and prey.

From the edge of her vision, she saw it. A barrage of autocannon rounds passed by her from behind and exploded in a crackling pattern on the forest in front of her.

The *Phoenix Hawk IIC* was behind her. *That* was why she'd lost track of it.

Glancing to the right of her compressed display, she saw it: the top of the *Phoenix Hawk IIC* obscured by tree cover, smoking from the launch of the missiles. Somehow she and her opponent had covered the entire distance and traded places on each other's side of the map.

"Clever."

Alexis' targeting computer instantly tagged the 'Mech now that it knew where it was, but she didn't stop to fight. Instead, she pushed the *Savage Wolf* back down into the system of red-rock ravines and sprinted through them. She had to outthink the MechWarrior in the *Phoenix Hawk IIC*. No doubt they expected her to run headlong toward them, wanting to close the distance and get a sure shot. If she did that, the pilot might jump to try staying behind her.

Alexis took a gamble.

She was already a MechWarrior and had nothing to lose, but if she read her opponent's mind sufficiently, she should turn around and get ready for an ambush.

The turn was tight in the canyon, but she made it and stepped forward.

Her hands, slick with sweat, gripped the firing controls and throttle, ready for anything.

Alexis took a deep breath...

...and the *Phoenix Hawk IIC* landed right in front of her, the perfect range for her missiles *and* her PPCs.

"Yes..."

Her targeting reticle turned a rich gold, and Alexis let loose with everything she had the moment the *Phoenix Hawk IIC*'s feet touched the ground. Her target had the same idea and fired a barrage at her, too.

Her 'Mech listed forward, the damage indicators flashing hard and bright enough to cause a seizure. When her *Savage Wolf* started to topple forward, the control console in front of her went dark, all of the blinking lights and dancing displays shutting off.

The screen faded to black before she could see the fate of the enemy 'Mech.

All Alexis knew was that she had done her best, and she hoped her family would be proud.

COPPERTON
QUARELL
RASALHAGUE DOMINION
10 SEPTEMBER 3144

To Alexis, walking side by side with one of her new "parents," the whole place made her feel as though she were pulling the biggest grift of her life. She had somehow convinced them to take her in and let her become a warrior. That alone would keep her fed for the rest of her life. In the long run, the risk and the danger would all be worth it.

No matter how short her life would be.

The *ursari*, Star Commander Sasha, felt dangerous to a point, but Alexis assumed any warrior in Clan Ghost Bear would feel dangerous. They were trained from birth to kill. Weren't they?

"I admire what the Star Colonel is doing," Star Commander Sasha said as they walked through the long, brightly lit hallway.

But Alexis didn't get the impression the Star Commander wanted a response. She offered no question in her tone and no question mark on her sentence. Not even the odd *"quiaff"* or *"quineg"* the Clanners liked to use.

"I really do," the Star Commander continued, assuring Alexis she had made the right decision to not respond. "It is noble to try elevating a survivor like yourself to warrior status."

Alexis sensed a *but* coming, and it came soon enough.

"But you are at such a disadvantage. Not even taking into account that you are a freebirth, the Bearclaws have been together since their days in the nursery dens, a close-knit crèche from the beginning."

Silence crept back into their long walk, and Alexis felt moved to say something, to defend herself somehow. She had a chance. Of course she did. She was at least as smart as those kids, surely. They'd never had to survive like she had, and surely that counted for something.

Alexis raised her head. "I will do my best, Star Commander."

Star Commander Sasha smiled, but Alexis could not tell if it was full of smugness or simply patronizing. Perhaps she even meant it. "Do not get your hopes up. You have found yourself a place to land for the moment, but you will have many grueling days ahead, and you are behind in every way. You have had no formal education whatsoever, *quiaff*? These Bearclaws are the best of what Clan Ghost Bear has to offer, raised from iron wombs to be our best. If you can keep up at all, you will have my respect."

The words stung, but Alexis clenched her jaw, determined to earn the *ursari*'s respect. "I will work twice as hard."

"It will take at least that to catch up. We will do our best to help you overcome your disadvantages. The Star Colonel demands it. But take heart. Even if you make it all the way to a Trial of Position, you surely will not pass. But the life of someone in the paramilitary forces or even the local constabulary is a better life than you would have had on the street."

"I will be a MechWarrior."

Star Commander Sasha smirked. "We will see, young one. Now, here we are."

They stopped in front of a classroom, a window looking in on the students. Another *ursari* was at the front of the class, reviewing holographic footage of a fight between two BattleMechs Alexis could not identify, but she knew that problem would be short-lived. She would learn everything there was to learn about piloting 'Mechs.

The door to the classroom slid open, and the eyes of all the students shifted from the instruction to her.

Star Commander Sasha stepped into the room and remained at Alexis' side.

"Bearclaws," she said, "this is Alexis. She is a freebirth snatched from the streets of Antimony. Star Colonel Aoi Bekker thinks she would do well in the Ghost Bears, and has insisted we accept her into the Bearclaws."

A murmur from the assembled class of children—all about her own age, dressed in matching light-blue uniforms and short haircuts—worried her.

"They will just let anyone in now, *quiaff*?" a kid in the front row sneered.

Half the class snickered with him until the instructor shushed them and scolded the student responsible. "Daniel," the instructor said. "Hold your tongue."

"*Aff*, Star Commander," he said with a complete lack of remorse in his voice.

Alexis knew she would have to keep an eye on that one.

The instructor, a man with darker skin and a kindlier face than Sasha, smiled at Alexis, a balm on her heart after the terror of being made fun of. "Welcome, Alexis. Please take a seat, there is one in the back. We will see about catching you up as best we can." Then he turned to Star Commander Sasha. "Thank you for bringing her here, Star Commander. We will take good care of her."

"I am sure." Star Commander Sasha tried to mask her expression, but Alexis was positive she almost rolled her eyes.

She looked around for the empty seat and found it right at the back of the room.

The march all the way there was mortifying and terrible. She had to put her back to those who had made fun of her, and that felt wrong somehow. It was a relief to have her back to the wall as she settled into her chair between two other students, a boy and a girl.

"Pay him no mind," the boy leaned in to say to Alexis as the instructor readied to restart the lesson.

"Yeah," the girl said from the other side.

"They think they are great because they have the best test scores, but test scores are not everything." The boy left her unconvinced, but at least he was willing to be friendly. "I am Thomasin. It is my pleasure to meet you, Alexis."

"I am Sophie," the girl said.

Alexis looked over to Sophie and found a piece of home in her face. This could be a family.

"No matter what they say, you are a Ghost Bear now," Sophie said.

"They don't seem to act like it," Alexis said, waving her hand to indicate the front of the room.

"You will see," Thomasin said.

The difference between Star Colonel Bekker's demeanor and Star Commander Sasha's, between the treatment from Daniel and his ilk compared to Thomasin and Sophie, was so great that Alexis found it difficult to reconcile. It hurt her head. The confusion between being welcomed and reviled all at the same time hurt her heart.

She knew she would have to be better than the best if she wanted to survive. And if the life of a street thief had taught her anything, it was how to go unnoticed when she wanted to.

Maybe she could just disappear until she became a MechWarrior.

From the front of the classroom, Daniel snickered again. "She could never be better than me. That freebirth will wash out fast, mark my words."

The *ursari* did not correct him.

HAMMARR
SUDETEN
JADE FALCON OCCUPATION ZONE
9 JANUARY 3152

Alexis stepped out of the simulator pod, shocked by the applause and happy faces.

The din of voices confused her.

"I cannot believe she did it—"

"—amazing—"

"What a shot—"

"Did you see that?"

"Wow!"

Bewildered, Alexis sought the friendly faces of Thomasin and Sophie and found them near to bursting with excitement. "What is everyone so happy for?"

Neither Thomasin nor Sophie had an answer for her.

Daniel muscled through the crowd and put a victorious hand on Alexis' shoulder. He strained to smile through the sting in his pride. "I knew you would do it."

Alexis figured it was not worth reminding him that, until up to six months ago, he had told her at every available opportunity that she would *never* be a MechWarrior—ever, no ifs, ands, or buts.

The crowd of onlookers parted and silenced at the arrival of Star Captain Dawn, her face solemn and stern. "Let me be the first to say congratulations..."

She paused for a moment, and time stood still for Alexis. The next words out of the Star Captain's mouth made no sense.

"...Star Commander."

Alexis looked behind her, wondering what she had missed. "Who?"

Dawn gripped Alexis' hand as if to shake it, but she could no longer contain herself and gripped Alexis into a bear hug instead. "I am so proud of you, little bear."

For her part, Alexis remained puzzled.

It wasn't until later, when they showed her the holographic battleROM footage, that she understood what had happened. And when she saw, it truly took her breath away.

From the cockpit of her *Savage Wolf*, all she had been able to see was the explosion and the blackness when her 'Mech's systems had seized. But on the battleROM replay in the dimmed lights, she saw an exterior view of the fight.

Her *Savage Wolf* pushed forward, and the *Phoenix Hawk IIC* dropped down from the sky. There was a pregnant pause, and Alexis couldn't tell if it was something created by whoever manipulated the battleROM on the screen, or if time had stopped on the battlefield, too.

Both 'Mechs unleashed everything in their arsenals. Alexis watched the *Phoenix Hawk IIC*'s Ultra autocannon shots smash into her *Savage Wolf* as her own missiles corkscrewed from their launch tubes and the dual PPC shots slashed blue across the field.

Her eyes focused on the *Phoenix Hawk IIC*.

The missiles clustered tight, crackling all over the *Phoenix Hawk IIC*'s cockpit.

Then the PPC strikes.

Right to the 'Mech's face.

Headshot.

Headshot.

As her *Savage Wolf* tilted forward, succumbing to the damage, so too did the *Phoenix Hawk IIC*.

She knew she'd wanted to hurt the *Phoenix Hawk IIC*, and every MechWarrior aims for the best shot possible, but it was never easy. And even when one's aim was solid—assisted by the targeting computer or not—the chances of two shots in the same salvo cracking the canopy of a 'Mech simultaneously was astronomical.

No wonder they kept calling her Star Commander.

She had made two kills.

She *was* a Star Commander.

Salty tears welled at the edges of her eyes, and her heart fluttered to the top of her chest.

She was a *Star Commander*.

"Well done, little Ghostbird," a booming voice said from the edge of the room.

The battleROM winked off, the lights brightened, and everyone in the room snapped to silent attention.

From her own vantage, Alexis could not see what everyone was reacting to, but did an about-face to see.

And there he stood just inside the room, his hands kept close behind his back.

Jiyi Chistu.

Khan of the Jade Falcons.

The normally pensive look on his face had been replaced by the hard, uplifting lines of celebration. "I knew from the moment I heard you challenge me over the comm that you would make something of yourself. I can see your spirit, and it is bright."

Alexis bowed slightly, unsure of the protocol now that she was a Star Commander. "Thank you, my Khan."

"Dark days are coming. Our greatest trials are ahead of us. But I am glad you will be a fully fledged warrior in my *touman*."

Alexis bit the inside of her lip, hoping it would keep her from blushing at the compliment from the leader of her Clan.

"You shall earn your Bloodname yet, little bird. Star Commander Alexis Zarnofsky. I like the sound of that."

Alexis could hardly believe he remembered her first name, let alone the surname she had been forced to abandon when entering the Clans. Jiyi Chistu was too important, too busy to remember such a thing.

And yet he had.

The Khan turned to the ranking falconer in the room. "Star Captain Dawn, see to it that our new Star Commander has her choice of MechWarriors for her Star. And I am assigning her to your Binary."

"*Aff*, my Khan."

"Also, as her ransom, she will need a 'Mech." He smiled, devious twinkles in his eyes. "See to it that she is given a *Turkina*."

"*Aff*, my Khan."

Jiyi Chistu looked back to Alexis, the pride evident on his face. "The family of our Clan matters, *quiaff*?"

"*Aff*," Alexis said.

"We never want to forget where we come from, do we?"

"*Aff*," Alexis said.

"In the coming days of challenge, we will all need the reminders of our past and the new paths we forge. May the stars light the way of our future."

The Khan looked back to Star Captain Dawn and nodded at her in appreciation. Then, he turned back to Alexis, and his smile grew even wider.

"Welcome, Star Commander Alexis, to Clan Jade Falcon."

She bit down on her lip even harder, this time to keep from smiling and crying. She looked back and forth to the family around her, new and old—Thomasin and Sophia, Daniel and Dawn—and she knew she was in the right place.

And as for that *Turkina*, she knew exactly what she was going to name it...

COCKPIT AMENITIES IN MODERN BATTLEMECHS

[OR WHEN YOU GOTTA GO, YOU GOTTA GO]

WUNJI LAU

A Ceres Metals Industries InfoTrid
[*with actual useful info from me, Chief Tech Agnus Sitompul*]
August 3151

For more than seven centuries, the armies of humanity have benefited from the strategic flexibility of fusion-powered war machines that can march tirelessly across a planet without rest or refueling.

Less enthusiastic about the prospect of weeks-long treks through hostile territory are those machines' pilots, who are invariably far less self-sustaining and indefatigable than their stoic avatars. [*Put simply: 'Mech strong, meat weak.*]

MechWarriors can find themselves stuck in their cockpits for hours, or even days, and in many cases don't know how long they'll be buttoned up when they launch. In hostile-environment operations, deep-recon missions, or extended pursuits, cockpit time has been known to stretch into weeks. The strain can be enormous, both physically and mentally.

Most BattleMechs can keep a pilot alive in a sealed cockpit for about 96 hours, in terms of oxygen, hydration, temperature, and pressurization. [*"Alive" doesn't mean comfortable, healthy, or sane.*] Generally, cockpits provide a basic suite of pilot comforts. [*Emphasis on "basic."*] This usually includes some storage space, a foldaway toilet, a water source, waste isolation or disposal, and enough space for an average-sized person to stretch out and at least partially recline. The quality of these features varies widely, but numerous manufacturer options, aftermarket modifications, and unofficial alterations are

available, some of which are described in this presentation. [*It's almost always less expensive and more effective for owners and operators to rig their own bespoke modifications—assuming they have a good relationship with their hopefully competent techs.*]

Pilots often supplement built-in amenities with their own personal accessories, such as inflatable pillows, toiletry packs, chemical-shower bags, stim crunchies, and so on. These are highly varied and outside the scope of this trid series. [*Although wet wipes are so universally useful that a lot of tech crews just toss a pack in the storage bin before every sortie. Better to have 'em and not need 'em...*]

CLAN COCKPITS

Pre-Republic Clan cockpits tend to have few (or sometimes none) of the features mentioned in this presentation. With little need for spare clothes, survival packs, or even toilet facilities, given the nature of most combat trials and Clan-style deployments, storage space is meager, and ceiling clearance is only a few centimeters (despite some dramatized media depicting Clan 'Mechs as having cavernous accommodations). Jump-seat space in Clan 'Mechs is often little more than an unpadded maintenance crawlway.

When Inner Sphere troops first captured Clan 'Mechs in 3050, their elation at inspecting the wondrous, advanced machines was quickly leavened with dismay at the prospect of spending more than a few hours sealed inside their coffinlike cockpits. [*After the Battle of Wolcott, Combine techs busted their butts trying to modify Clan cockpits, but didn't get far. For much of the last century, pilots of Clan 'Mechs on long sorties pretty much accepted cramps, insomnia, panic attacks, and awkwardly located infections as the price of technological edge.*]

The Sea Foxes now offer [*Expensive!*] services to reconfigure older Clan 'Mechs with larger cockpits, and due to the Clans' adaptation to Inner Sphere warfare (and markets), most new Clan-manufactured 'Mechs are constructed with increased crew space. However, the cockpits of Clan-exclusive chassis are still noticeably spartan compared to Inner Sphere machines.

ERGONOMICS

Claustrophobia is an exceedingly common root cause for MechWarrior training washouts, but the necessities of building a battleworthy machine almost always prioritize sturdiness and compactness over comfort.

Seat Mobility: A requirement for spending more than a few hours inside a cockpit is the ability to stretch and reposition. Even the smallest Inner Sphere-built cockpits have enough space for most people to straighten either their arms or legs, if not both. Most seats recline and slide, and top-end models (common on assault and command 'Mechs like the *BattleMaster* and *Atlas*) also rotate and convert to full-length sleeping modes.

While Clan command couches are comfortable, exceptionally shock-resistant, and minutely adjustable to perfectly fit their occupant (albeit with specialized alterations for the occasional Elemental or aerospace-phenotype MechWarrior), they are not designed for relaxing or stretching, making them excellent for short, high-stress excursions but extremely restrictive for anything longer than a few hours. Panels and controls are placed for maximum accessibility, greatly improving pilot efficiency in battle, but are painfully obstructive when trying to nap or stretch.

Although ejection-seat mountings are by no means universal, enough commonality exists for pilot seats to be generally transferable between 'Mechs, with sufficiently skilled techs and adapter parts. There are also numerous aftermarket kits and informal modifications to add features to basic seat models. [*The trick is getting the modifications to work without impacting the function of the ejection-seat system. This is delicate and time-consuming work, since it's literally holding the pilot's life. A full lay-back hinge-and-slide system isn't worth it if fails during an ejection and makes the pilot kiss their own toenails.*]

Container Holders: Surprisingly rare in stock 'Mech cockpits, these come in a wide array of aftermarket add-ons and kits, but all serve the same basic function: securing cups, mugs, bowls, and other containers while the 'Mech is in motion. For most uses, a simple wire clamp suffices, but given the rank and prestige of many MechWarriors, it is no surprise that options exist for temperature regulation, gyro-linked position-keeping, and automatic refilling. [*At this point, it's assumed they don't bother including these stock because there are so many ways a tech crew can rig one up. The first mod most apprentices solo is some kind of cupholder. Materials are usually easy to find or adapt, but sometimes, folks have to get really creative. Saw one made out of stacked, hollowed-out hooves on a busted-up pirate 'Mech a while back. Guess that was the only part of the horse they couldn't eat.*]

Folding Work Surface: Monitors and noteputers are staples of information delivery and analysis, but millennia of advancements have still not replaced the jotting down of notes as the go-to thinking aid for soldiers under pressure. Standard in command 'Mechs and occasionally seen in other machines, these items usually incorporate a small pocket to hold paper, writing utensils, and a noteputer. [*Cut a hole in the corner of the desk. Attach an end section of PC562 covering.*

Voila, a collapsible, insulated cupholder. You can even add a locking hinge to the desk, making the cupholder usable while the rest of the desk is stowed. Some techs like to round off the desk's edges in case it busts loose in combat, but I've never heard of that actually saving anyone's life. If the cockpit's bouncing hard enough to pop the desk brackets, the pilot's probably already halfway to the consistency of a cheese blintz.]

SUSTENANCE

While pilots can and do survive on ration bars and recycled water, access to tastier fare does wonders for morale and combat performance.

Hydration Systems: Heat is a critical concern for MechWarriors, even out of combat, making hydration an oft-mandated checklist item during sorties. The still-common head-and-shoulders neurohelmet designs often incorporate a flexible drinking tube fed from one or more onboard reservoirs. More streamlined neurohelmets, such as those of Clan design, often lack this feature but usually have movable faceplates that sidestep the problem. A few available kits add switchovers, enabling the dispensing of various beverages through the helmet drinking tube.

[*Unnecessary distractions. You want a naranji smoothie, wait till it's safe to take your helmet off. A more useful mod for the hydration system is to move the reservoir to take advantage of any onboard cold areas, like the three big, chilled coil chambers on a* Thunder Hawk, *or the independent cooling unit on a* Cyclops' *computer bay.*]

Storage: It's essentially impossible to keep an entire 'Mech or even its cockpit cool, but it's less of a problem to chill small spaces and isolated areas like Gauss coils and laser capacitors. Made from high-efficiency insulation wrapped in an impact-resistant polymer shell, a combat refrigerator like the Quikscell CryoCrate will keep about 3,000 ccs of material chilled to just above 0° C. It draws power from the same sources as other cockpit systems and expels its minor waste heat into the main heat-exchange system. It is small enough to fit in most storage spaces, even in the tiny allotment provided in Clan cockpits (if only barely). [*People ask me, "Why don't they just make the whole cockpit out of the same stuff they make my drink cooler out of?" Those people are dumb. That said, I've seen some cockpits rigged with emergency switchovers that flush the CryoCrate's output into the pilot's cooling suit. It's not much, but there are times when ten extra seconds of consciousness is worth losing a six-pack of Timbiqui Dark.*]

Food Preparation: Small microwave and convection cookers are not uncommon in 'Mechs; the smallest examples fit only compact ration packs, but also take up less space than a box of spice crisps. Best used when the 'Mech is stationary (and preferably in auto-balancing maintenance mode so that the pilot can remove their neurohelmet), these devices can be quite large and elaborate, and combined with other cockpit amenities, enable the preparation of surprisingly complex dishes, pastries, and even cocktails. [*People joke about the Lyrans, but every military has people who insist on treating their cockpit like a mobile liquor lounge. They'll never admit it, but even the Clanners have a few combat alcoholics.*]

At the top end of the cockpit culinary hierarchy is the TharHes AuroChef, a set of armored cabinets totaling over 90 kilos that fold out into a multitiered array of prep boards, cooktops, high-grade utensils, and individually climate-controlled storage bins. The AuroChef, used in conjunction with a fully rotating pilot seat, replaces a cockpit's usual jump-seat area, and it must be hard-mounted to the cockpit bulkhead. [*The adverts claim the included utensils double as combat tools and weapons. Ha! Imagine a 130-kilo Duke of Whatsit heaving himself out of an* Atlas *cockpit to stab a Clan Elemental with an escargot fork!*]

The ever-popular *Fusion Casing Cookbook*, currently in its ninth edition, provides techniques, recipes, and safety tips for using various parts of a fusion-powered vehicle's power system for cooking, but the reality is that such meal-preparation opportunities are rare. Usually, if a more convenient canteen or camp meal is unavailable, a pilot is buttoned up in their cockpit due to combat readiness or hazardous environments. Still, the book is a perennially popular gift for academy graduates and troops on extended deployments. [*I'd recommend a cheap copy of a cookbook for itinerant workers or dormitory residents. They have many of the same space, ingredient, and equipment restrictions as MechWarriors. There's a kinship in cutting random vegetables with a multitool to make reconstituted noodle soup with a hotplate or boiling vessel while stuck inside a room the size of a broom closet.*]

HYGIENE

The smell in a cockpit becomes unbearable after only a few hours of combat. Soldiers learn to adapt, of course, but there is no question that such unpleasantness is detrimental to alertness, morale, and overall health. Some 'Mechs with upgraded life-support equipment feature dedicated space for waste disposal and dispensing of potable water (gathered or recycled from reactor reservoirs), enabling the use of water for washing, disinfecting, and even minor laundering. Most MechWarriors, however, must rely on using their cockpit storage to bring cloths, sanitizers, deodorant, and other necessaries. [*For any number of reasons, some pilots just need more space for privy usage. Since most MechWarriors don't get to pick their ride, we have to do what we can to help them use what they've got. Usually it's pretty simple, like shifting some storage bins to allow more legroom. Sometimes, though, we have to rebuild a whole bulkhead and reroute nearby systems, which can be a bear in machines like a* Vindicator *or* Grasshopper*.]*

Clan cockpits and many smaller Inner Sphere cockpits lack space for a separate toilet, prompting creative solutions. Diapers and waste packs are an option, but only as a stopgap. A common retrofit to older designs places a retracting waste tube under the pilot seat itself. The pilot slides forward in their seat, extends the tube, and after defecating, flushes the tube with water. [*We call it the Skidmark, because, well, that's what you get. Most tech crews cut a custom-fit seat cover out of spare materials and store it in the back of the pilot's seat. Placed properly, it catches any...excess, and the pilot can then just roll the thing up and stuff it in a sealable waste bag for cleanup back at base. It takes up extra space, but it'll get a pilot through a couple more days in the sarcophagus.*]

MICROGRAVITY

All of the systems described above are available in versions useable in microgravity conditions. [*In fact, most of this stuff is actually derived from ancient aerospace cockpit systems. Long before BattleMechs, space pilots were already used to dealing with long hauls in cramped compartments.*] Costs vary, but since the systems must usually be designed from the ground up for use in space, a tenfold (or greater) price increase is not unusual. Snow Raven 'Mechs in particular are notable for having zero-g cockpit equipment. While space-operation modifications are available from nearly every 'Mech and aerospace manufacturer, equipment imported from the Raven Alliance is often considered the most reliable. [*This is one area where you really don't want to mess around. A water leak on the ground is a mess. The same leak in space can drown a pilot in less than a liter of liquid. Buy the good stuff.*]

This concludes this introductory presentation. For more information on the products and topics introduced here, please proceed to CMETTE Volumes 733–984. [*And if you actually plan on selling this stuff to anyone in the field, come on down to the bays for a few weeks. After a stint scrubbing waste filters, you'll be ready to preach to any customer who's waffling about springing for a high-end toilet system. Just remember to bow instead of shaking hands for a few weeks, until the smell fades.*]

UNIT DIGEST: FIRST KEARNY HIGHLANDERS

ÉTIENNE CHARRON-WILLARD

Nickname: Tradition's Weight
Affiliation: Mercenary
CO: Colonel Cadha Jaffray (*Highlander* HGN-732)
XO: Lieutenant Colonel Luis McNamara (*Grasshopper* GHR-8K)
Average Experience: Elite/Fanatical
Force Composition: 1 reinforced heavy 'Mech regiment, 1 battle armor battalion, 1 medium aerospace fighter wing
Unit Abilities: Esprit de Corps, Highlander Burial, Forcing the Initiative
Parade Scheme: When not in appropriate camouflage, the First Kearny paints its units in a flat green. The Stuart Tartan is always proudly displayed on the right torso, shoulder, wing, or side of any combat unit. Family crests may be displayed on the right leg, right wing, or front of a vehicle.

UNIT HISTORY

In late 3150, a two-pronged invasion of Northwind came to an explosive end: Northwind had prevailed. Barely taking time to rearm, many of the most loyal defenders—the First Kearny and over a battalion of the newly formed Grey Watch—immediately joined Countess Tara Campbell in departing for Terra, ready to fight in its defense. Their return a few months later was not celebrated with parades and fanfare. Veterans of the Battle of Terra grimly relayed a tale of bloody, planet-wide fighting and of their countess forced to swear fealty to a man now styling himself ilKhan. Tara Campbell had held the Highlanders together after the chaos of the Blackout, but now-Colonel Cadha Jaffray explained the hard truth of the situation: Exarch Devlin Stone and the

Republic of the Sphere had taken their last breaths. Campbell wasn't coming back, and Northwind was truly alone once more.

This news was taken by clan elders and Luis McNamara, CO of the Twelfth Hastati Sentinels, with a combination of soft grief and hard pragmatism. Though the loss of their beloved countess was distressing, Tara's younger sister, Arabel Campbell-Stewart, bravely stepped forward to fill the large shoes that had been left behind. Even so, Northwind was now a solitary, injured planet besieged by predators on all sides. Not only were renewed Liao or Kurita assaults stark possibilities, but the so-called ilKhan could just as easily launch an offensive to capture worlds that had once belonged to the Republic. Northwind had no allies left to call on, and its HPG, heavily damaged months prior, could not be used to seek help. In addition to the devastation wrought across Northwind's cities, morale was low and the world faced significant economic decline.

Cadha Jaffray refused to let civilian malaise push her Highlanders toward a tired sense of defeat. She had briefly commanded the First Kearny before the Republic's formation, and her fiercely ambitious vision for the unit saw her take action to return it to its elite roots. She conferred with Brigadier General McNamara, convincing him that with no state left to vow loyalty to, his regiment should be brought under her command for the sake of Northwind. Many in the Twelfth Hastati had served in the First Kearny years earlier, so for them, this operational transfer was a welcome return home. Hastati infantry and 'Mech forces were fully integrated, and the boom in materiel and personnel allowed Jaffray to re-form the First Gurkha battle armor battalion, which was immediately plunged into an intensive training regimen. The Twelfth's armor assets were folded into the Grey Watch as part of a compromise made with Northwind's clan elders: the regiment would remain defensive in nature, always ensuring Northwind had the protection it deserved.

The First Kearny, barely more than a battalion before the Battle of Terra, was now over a regiment in size, and filled with some of the most experienced soldiers in the Inner Sphere. Countess Campbell-Stewart knew, however, that Northwind, regardless of the skill of its defenders, could not hope to stand strong as long as it remained alone. The Highlanders needed allies who could lend their support to the planet and its people. The Capellan Confederation and Draconis Combine were out of the question, as the recent fighting for Northwind was still too raw a point for anything but hostility to come from either state. Likewise, any feelers sent anti-spinward would inevitably draw the eye of the ilClan and its troops, whom no one wanted business with. Traders passing through Northwind, however, brought up an unusually tantalizing prospect: a certain Duke of Tybalt, rumored to be looking for alliances of his own.

Countess Campbell-Stewart ordered Cadha Jaffray to Tybalt in late 3151, only for the stunned Highlander to find someone she had met before: Loren Hansen, colonel of his eponymous Roughriders and newly minted duke. Though Jaffray's time on Terra had brought the two into amicable contact, Hansen had never suggested being a man of any power or influence within the Federated Suns. One thing was clear, though: unlike the Highlanders, his Roughriders had not departed Terra intact. Their forces had been smashed, and many of their soldiers captured, leaving the duke with few forces to secure his new holdings. His late uncle Ludwig, however, had taught him the importance of building strong alliances during the creation of the Galatean League and the mustering of its forces. Loren aimed to do the same with the worlds surrounding Tybalt, and Northwind and the First Kearny were a more-than-welcome foundation with which to start.

After swift negotiations, Cadha Jaffray and the First Kearny accepted a short-term contract with the Duke of Tybalt. Jaffray believes if anyone will understand the needs of her mercenaries, it will be a fellow mercenary. Some of the duke's Roughriders have lambasted her soldiers for their capitulation on Terra, but the Highlanders are secure in the knowledge that they, unlike so many others, left the planet with their freedom—and their lives—intact. Tara Campbell's actions allowed them to continue as one of the oldest continuously serving regiments in the Inner Sphere, and they are grateful for it. Now, under Jaffray's leadership, the Kearny is being chiseled into an immovable command once more—one that will give no ground in the defense of Northwind and its people. Through chaos both past and future, Northwind remains.

COMPOSITION

What the Inner Sphere offers, the First Kearny has. The past twenty years of combat have pitted the regiment against splinter Republic forces, Kuritan and Liao invaders, and the massed weight of Clans Jade Falcon and Wolf. The regiment has barely needed to requisition or purchase BattleMechs for more than a decade due to extensive salvage efforts, so it is a common sight to see a cutting-edge *Grand Dragon* march alongside a captured *Shrike* and an ancient, family-owned

Warhammer. Even so, when given the option, the regiment favors resilient, durable 'Mechs above all others.

Of particular note is the heavy concentration of *Gunslinger*s in the Highlanders, as several of the new -3ERD variant, the result of a pre-Blackout partnership facilitated by the Republic, were sent to the First Kearny for thorough field testing. Though the Blackout prevented further variants from reaching the First Kearny, the mercenaries have taken to the toughness offered by the -3ERD's reinforced armor.

UP CLOSE

W. T. BROWN

BEEVALE
UMKA
FREE WORLDS LEAGUE
18 MAY 3061

Will took a second to stare at his ring finger as he pulled on a rubber glove. It had been nine years since Anna's death on Tukayyid, but he still wore her ring beside his own. He sighed, pulling the glove on with a snap, and picked up the paint roller.

It was a quarterly ritual, getting out the tins of purple paint and going over his 'Mech. Everyone on the team was doing the same. Will shared a hangar with Kentavious Kane, Kent for short. He'd turned up a year earlier with a 'Mech that was literally falling to pieces. *Definitely not short on bravado, that guy. Thinks he's on Solaris VII. His in-your-face* Wolverine *suits his in-your-face personality.*

Will looked over at him chatting up one of the newer techs, shades on indoors, a cigar hanging from the corner of his mouth. *He isn't going to do it again this time. He can do his own work.* "Hey, Kentavious. Over here!" he shouted from the other side of the hangar. "You're not gonna convince the poor girl to paint your damn 'Mech for you!"

Kent feigned shock, lifting the shades from his eyes. "Me? I'd never think of such a thing. I always pay attention to a beauty like this—and the 'Mech too," he said with a wink.

Will rolled his eyes.

Kent's laugh echoed in the tall hangar, and the tech blushed so hard her face turned beetroot.

Will turned back to his work. *Damn him if he isn't battle ready. I will be.*

He got to work. It would take all day, but it was necessary. The seemingly never-ending downpour on Umka would eventually strip the paint every few months, sometimes wearing at the more delicate parts of exposed systems. Painting the legs was the most important, as was checking the water seals.

Umka was nearly all water, but a lot of the sea between and around the islands was shallow, and Will had convinced Commander Azzat that, where possible, retrofitting all the 'Mechs so their heat sinks were in the legs would make sense for defending this world. Azzat had agreed with Will, and let him take charge of the work. That was years ago. Now, fording the shallow seas was standard practice for their team, although they trained less frequently than Will would've liked. Definitely much less than he did in ComStar. In Azzat's own words, "*Who would want to attack us? They'd lose more armor plating fighting us than they could take away.*"

Still, best be prepared, just in case. Will had just finished a leg section and went to move his scaffold. He glanced over to the other bay, and saw Kent was still chatting up the young woman.

"Kent!" he shouted over. "This isn't a holiday camp, it's a military base. Get some work done!"

Kent picked up a glove, winked at Will, and finished smoking his cigar as the tech walked away.

BEEVALE
UMKA
FREE WORLDS LEAGUE
21 MAY 3061

Kent couldn't sit still, Commander Azzat was frowning, and everyone else was looking at Will, who felt uneasy in his purple militia jacket.

"You've fought Clanners before, haven't you?" asked Adetutu Njoku, the Static Defense Unit's *Spider* pilot. "We should be okay?"

Will didn't know what to say. The sum of his combat experience had been watching his wife die while fighting the Diamond Sharks. He didn't want to say that this bunch of nobodies who just happened to own 'Mechs would be no match for the Clans. He felt nauseous, and gripped the chair in front of him tightly. All he wanted to do was go and hide.

"Commander, play the recording again please?" he asked Azzat.

Azzat clicked a few buttons, and the blurry, tattooed face of a fat man came to life.

"*I am Star Leader Chris Moon of the Clan Jade Falcon. We have come to take your world. Surrender now or face our challenges. We bid you five Stars!*" Then the recording cut off.

"There is one DropShip incoming, ETA three days," Adetutu said. "How much can they accomplish?"

"Clan 'Mechs are supposed to be way better than ours, isn't that right, Will?" said Rook Davies, who was a rookie pilot with a *Panther*. Her 'Mech was on its first coat of purple paint.

"They are," replied Will. "But something about that message just doesn't seem right. How could Clanners get so far into Free Worlds space without us hearing about it first? And the name Moon—does that mean anything to any of you?"

Kent slammed a fist on the table in front of him, ignoring Will's questions. "It's just one DropShip. We have *six* 'Mechs. We can beat their asses back into space. Even if they do challenge me personally, I am ready for it! Just trust me on this."

Nobody replied to Kent. Zhang Ming, the *Locust* pilot was crying.

After an awkward minute of everyone looking at the floor, Commander Azzat coughed into his hand. "In any case, the capital is not sending reinforcements. They say if we lose at Beevale, they have to keep their assets to defend Shenville. So we have six BattleMechs. We will be the front-line defense. The infantry and artillery will stay put in Beevale to protect the civilians in case we fail."

"More like they'll be protecting the Kerr-McGinniss factory," quipped Kent.

Azzat glared at Kent. "This is a military unit, and we follow orders. Dismissed."

Will didn't wait for anyone else. He left the briefing room and headed straight for his bunk. He couldn't believe he had traveled so far to get away from the Clans, and they had still found him. He just couldn't get the idea out of his head that there was something wrong about the Bloodname of the warrior giving the challenge. He'd tried his hardest to forget the Clans even existed, but now he was struggling to remember his thorough ComStar training.

He heard footsteps behind him as he reached his door. It was Adetutu.

"Hey, look…" He sighed. "I fought Clanners once and only once. I came here so I didn't have to do it again. I really need to lie down, so can you save your questions for later? We have three days for this."

As he opened his door, Adetutu pushed him through and shut the door behind him. Will was shocked by how strong she was for being a head shorter than him.

"Look, Broadoak. Let's get something straight here. Out of the six of us, you're the only one with real combat experience. We need you, we really do. But that's not why I'm here."

Adetutu pushed Will onto his bunk gently and sat next to him. She held his left hand, and softly touched both wedding rings. Will felt a rush of sadness. His throat dried up.

"You never told any of us what happened on Tukayyid. We know the general story. We don't know anything about this." She held up his hand. "But you need to open up."

She pulled him in close. Her body heat felt good against him. It was a different type of heat than a BattleMech that had been pushed too hard, something he hadn't felt since he'd left Tukayyid.

And he did open up. He couldn't get his words out at first, but eventually he spoke, and told Adetutu his life story, and she told him her life story, and by the next morning, it was like a weight had been lifted.

VILLAGE OF TENELID
UMKA
FREE WORLDS LEAGUE
25 MAY 3061

They were a day late. Tenelid was in tatters. The small fishing village was burning. Dead bodies littered the streets—men, women, and children.

Why would Jade Falcons come here and do this?

"This is very wrong," Will said over their unit's radio. "The Clanners I knew fought challenges and had honor. They didn't run around murdering civilians."

Kent had taken point in his *Wolverine* with its rushed paint job and led the way up the main thoroughfare. "They must've soaked the place in flammable fuels, or the rain would've put the fire out by now."

"Agreed," replied Zhang, flanking Kent in her *Locust*. "Does anyone see life signs?"

"I've got some on thermal," said Adetutu. "In Storage Tank G. I'll go take a look—"

"Wait," interrupted commander Azzat. "It's my responsibility. I'll go. Will, you're with me."

They had parked their 'Mechs outside the metal storage tank. The dome was essentially a giant chiller and full of fish, and a family had managed to hide out in there. Will waited at the doorway, keeping an eye on their 'Mechs more than anything else, while Azzat spoke to the elder of the family. They were reluctant at first, but eventually the grandfather and Azzat had a short conversation.

"Well?" prompted Will when Azzat was back outside.

"BattleMechs, painted in tiger stripe. Orange with green. Ten of them. And a host of warriors in wheeled vehicles. They came from the north-road bridge and headed back that way after destroying the place. They didn't have any demands, just started torching the village. The elder said it was like they were trying to find something, and got angry when they couldn't. They left less than an hour ago."

"If they came for something, it clearly wasn't fish. What else is here?"

"Nothing." Azzat shrugged. "And they seem to be heading away from the factory islands. But I know one thing. If they have wheeled vehicles, they're stuck on the road. We can outmaneuver them. Let's take a shortcut."

The island chains around Beevale were home to a multitude of fishing villages connected by a single-bridged highway. Most of the populace used boats, but road vehicles were still in use. The militia had their walkers, as some of the locals liked to call them.

The Umkan seas near the islands were always calm this time of year. Will once thought it had something to do with the rain, but Azzat had taught him to read the weather better over the years. They weren't deep, either. As long as they kept to within three kilometers from the coastlines, they could ford the barrier reefs and never enter water deeper than two or three meters. Thankfully it wasn't typhoon season.

It was a good plan. Azzat had no combat experience, but Will respected his cool head and local knowledge. He was a good leader.

Adetutu's *Spider* was in the lead, its nimble legs plotting a course through the sea, making sure nothing dangerous was underfoot. Will stayed at the back, protecting the rear of the commander's *Awesome*. They would need his assault 'Mech in the coming battle if they were to have any chance against the Clanners, especially if they were outnumbered.

The radio buzzed. It was Adetutu. "Contact ahead. Two klicks northeast. The enemy is still on the bridge."

"That's good," said Azzat. "We can stop them before they reach the next village. Remember, we are here to save lives."

"And kill those bastards!" Kent shouted as he maneuvered onto a small atoll, bringing his 'Mech fully out of the water. "They're mine!"

His *Wolverine*'s thruster jets thundered and the medium 'Mech blasted off over the sea, water evaporating into steam around him. *He thinks he's a Solaris gladiator. Doesn't he know this is real? Life or death?* Will could feel the weight of Anna's ring pressing on his finger.

"Kent? What are you doing? Get back into formation." Azzat's tone was flat but hard. Will could hear the anger trying to creep out, but the man kept it in check. When Kent didn't reply, he gave new orders. "Adetutu, follow Kent. You can keep up. Everyone else, form up on me."

Will watched Adetutu expertly bounce away. She had exceptional control of her machine, but he knew the light armor of a *Spider* was just a practice target for a Clan 'Mech.

Azzat pushed his *Awesome* forward, Will's *Shadow Hawk* was behind and to the left. Zhang Min's *Locust* and Rook Davies' *Panther* flanked the commander's 'Mech on either side. They were a pretty light lance, and being in the sea hampered their only asset, their speed. Still, they had cut off a good amount of distance with the shortcut.

Weapons fire flashed on Will's sensors, too far away to see or hear. Kent had gotten into range. His *Wolverine* was efficient in combat, but Kent was a hotheaded pilot.

Will's restraints felt very tight all of a sudden, like he was trapped. With every step closer, he could hear the actual sounds of battle. Visibility through the rain was difficult, but he could catch the odd flash of laser fire.

Kent's voice came through full of static. "They're getting away—the Clan 'Mechs, I mean. I've got the vehicles trapped."

Closing to 500 meters, Will was gaining some visibility through the downpour. Kent had managed to destroy a section of the bridge, cutting off the road to the north, and had jumped his 'Mech onto the bridge behind the enemy, cutting them off to the south. He was pummeling the vehicles with lasers. It was like blasting fish in a barrel.

Adetutu was following the enemy 'Mechs at a distance. One was left behind in the sea, struggling to keep steady. It looked like an *Enforcer*, but with only one arm. Azzat stopped 300 meters from it, aimed, and fired with all three of his particle projection cannons. The Clan 'Mech was blown to bits by the PPC discharge before Will could get a proper reading on it, but something about it looked wrong. *More like a junker than a Clanner...?*

"Adetutu, keep your distance. Don't take any risks," the commander ordered. "Kent. You have them. Cease firing. Please."

It was a full minute before Kent stopped. The vehicles were burning husks.

"Okay, Kent, you had enough killing now?" said Rook with venom in her voice.

"Ha! Have I had enough? They murdered people, Rook. What do you think? We should just let those bastards go? We all have families on this rock. Well, except Will. But he knows all about revenge, don't you, buddy?"

Will walked his 'Mech up to the bridge. He didn't know how to answer. The road was strewn with bodies and burning vehicles. The strange thing was, they didn't look like Clanners. They just looked like people. Regular people, just dead.

"I think you overdid it, Kent." Will wanted to say more, say how he never really had revenge, and how killing the Clanner that had killed his wife had made no difference to him, but he couldn't. He felt his wife's ring on his finger, and he could picture all the dead families in the village of Tenelid. "We need to get after Adetutu, in case they turn on her. We can't let her fight them alone. We need to get closer."

"Copy that," said Azzat. "Will, take the lead. Kent, stay near me this time. That's an order."

**ISLAND OF GREATROCK
UMKA
FREE WORLDS LEAGUE
21 MAY 3061**

The enemy 'Mechs had gained distance from the militia by being on the road, and only Adetutu could keep up with them while in the sea. The next island in the chain was Greatrock. It was sparsely populated. Will had been there once, and remembered it being like a rock forest. Spires of reddish-gray rock shot out of the ground like great trees, worn into points by the rain. The road cut a winding path through the island. If the Clanners wanted to make a stand on this island, it would be good defensive ground. Will just couldn't help thinking this wasn't how Clanners were supposed to fight.

"We should challenge them," he said, as they drew close to the island. He could now see Adetutu's *Spider*, waiting at the end of the bridge.

"What do you mean?" asked Zhang.

"Don't you read military history?" snorted Kent. "Clanners are supposed to fight in duels. Like one-on-one. You challenge their leader, and if you beat them, they all leave. Isn't that right, Will?"

Will thought for a moment. "I was in one battle, Kent. I went where I was told and fought who I was told to fight. I'm not an expert on the Clans. But I think you're right this time. I should challenge their leader."

"Why you?" asked Kent. "I've been in a battle now too. *I* should be the one to fight—"

"That's enough," Azzat interrupted. "I know you guys don't care, but we are a military organization, and *I* am in command here. If anyone is to issue a challenge, it's me. Form up on Adetutu. Radio silence from now on."

Will knew Kent would be raging, itching to fight. If it was up to Will, he would be overly cautious. Anna had been in her *Warhammer*, and the Clanners took her out with one shot. Even Azzat's *Awesome*, assault 'Mech though it was, was vulnerable to Clan weaponry.

Once they all reached the island, they formed up: Azzat in the center, Kent and Will flanking him, Rook and Zhang just behind Azzat, and Adetutu at the back, making an inverted wedge. Azzat was moving slowly, trying to keep his heat levels down in his heavier-tonnage 'Mech.

In the forest of rock spires, Will couldn't get any helpful readings on his instruments. Infrared was useless. The first sign of the enemy was when a missile exploded against the commander's front armor. Will saw the *Awesome* stop for a second before returning fire, chunks of rock flying everywhere.

"Contact, battle formation," said the commander. Will was impressed at how cool the man sounded under fire. Then his attention was stolen by the purple *Wolverine* running past him.

"Damn it, Kent, you're going to get yourself killed!" Will shouted through the radio. He didn't expect a reply.

"I'll follow him," Adetutu said.

Before Will could object, an enemy 'Mech sidestepped around a spire. Green and orange, it fired lasers that burned armor from his right leg and torso. Will turned his 'Mech to face the enemy and fired his PPC. The charged-particle blast fizzled the air and took the enemy 'Mech in the torso, cratering a pit out of its midsection.

Will took a good look at its design. It looked like a standard *Catapult*, but the missile launchers had been replaced by lasers. It returned fire but missed, the shots going wild. *Bad shooting for someone supposedly so highly trained.*

Will advanced and shot his PPC again, scoring another torso hit. The enemy BattleMech collapsed in into a heap, like someone having a heart attack. Must have been an engine hit. It was a lucky shot, but seemed too easy. *This unit must've been in some bad scrapes, to come to this planet in this state, to fight for no reason we can understand.*

A glance at his tactical map showed the battle formation was long gone. Kent and Adetutu were halfway across the island, at least two kilometers away. Azzat and the others were steadily advancing. Enemy blips were disappearing from the map. This was way too easy. This was not the same enemy Will fought on Tukayyid.

"Commander, permission to go after Kent as well? It seems you are doing all right here."

"Permission granted, Will. Just don't do anything stupid."

Famous last words.

Will was getting closer. Adetutu's green blip hadn't moved for over a minute. That wasn't good news for the agile *Spider*. The knot of fear in Will's stomach was building again. He just knew she was dead. *Damn you, Kent. It's all your fault.*

Two red blips and a green blip appeared 300 meters to the north. Will fired his jump jets and came down in a clearing. At the far side, two enemy 'Mechs, a *Hatchetman* and a *Firestarter*, were circling Kent's purple *Wolverine*. The *Hatchetman* was lunging in close, trying to hit with its primitive namesake weapon, and the *Firestarter* was blazing away with its flamers. Will could see Kent's paint peeling away all over. *He must be overheating. His 'Mech is shutting down.* "Retreat, damn it!" he shouted. "You're going to die!"

"I'm not a weakling," Kent replied, although his voice was unusually wavering.

Will opened his radio to a public catch-all frequency. "I challenge you! Leave him alone."

A semi-familiar voice replied. "What's it got to do with you? We have what we came for. Revenge on Kentavious Kane!" There was a throaty chuckle before the transmission cut off.

A bounty on Kent? This makes no sense.

Kent turned toward a hatchet strike with his 'Mech's shoulder guard. It was a well-done defensive move, saving his 'Mech from any critical damage, but he wouldn't be able to take another hit like that.

Will got a lock on the *Firestarter* and triggered his PPC and a rack of long-range missiles. He was still at least 200 meters away, so he missed with the PPC, blowing chunks off of a rock spire behind the target, but at least half of his missiles hit. The *Firestarter* went up like a fireworks celebration. *Must've hit its ammo cache. More good luck, or these 'Mechs are badly maintained.*

When he turned his attention back to Kent, the *Wolverine* was down, and the *Hatchetman* was going at it hard.

"Fight me, I challenge you!" Will shouted over the radio. "You're nothing but a murderer!"

"You're right." came the reply into his private channel. "And I've already downed two of your guys. You're next! Kane left us with nothing, to die in dirt. Now he can do the same."

The *Hatchetman* rotated and pointed its melee weapon at Adetutu's *Spider*. It was lying face-down atop a rocky plinth, almost like an altar. One of its legs was missing, and electrical sparks were shooting from its back. "I might finish that one off now," cackled the enemy leader.

Will saw his wife, lying in her cockpit. All red.

"No. You don't get this one." He closed his eyes, cracked his neck and shoulder muscles, and started to count to five.

Before he got to three, he was rocked by autocannon fire.

Will tried to fire back with his missiles, but they didn't go. *Bastard damaged something in my firing control*. He tried firing his PPC, and it worked, but the shot missed. The *Hatchetman* was coming at him fast, zigzagging around small rocky mounds. It was firing its arm lasers as it ran, but missed every shot.

Then Will saw what he needed to see. The green-and-orange paint on the enemy 'Mech was washing off in the scouring rain. Underneath it was black, with white striping.

Everything suddenly made a lot more sense to him. *Periphery pirates pretending to be Clanners, trying to scare us into not engaging them with all-out force. They might've gotten away with it if they didn't have such poor equipment. It's time to close up and finish this.*

Will fired his jump jets and came down right in front of Chris Moon's 'Mech. The pirate leader's forward momentum brought it into a collision with the *Shadow Hawk*.

Will bounced around in his command couch, the safety restraints biting into his chest and shoulders. The *Hatchetman* was practically on top of him, and Will could see the large, ugly body of Chris Moon inside the other cockpit. *If that is really his name. Moon isn't a Jade Falcon Bloodname, is it?*

The pirate was shouting inaudibly in frustration. Will grabbed the haft of the hatchet in his 'Mech's left hand and grabbed the pirate's autocannon barrel with his right. Metal groaned as he bent both weapons out of shape.

The *Hatchetman* raised its left arm to fire its underslung laser, but Will managed to bat it aside, destroying the laser. The *Hatchetman* was trapped. It struggled to break free, but the *Shadow Hawk*'s grip was too strong for the lighter 'Mech. Will could see Moon going wild in his command couch.

Then Will grabbed the *Hatchetman* tighter so he had a firm hold on both of the pirate 'Mech's arms. *This was the stupid thing the commander warned me not to do.*

He lowered his PPC barrel over his 'Mech's shoulder until it was touching Moon's cockpit. He glimpsed the ComStar tattoo on his forearm as he squeezed the trigger. *This is for Anna, and Adetutu, and all the people on Umka who died today.*

Will's cockpit faded to black, and his instruments went out. He could feel his gyro kicking up to try keeping the 'Mech balanced. There was a muffled cacophony of explosions, and when his viewport regained clarity, there was only half a *Hatchetman* left burning in the rain.

Will looked around to see steam rising from Commander Azzat's PPC barrels. Zhang's *Locust* was running to Kent's position, Will slowly walked to Adetutu's *Spider*, his *Shadow Hawk* protesting every step.

His cockpit was burning hot, most of his heat syncs were nonfunctioning, but he was too determined to care about a bit of sweat now. His 'Mech was struggling, but he made it there. His *Shadow Hawk* took a knee, and Will popped the cockpit hatch. The cool rain refreshed his skin. He jumped down, almost losing his footing on the wet ground, and ran to the *Spider*, scrambling up the rocky plinth to the cockpit. His stomach was turning. He could see her inside, unconscious, but not red. He pulled the emergency hatch release.

Adetutu was hanging facedown from her harness, limbs dangling. Thankfully her chest was rising and falling. Will took her weight and unclipped her. She fell on top of him, and the jolt woke her up.

"W-What happened?" she asked, slurring her words, her eyes only half open.

Will held her in his arms. "It's okay now. You're safe."

"We got the Clanners? We saved the people?"

"We did."

SHENVILLE
UMKA
FREE WORLDS LEAGUE
24 MAY 3061

Kent sat in the reception area of the Governor's Hall, fresh out of the medical unit. He propped his encased leg up on a folding chair. People, civilians, were actually forming a queue to sign his cast.

Will sat a row behind him, ready for the press conference. "You're loving this, all this attention," he said to Kent.

"What gave it away?" Kent was beaming. He had a smile from ear to ear.

"We need to have a talk when this is all over. I need to know why they came. I need to know who you are."

Kent didn't reply. He just winked at Will and lowered his shades.

Adetutu leaned into Will. Her eyes were puffy; the concussion had taken it out of her. Will looked at both wedding rings on his left hand. Then he looked at the way Adetutu was nestled into his chest.

Anna would be happy that he was happy. Hopefully, if she was somewhere looking down on him, she would understand him for moving on with his life.

INNER SPHERE INGENUITY

MATTHEW CROSS

**SHIVER SPECIAL LECTURE ON
  INNER SPHERE TECHNOLOGICAL DEVELOPMENTS
STAR COMMANDER ARIADNE
CDS *KRAKEN*, FOX ARCSHIP
30 OCTOBER 3125**

Begin Transcript

Hello, little Shivs! It is my pleasure to bring you all the latest and greatest information I have acquired from our good friends down at the New Avalon Institute of Science! I recognize most of your faces here, but in case any of you do not know who I am, I am Star Commander Ariadne, *ristar*, and member of the Faulk Bloodline. I welcome you all to my special lecture on the advancements the Spheroids have made over the last fifty or so years, hopefully educating you little Shivs in the basics of their newest technologies. [*Transcript note: I, the assigned transcriber, and the rest of the attendees do not appreciate being referred to as "little Shivs."*]

I have spent the last three weeks in the company of one Dr. Kiran Suzuki, who would fit well in our Clan customs with his grumpy demeanor and common threats of violence. He has taught me a great many things, but today we are going to go into detail on the various weaponry the Inner Sphere has developed since the 3070s. I'm going to cover them in the usual order: lasers, missiles, and ballistics.

The biggest advancements in Inner Sphere laser technologies came in the form of pulse lasers. While our pulse lasers are fantastically perfect with a wide variety of ranges, Star League-era pulse lasers were unfortunately quite short ranged, with the medium-class pulse laser not being effective to 200 meters. While our scientists were able to double that range while increasing damage output, the Spheroids have taken different approaches that are quite ingenious, given the limited tools and technologies available to them.

Their first foray came in the form of the X-Pulse laser. While sounding very fascinating and very powerful, these weapons simply increased the pulse-laser's range at the expense of 50 percent more heat. When compared to our pulse lasers, it is more of a waste of tonnage than anything, but is still an interesting data point, and every once in a while, you will encounter an X-Pulse laser on the battlefield.

The next and much more interesting piece of technology was unfortunately created by those pesky Blakists and their kooky secret labs. Oh! Kooky! I learned that word from the NAIS students. Apparently, it means "very interesting but a little strange." I think. What a kooky word! Kooky! [*Transcript note: Once the Star Commander is able to calm herself from giggling for far too long, she continues.*] Anyway, the Blakists invented the variable-speed pulse laser. And while it sounds as if it is a single laser with advanced software control, it is far more than that. Each laser has a set of lenses that rotate into place, selecting a different lens based on the range to the target. These lenses rotate quickly, but this can present some issues in manual targeting environments. No matter, the system works effectively, increasing damage and accuracy at close ranges, but extending the range of the weapon beyond normal pulse lasers at the cost of accuracy and damage. While the range extension matches X-Pulse lasers, the increased damage and accuracy at knife-fighting ranges made these weapons extremely deadly. While rare, these weapons occasionally do make it onto the modern battlefield. Treat them with extreme caution, and make sure to claim as *isorla* each one you encounter, because they will fetch a very nice price, and you simply cannot skip making such a great sale!

There are rumors at NAIS that the researchers are trying to mate the advanced power of Clan heavy lasers with pulse technologies, which we have tried and explosively failed at, but if the rumors are true, there may be one more type of laser debuting in the next few years. We shall see. Dr. Suzuki was very cagey whenever I asked about their "new super laser," and I never got anything valuable out of him. So sad.

Oh! And to save some time on this lecture, I have included Dr. Suzuki's lecture on Inner Sphere PPC technology to the ship's data net, so please download that at your earliest convenience.

Now, missile weapons! My favorite! Well, I pilot a *Nova Cat*, usually a Prime configuration, so, maybe not my favorite. But I did have it in the Beta configuration once! It was great fun. Remind me to show you the battleROMs later.

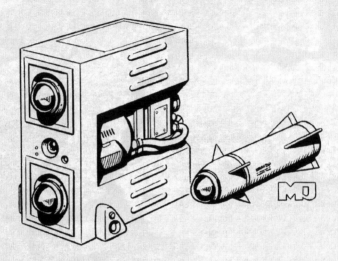

The Inner Sphere's efforts in improving missile weapons have mainly focused on trying to make their LRM launchers be less inferior to those of the mighty Clans. Almost every effort they have produced has yielded improvements, but nothing quite as effective as our enhanced software and materials engineering improved on Star League-era LRM launchers. While Spheroid SRM launchers have remained relatively static, with their Streak launchers being fully developed, most of the advancements have created weapons that are effective either at all ranges or at longer ranges.

The first major efforts yielded Enhanced LRM launchers and Extended LRM launchers, abbreviated NLRM and ELRM, respectively. While the NLRM launcher simply reduces arming and/or lofting requirements to reduce minimum effective range, the launchers are simply heavier versions of the traditional launchers.

ELRMs are a different story. Using a two-stage rocket system, the Extended LRM is a ludicrous technology that extends the missile's range to more than twice that of a standard long-range missile. For Kerensky's sake, it outranges our advanced tactical missiles by 40 percent! This comes at an extreme cost of tonnage, with an ELRM 10 massing a full 60 percent more than either a Spheroid LRM 10 or one of our ATM 9 launchers. It is amazing what these people come up with in the absence of our advanced technologies. I have often considered whether it would be honorable to engage at such ranges, but honor is a funny thing...

The other two major advancements are both a bit more unique. The multi-missile launcher melds an SRM launcher and an LRM launcher into a single device, in a crude attempt to mimic our advanced tactical missiles. On the other side, there is the Thunderbolt missile system, which attempts to pack the explosive power of many individual LRM warheads into a single powerful missile, which is more effective than most of you would guess.

MMLs are straightforward, and do not require much explaining. The circuitry, loading mechanisms, and software for a Star League-era SRM and LRM launcher are quite similar. By expanding the loading mechanism and messing with the missile-flight sizes, the Spheroids have created a line of missile launchers that cover their minimum ranges and deal some substantial close-range damage without harming long-range performance. The launchers themselves are bulky, but they transplant quite effectively into older 'Mechs with original, low-bulk hardware.

Thunderbolt missiles, on the other hand, are an interesting solution to the problem that is the Inner Sphere LRM. By combining the firepower of a flight of missiles into a single large projectile, Spheroids have effectively created a launcher that can rival many autocannons. The missile itself has an explosive payload, but a kinetic factor also allows the weapon to hit very hard and do substantial damage to the modern ablative armor common throughout the known galaxy. When the launcher fires, the missile experiences extreme acceleration that is difficult to guide with its limited control abilities, and protection circuitry disables most of the warhead's deadly power to prevent early detonation. All of these factors still give Thunderbolts a minimum-range issue and reduced damage output when hitting within that minimum range. Most of the other drawbacks are more typical of 'Mech-scale weaponry: heat, bulk, and tonnage. The missiles themselves only provide 60 percent of the ammunition of a typical LRM launcher per ton. They weigh more than the equivalent LRM launcher, but surprisingly weigh typically less than an equivalent advanced autocannon. And while the missiles are quite vulnerable to anti-missile systems, I would like a show of hands around the room on who has actually piloted a 'Mech with an AMS? [*Transcript note: the number of raised hands represented about 40 percent of the room.*]

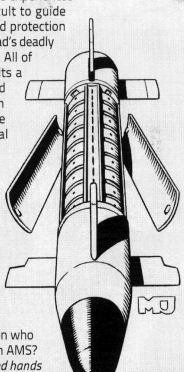

See? Not many! These weapons can be very, very deadly in the hands of the right warrior.

Finally, we are going to review their advancements in ballistic weaponry. While their Gauss rifle technology has yielded a variety of range and damage profiles, their work is mostly uninteresting and over-engineered. To prove that, I have attached a second article to the data net on their Gauss technology, also from Dr. Suzuki. So, read that and see why the only interesting Gauss rifle from the Inner Sphere is the improved heavy Gauss rifle. More interesting is their work with light autocannons and hyper-velocity autocannons.

Light autocannons likely spawned from previous work on rotary autocannons. As our Diamond Shark predecessors worked to create a Clan analogy of the rotary autocannon, we haven't found a need to use the light variants, but essentially, the Inner Sphere back-ported improvements—or, rather, necessary cutbacks—from the rotary cannons and integrated them with traditional single-salvo autocannons from the Age of War. What they got was a Class-2 and Class-5 autocannon with the range profile of a Rotary-2 and Rotary-5, respectively, but at nearly a 40 percent mass reduction and removal of any minimum-range concerns. I mean, even the Blood Spirits saw this was a good idea and created the ProtoMech line of autocannons. If a Blood Spirit can see this is a good idea, you know it has to be somewhat okay. No offense to anyone here who may have Blood Spirit genes, of course!

The hyper-velocity autocannons, on the other hand, take the technology in the opposite direction. At the expense of reinforced barrels, specialized munitions and propellant, and the risk of catastrophic explosion, the Inner Sphere added a full one-third more range over our Ultra-class autocannons. The hyper-velocity cannon can fire extended salvos of autocannon rounds at higher ranges, but with similar damage profiles to standard autocannons. An interesting side effect of the cannon is large plumes of white smoke generated from burning the specialized propellant. While mostly a downside, some skilled warriors have used such smokescreens as a tactical advantage, creating cover while delivering damage to their enemies at the same time.

Now, all of these technologies, are they necessary? Not really. Are they niche? Definitely. Are they something you should be concerned with? Undoubtedly. These weapons are appearing on battlefields throughout the Inner Sphere. We have even put some of these silly technologies into our own products! Or at least, some scientists have put forth proposals to do so. Our customers are using this tech, as are their enemies, who are also our customers. And the current demilitarization of the Inner Sphere has called for more advanced technologies and niche weapon systems. Their effectiveness can be doubted at times, compared to their traditional counterparts—or especially, the superior Clan counterparts—but a Thunderbolt 15 to the cockpit will make you as dead as the next MechWarrior, mind you. I have put a list of all new production hardware on the net for you all to download and study over the next few days.

Now, who wants to watch me and my Star destroy some Snow Ravens with a hail-fire of missiles from my trusty *Nova Cat*? Anyone?

COMIN' TO TOWNE:
A ROLE-PLAYING ADVENTURE

ERIC SALZMAN

This adventure is for use with *A Time of War: The BattleTech Role-Playing Game*.

MISSION OVERVIEW

The Republic Armed Forces destroyed the Towne Guard in 3149 during Operation Eruptio, collapsing the planetary government and triggering civil war between Republic and Draconis Combine partisans. Terror attacks subsequently destroyed medical supplies, allowing a virulent outbreak of Hyborian Blood Plague to spread across the planet.

Townians eagerly anticipated the arrival of Santana's Slayers—not only because the famously philanthropic Klaus Santana was known for lavish spending and charitable donations on worlds he visited, but also because he was escorting an antigen resupply to treat the plague. However, as Santana's DropShip descended toward Port Howard on 24 December, a tremendous snowstorm shifted course and caught the ship in gale-force winds. Traffic control received a broken report from the ship's captain of their guidance system having failed before the ship crashed on the Hyborian Plateau.

A team dispatched to the site found the ship had executed a successful emergency landing. However, the bay doors had been torn open from the outside, and the Slayers were missing. Enormous footprints and drag trails led toward the Eiglophian Mountains.

ASSETS

The players are freelance mercenaries trapped on Towne by the plague. They have been granted release from quarantine to recover the medicines.

In addition to any vehicular units the players' team possesses, the Port Howard authorities have attached a pair of wilderness guides.

OPPOSITION

The wilderness guides note that the Hyborian Plateau and Eiglophian Mountains are home to some of Towne's largest megafauna, including flocks of rodans—winged predators large enough to carry off a two-ton whiffle-tail—as well as territorial packs of shaggy, six-legged, ten-meter-high eiglotheriums.

The guides say the tracks lead toward the ruins of a Star League-era bunker. Settlements in the Cimmerian foothills have reported bandits using trained megafauna in recent years, and the trail suggests the raiders, calling themselves the Beastlords, have made the ancient bunker their base.

TACTICAL ANALYSIS

The team must ascend the Eiglophians via the service road, risking encounters with wildlife, avalanches, and bandit patrols. The players will need to decide whether to launch a frontal assault on the bandit enclave, or to try infiltrating the bunker without alerting the Beastlords.

OBJECTIVES

1. **Climb Every Mountain.** Work with your guides to reach the Star League bunker without alerting the bandits. Following the Beastlords' trail through the snow is possible, but there are sure to be guards on the main route.

2. **Jailbreak!** Only a few bodies were found at the landing site; the rest were probably taken prisoner. If you can rescue them from the Beastlords' dungeons and get them to their BattleMechs, they could help you destroy the bandits.

3. **Race for the Cure.** Recover the shipment of antigens and end the plague.

Completing Objective 1 is a prerequisite for attempting the other two. Completing Objective 3 without losing more than 50 percent of the player characters is counted as a mission success. Completing all Objectives without losing more than 50 percent of the player characters and Santana's Slayers (Klaus must survive) is counted as a huge success. Eliminating the Beastlords will significantly raise the players' reputations on Towne.

GAMEMASTER SECTION

ENEMIES

The Beastlords responded to Republic limits on 'Mech ownership by domesticating megafauna for combat, using *CattleMaster*s to train and control the beasts. Lesser rodans are used like hunting falcons, launched from *CattleMaster* forearms, while larger rodans can be ridden. Domesticated eiglotheriums are used for brute labor, and to take on militia BattleMechs.

The Beastlords have a quartet of *CattleMaster*s they use for megafauna training, as well as *Krampus,* a BGS-2T *Barghest* the eiglotheriums see as their pack leader.

LOCAL CONDITIONS

The storm raging over the Hyborian Plateau precludes aerial support. Ongoing snow squalls may obscure the trail if the team doesn't move quickly. While climbing up into the Eiglophian Mountains on a crumbling Star League-era service road, visibility will decrease to nearly zero (a boon to players attempting a stealthy approach), but high winds, icy footing, and Beastlord guard posts will need to be overcome, along with the ever-present risk of an avalanche. The storm will begin to clear as the players near the ridge where the bandit squat in their fortress.

The wilderness guides can provide the team with information about the conditions and known passes. They had been inside the abandoned bunker before the Beastlords took it over, so they know the general layout, but claim anything of value was stripped by *lostech* prospectors centuries ago.

The bunker lies at the base of a shattered peak, blasted into ruin when Star League WarShips bombarded the base. The facility has three entrances: (1) a large door opening into a 'Mech bay, (2) a similar vehicle-garage door, and (3) the main personnel entrance. Security tunnels connect the 'Mech bay and the vehicle garage to the main complex.

The 'Mech bay holds Santana's Slayers' equipment—an RDS-2B *Red Shift*, *Fire Moth* H, *Incubus 6*, Comet Light Strike Fighter, THR-2L *Thunder*, and an LHN-C5 *Lightning*—and the Beastlords' four *CattleMaster*s. If the team takes longer than a day to reach the site, the Beastlord techs will have cracked the Slayers' security systems. The vehicle bay door is generally left wide open, as the bay serves as a lair for the eiglotheriums, which roam nearby valleys foraging for food, then return to the bay for shelter and sleep.

The shattered peak now serves as an aerie for a flock of rodans. An underground maintenance tunnel still runs from the bunker up to the ruins. The rodans nest here and emerge when summoned by the bandits.

The main facility interior features a dormitory, armory, kitchen, and infirmary, mostly equipped with gear stolen from nearby settlements. The control center has been converted into a throne room, while the Slayers and DropShip crew may be found in a storage room/makeshift brig. The antigens are in the infirmary, while loot from the DropShip and other raids are in several storage rooms.

OBJECTIVES

Attempting to penetrate the 'Mech-bay door or personnel door will certainly alert the Beastlords to the team's presence. However, it may be possible to sneak in through either the vehicle bay (tiptoeing past a shaggy pile of slumbering eiglotheriums) or through the rodan nest in the peak. The bandits inside the facility are either celebrating or cataloguing the haul, and will only be expecting trouble if they are forewarned.

DIFFICULTY

If the Beastlords' guards spot the team during the ascent and put the base on alert, the full might of the brigands will be awaiting the team at the top of the pass. If *Total Warfare* (*TW*) rules are used to play the resulting battle, statistics for eiglotheriums and rodans as beast-mounted infantry (see pp. 106–108, *Tactical Operations: Advanced Units and Equipment*) can be found in the *Bestiary* section below.

If the team took more than a day to make the ascent, the bandits will field the *Thunder*, *Lightning*, *Incubus*, and *Fire Moth* instead of their *CattleMaster*s. The bandits have ten eiglotheriums, five greater rodans, and eight lesser rodans.

AFTER THE MISSION

If not eliminated, the Beastlords will pursue the team back to Port Howard. Even a successful extraction raises the question of who gets the valuable medicine. Players will face pressure to choose between Combine and Republic partisans, while Santana will push to distribute the cure to all.

BESTIARY

Eiglotherium

The shaggy, six-legged eiglotherium is a massive, herbivorous herdbeast, standing ten meters high at the shoulder. The Beastlords have tricked the dimwitted beasts into regarding a *Barghest* as their pack leader.

Mass (kg): 20,000

Attributes (S/B/D/R/I/W/E): 75/90/1/2/1/3/1
Size Class (Modifier): Monstrous (+5)
BAR (M/B/E/X): 3/3/2/3
Damage (AP/BD): 4M/10
Move (W/R/S): 3/15/25
Traits: Domesticated
Skills (A/P/T): +3/+2/-1
Notes: This creature can ram; multiply AP by 2 and add 10% of creature's BOD to BD per meter charged (to max 100% BOD).

As Infantry:
Size: Monstrous
Weight: 20 tons
MP (Type): 2 (Ground)
Bonus Damage vs. Infantry (Vehicles): +5D6 (2)
Damage Divisor: 3.0
Terrain Restrictions: Water (Depth 2+)

Rodan

This aerial reptilian predator rides the winds, its keen eyesight seeking prey below. Fully grown lesser rodans have a four-meter wingspan, and mountain-dwelling greater rodans are much bigger. The Beastlords use lesser rodans as enormous hunting beasts, launching them from the forearms of their *CattleMaster*s, while riders on larger ones serve as aerial scouts.

Lesser Rodan:
Mass (kg): 300 kg
Attributes (S/B/D/R/I/W/E): 12/10/2/6/2/2/2
Size Class (Modifier): Medium (+0)
BAR (M/B/E/X): 1/1/0/1
Damage (AP/BD): 1M/4
Move (W/R/S): 8/24/140
Traits: Aggressive, Night Vision (+2), Pack Hunter (3-6), Flight (+1), Offensive Adaptation (Talons/Bite), Good Vision (+1), Domesticated
Skills (A/P/T): +2/+6/-1

Greater Rodan:
Mass (kg): 880 kg
Attributes (S/B/D/R/I/W/E): 25/20/2/6/2/2/2
Size Class (Modifier): Large (+1)
BAR (M/B/E/X): 2/2/1/2
Damage (AP/BD): 1M/6
Move (W/R/S): 6/18/110
Traits: Aggressive, Night Vision (+2), Pack Hunter (3-6), Flight (+1), Offensive Adaptation (Talons/Bite), Good Vision (+1), Domesticated
Skills (A/P/T): +3/+6/-1

As Infantry:
Size: Large
Weight: 0.88 ton
MP (Type): 5 (VTOL)
Bonus Damage vs. Infantry (Vehicles): +2D6(1)
Damage Divisor: 1.0
Terrain Restrictions: As VTOLs (see *TW*, p. 54)

HELL'S HIGHWAY

JAMES HAUSER

**VESTRED STABLES
CSESZTREG
HELL'S HORSES OCCUPATION ZONE
7 APRIL 3130**

Rafeny heard the call as his unicorn jumped the short fence. The beast he rode bore a fairly close resemblance to the mythical Terran creature, but the Meinradian unicorn had a pair of curled, ram-like horns on the sides of its head to complement the single curved horn on the top of its skull. Its bronze skin had an almost metallic sheen.

He wiped the sweat from his olive skin with his shirt sleeve as he turned his beast back toward the barn. The sun bathed the landscape in a warm glow as it slowly sank to the horizon. The unicorn galloped across the field, through the fence, and among the buildings until it arrived at a small herd gathering before the stable doors.

One of the stallions queuing at the stable turned his head toward Rafeny's stallion and stood on his rear legs, roaring a challenge. Rafeny's unicorn reared up, and both animals bashed their heads together, throwing Rafeny from his saddle. Dismounted riders and other nearby laborers grabbed the reins of both animals and pulled them apart as Rafeny scurried out of the struggling beasts' way.

As the laborers ushered the unicorns away, Rafeny dusted himself off and raked his dark hair back into place. Unease swept through him as he considered the possibility he might be relieved of his duty assignment here and have to return to the more mundane tasks given to the other members of his *sibko*. *Sibkos*, or sibling companies, were groupings of selectively bred Trueborn children. Trueborns were not often permitted to mix with the other castes as extensively as they did here, but stable duty was a special assignment given to those cadets who demonstrated exceptional performance in their studies and duties. It was considered a patriotic duty that reinforced the spirit of Clan Hell's Horses.

The unicorns were settled into the stable, and the assemblage of workers headed to a series of wooden benches and tables in a nearby grassy field.

"Rafeny, are you injured?"

He turned toward a tall, strongly built, gray-haired man. "Stablemaster. I apologize for losing my control of my steed."

"There's no need for an apology. Are you injured?"

Rafeny shook his head. "Just a little sore where I landed. No real pain."

"Good, but your eyes say you're a little shaken up. Eat with me."

They sat and were soon joined by two boys and an adolescent girl. The stablemaster introduced them as his own offspring. Greetings were exchanged, food was brought over, and the meal began.

As they ate the lizard burgers that tasted like chicken, the stablemaster paused. "Don't worry about what happened with the two stallions back there. Everyone who's ever ridden a unicorn stallion near another has had an experience like that."

"Why?"

"Mating rights." The older man paused to chew his food. "Whether they realize it or not, all life forms seek to preserve their genes. Everything life does leads ultimately to that. Stallions can't rely on iron wombs, so they need to fight with the other stallions for access to the mares."

He gestured around the table. "These are my children. I would lay down my life to protect them. It's no calculation on my part, but you know that's what's behind it."

The conversation went in other directions as Rafeny and the family chattered about anything and everything as the shadows gradually lengthened. For the next hour, he felt like he was part of this family. And when the light faded and the tables were cleared, he knew he would cherish these memories of the stablemaster's family in the years to come.

OUTPOST-CLASS DROPSHIP *LAUREN BOURJON*
ORBITAL APPROACH
DENIZLI
JADE FALCON OCCUPATION ZONE
1 FEBRUARY 3141

Eleven years later, Rafeny sat at a mess table, surrounded by other warriors. Sitting on his right was the gunner of his Epona hovertank,

Arismaily. Like Rafeny, she was a Trueborn who had failed her initial Trial of Position and tested into an armored-vehicle crew. Bred as an aerospace pilot, she had a small body topped with a normal-sized head, dark brown hair falling loosely around her neck. Skarleth, the tank's driver, was seated on his other side, but being of MechWarrior lineage, was of normal proportions with long, reddish hair. The freeborn Brayden, pale with blond hair and light brown eyes, rounded out Rafeny's crew.

Sitting across the table from them was the crew of a Svantovit infantry hovercraft they would be competing against. Dark-skinned Kaliyah commanded the vehicle. Jairo, with Asian features, served as the driver. Agam, sporting long dark hair, was the vehicle's gunner and the most talkative of Kaliyah's crew.

"So, we are not going to be in your Point?" she asked.

"*Neg*, Agam," Kaliyah corrected. "We will be paired with Meyli's Hephaestus."

"We," Rafeny gestured to his crew, "will also be paired with a Hephaestus, but ours will jump. For the Mad Stampede, a faster vehicle is paired with a slower one so that no team has a better chance of winning simply because of what they are driving. We must finish with our Starmates, assuming they are still alive. Losing too many brings shame."

Their losses occurred because Mad Stampedes were always held on hostile worlds while under fire from the local forces.

"We are competing in a Branding ritual of sorts," Kaliyah continued. "Except that paired vehicles cooperate and share the honor or the shame and compete against the other four vehicle Points.

"As any good Hell's Horses warrior, I want to share the victory with your crew." She reached out to Rafeny's crew. "But this is a competition between Points. Honestly, I like you better than the crew we have been paired with. So I hope you finish the race too, but at least several seconds later than us."

Rafeny smiled. "I hope the same for you. And perhaps we can kill some Jade Falcons while we are at it."

"Has anyone thought about what you want said about you in *The Book of Barding* should you win?" asked Agam.

The Book of Barding was an unofficial offshoot of *The Remembrance*, chronicling the achievements of Hell's Horses vehicle crews. As it was not a part of the Clans' founder Nicholas Kerensky's original grand design, it could not be officially recognized by the Clan leadership. Unofficially, the Horses' leadership, both warrior and scientist, read continuously updated copies. Rumor had it that readership extended beyond the warriors of the Hell's Horses to the vehicle crews of other Clans. Its name had a double meaning in old English: the recitation of epic poetry and the armor of a warhorse.

Each of the warriors shared daydreams or even had prepared lines. Rafeny simply said, "The details are unimportant. As long as it inspires the geneticists to use my DNA to seed new *sibkos*, I will be pleased."

JADE FALCON COMMAND CENTER
DENIZLI
JADE FALCON OCCUPATION ZONE
2 FEBRUARY 3141

"Have they issued a *batchall*?"

"*Neg*, Galaxy Commander," responded Star Colonel Robert of the Twelfth Falcon Regulars. "Nothing beyond the request for *safcon*."

"Hmm." Clarence Pryde grunted and brushed at his green tunic. "What has emerged from that DropShip?"

"So far, just a Star of vehicles. I have satellite imagery."

"On the holotable, please." Pryde sipped his coffee. He sat at one of the stools around the holotable dominating the center of the room. He was flanked by his Star Commanders, all either standing or on stools. The rest of the communications and analytic staff manned stations along three of the walls. The fourth wall, transparent, revealed the ready room. The rows of seats were filled with green-clad warriors staring up at monitors along the top of the wall. Some perused data tablets. A few black-uniformed warriors clustered gloomily to one side.

Their uniforms had significance. The Jade Falcons were long known as a Clan characterized by its ferocity in battle, and sometimes the harsh treatment of its lower castes. With the ascendancy of Malvina Hazen nearly a full generation earlier as the Clan's leader, the Jade Falcons' worst instincts had been unleashed and encouraged. The traditional green uniforms were now only worn by those warriors who did not approve of the brutality Khan Hazen demanded from her warriors. The new black uniforms were worn by warriors who either embraced her wholeheartedly, or were afraid to be seen as dissidents. They proudly referred to themselves as Mongols. Green-clad warriors found themselves disfavored, at best.

As a traditionalist, Galaxy Commander Clarence Pryde and Star Colonel Robert had both found themselves exiled to this backwater world and on a downward trajectory in their careers. As a Bloodname holder, Clarence Pryde had a decent chance that his DNA would survive to the next generation, when it would be used to create a new *sibko*. Robert, on the other hand, remained bitter that Mongol politics meant no one had supported his bid to win a Bloodname. On two occasions, he had tried to compete in Grand Melees, but was cut down. All these years later, he was uneasily fatalistic about it. He consoled himself with his hobby of breeding Terran zebra finches.

Both were starting to show their age. Clarence Pryde's dark-brown hair was thinning considerably, which only made his mustache look bushier. Robert's brown skin was turning dark under his eyes, and the hair around his temples was streaked with gray.

Robert enlarged the rectangular box to show ten combat vehicles forming a line several hundred meters from the DropShip. "*Outpost*-class DropShip identified as the *Lauren Bourjon*. They should also have a BattleMech Star, an Elemental Star, and a pair of aerofighter Points... Curious that they have not unloaded them yet. They have had plenty of time."

"Have we detected any other Hell's Horses DropShips?"

"*Neg*, Galaxy Commander. Just this one."

Pryde's eyes remained fixed on the holoprojection. "Most of them are fast hovercraft." He glanced at his officers. "This is most odd. And totally out of character for the Hell's Horses. Any thoughts?"

He glanced through the wall to the ready room, and the warriors leaned forward almost in unison. He shook his head and waved them away. They leaned back in disappointment.

Robert grinned. "They all want a shot at the newcomers. There are not many opportunities for battle around here, *quiaff*?"

Pryde stepped next to Robert and whispered, "I suppose it is to be expected when you are a sane warrior in a Clan run by psychopaths."

Both men grinned and shrugged.

Raising his voice to normal, Pryde said, "Few have 'Mechs fast enough to keep up with those hovers. We will need to improvise a Star to pursue and destroy. We do not have enough fast units for bidding.

"Star Colonel Robert, put the Star together. 'Mechs and vehicles only. No aerospace fighters. I want them ready for when the real action begins. But tell the pilots I have granted the DropShip *safcon*."

Eight hovercraft and two wheeled vehicles kicked up dust as they idled on the grassy plain. To Rafeny, it sounded like a line of aircraft waiting to take off from a runway.

"Attention, Palomino Star," he announced, "you ride for the honor of yourself, your crew, and the Herd. The honor of one is not complete without the others. One reaches the finish line first, but only with the Herd. Anything else shames the Herd.

"Several possible routes have been loaded into your nav systems. When choosing a route, remember that this is a test of your ability to cooperate as much as anything else.

"Also, this world hosts a respectably sized Jade Falcon garrison, so you will need to remain sharp. However, in addition to your speed, you have a unique advantage on this planet. Look up and observe the green spheres in the sky."

Many of the clouds were green, and small fragments of them were scattered as far as the eye could see. The closer ones were clearly made of light-green ball-shaped objects. The sunlight shined through them, casting a pale-green glow on the ground.

"They are a kind of plant known as balaoverde. They extract hydrogen from water and store it in their main chamber, which keeps them aloft. Large concentrations of these plants will block satellite observation. IR cannot see through them during the day, but it can at night. Aerospace fighters typically will not fly through them. Use them to evade detection.

"We will meet you at the finish point. Let the Mad Stampede begin."

At the back of the line, Rafeny watched the compressed 360-degree display as the wheeled Odin and Zephyros at the front of the line peeled off. An Epona A and a Shamash kicked up the dust a heartbeat later. A paired Svantovit and Hephaestus C departed next, followed by a Hephaestus A and an Ashur.

Rafeny felt his Epona Prime lurch forward as Skarleth drove the hovertank alongside their jumping Hephaestus Pointmate. As the great form of their DropShip receded in the distance, Rafeny watched its base flash, and the ground smoke as the ship rose into the air. Unease nipped at the back of his mind as he watched their support and sole means of escape from this hostile world leave them.

He called up the maps in the navigation system again. The first route included a river valley. It was good for the hovercraft, but the wheeled vehicles would need to look for a road and a bridge through the region pierced by the river and wetlands. A second route passed through a forested area, which would favor the wheeled vehicles over the hovercraft. Both routes were shorter than the third route, which had a well-defined road system both kinds of vehicles could exploit. The problem was that it would leave them exposed in many places, and was significantly longer, giving the Falcons more time to hunt them. The choice of route was a test of its own.

Rafeny opened a channel to his own crew and the commander of the Hephaestus. "Palomino Ten, this is Palomino Nine. Do you have a route preference?"

"Pull up your weather maps." The Hephaestus' commander paused as the other crew toggled their maps. "The prevailing winds are to the east. Right now, we have a low-pressure area over us the balaoverdes ride around in. A cold front is coming in from the west with a high-pressure area behind it, so the skies are likely to clear when the front passes through. We have no more than thirty hours or so before all three routes become exposed to observation and aerial attack. If we take the first route, we are more likely to avoid the gap in cover."

"Then the first route it is."

The vehicles kicked up dust and road debris, still in a relatively tight formation. After a few kilometers, paired vehicles veered to the flanks to get out of the herd and pull forward.

Constant vibrations reverberated through the Epona's hull. Jolts tossed Rafeny as the hovertank passed over depressions or rises in the ground. His Point, and Point Two with an Epona and a Shamash, were pulling ahead of the others. They were in a good position for now. But Rafeny knew when they hit rougher terrain, their speed and Skarleth's driving skills would not matter as much. They needed luck in choosing the right path and avoiding dead ends or ground that could wreck their motive systems.

In his display, the images of the other competitors blurred from the rhythmic shaking of his Epona. The other vehicles shrank as they increased their lead. Two of the others broke off to the flank. The Odin and Zephyros were the only wheeled vehicles in a herd of hovercraft, and they were clearly headed for the second route. It would spare them the river crossing, but leave them without support.

Rafeny wondered if he would ever see them again.

JADE FALCON COMMAND CENTER
DENIZLI
JADE FALCON OCCUPATION ZONE
2 FEBRUARY 3141

Galaxy Commander Clarence Pryde watched the Hell's Horses DropShip depart for the northeast, flanked by its fighters. On the map, the vehicles disappeared under the cover of the balaoverde clusters.

"Robert, how is it going?"

"We are short on 'Mechs fast enough to intercept and keep up with what the Horses put down. But we have enough Donars, Skadis, and Nacons to make two Stars, if we include Serkan's *Piranha* and Kerbit's *Fire Moth*."

"Kerbit..." Pryde shook his head. He looked over to the ready room. As usual, the black-clad warriors sat in their own section, away from the greens. But sitting in his own isolation, a warrior with curly, blond hair beamed a big smile at apparently nothing. He was not staring at a personal device or a wall monitor. He just stared straight ahead with a disturbingly enthusiastic smile.

Pryde exchanged an uneasy glance with Robert. "In spite of him being a young and enthusiastic Mongol, even Malvina's officers did not want him in a front-line unit. The scientists need to give that Bloodline a rethink, *quiaff*?"

"*Aff*," Robert replied quietly enough for only Pryde to hear. "I thought he could do the least amount of damage in a *Fire Moth* before he got himself killed, so I assigned him the only one we had."

"Why not the *Piranha*? Serkan was worthy of an OmniMech."

Robert shook his head. "All those machine guns. I was afraid they might give him ideas."

Pryde sighed. "Good thinking."

HAMPSTEAD PLAINS
DENIZLI
JADE FALCON OCCUPATION ZONE
2 FEBRUARY 3141

The tsaran glided among the balaoverde with all four of its skin flaps extended. Its eyes darted over the floating plants, in search of the right color. The lightest ones had skin thin enough to punch a tiny hole through.

The tsaran's vigilance was rewarded with a plant hovering just below the formation. The furry creature banked and swooped, then grabbed the sphere with all four limbs. The balaoverde rolled slightly on impact, and the tsaran felt a light *thump* as a head popped over the top of the orb and hissed in its direction. Another tsaran was contesting the prize. Both climbed to the top and hissed at each other, their mouths wide open in challenge. They maneuvered back and forth, knocking off several balao-mites in the process. After several rounds of threatening push-ups, the first tsaran lost its nerve, jumped off, and glided away.

The victor sniffed the air as it scrambled around the orb, searching for other threats. Its sense of smell said the plant was already punctured and leaking gas. It gazed at the ground below and confirmed that the balaoverde was dropping at a safe speed. It scrambled down the side to the reservoir lip that circled the bottom of the plant and lapped up the pooled moisture. As the stricken balaoverde drifted down, the tsaran feasted on the many different insectoids that lived on the sphere's surface.

When the balaoverde landed on the ground, it sagged. The tsaran instinctively ate as quickly as it could. For now, there were few of its kind here. But the vast migration was already arriving, and their numbers would darken the skies. The multitudes would feed on the balaoverde, and the skies would clear.

Jairo watched the herd of large grazing animals massing on the opposite bank of the river. "How far back do you think they go?"

"Easily kilometers," responded Kaliyah. "The computer identifies them as grunes. Heavy and tough. They form herds with as many as ten thousand individuals."

They had muscular bodies, bare brownish-green skin with alternating black-and-yellow striping along their spines, and four legs covered in brown fur near the ankles. Their heads resembled a three-lobed stone with a series of black eyes ringing the head.

"Jairo, look off to the right. Do you see that opening on the far side of the rock formation?"

"*Aff.*"

"Take us there. Palomino Six, this is Five. Follow us."

"That is risky, Five. They may not give way to us."

"I think we can get across before they start crossing. The alternative could add half an hour to our trip."

"Acknowledged."

The Svantovit drove down to the river and blasted up a cloud of moisture as it slipped into the water. As the accompanying Hephaestus followed it, the grunes piled into the water on the other side and came on quickly. As the herd bore down on the other side, the Hephaestus turned parallel to the river and radioed warnings to the Svantovit.

Kaliyah shook her head. "We cannot outrun them. Push though. They will get out of the way when they start hitting metal."

As the hovercraft pushed into the herd, a grune climbed up onto it. Kaliyah looked up as she heard stomping that began at the front of the hull, then passed overhead and continued to the back. The Hephaestus wobbled as the grune jumped off. Soon, Kaliyah heard more stomping as other grunes climbed on.

An alarm screamed as the hovercraft rocked from side to side.

"*Horscat,*" Jairo cursed under his breath.

The stomping noises increased in frequency as more grunes piled atop the tank. The crew pressed on as Kaliyah noticed her hovercraft was tilting consistently to the right. Suddenly she was thrown to the side as the Svantovit flipped and sank.

"Bail out, now!" Kaliyah commanded as she announced their emergency to the Hephaestus.

Jairo released the hatch and pushed, but the inrushing water pushed the hatch back.

"Remember your training," Kaliyah told her crew. "Just before the water reaches the top, three deep breaths."

Time dragged as they all waited for the water to rise. They took their breaths and pushed through the murky water and out the hatch. They swam toward the light, but as they reached the surface, all was turmoil and grune legs.

The kick Jairo took in the head was the beginning of the end for all three of them.

HAMPSTEAD PLAINS
DENIZLI
JADE FALCON OCCUPATION ZONE
2 FEBRUARY 3141

Rafeny's Point was gaining on Point Two. They appeared as a pair of dust clouds a few kilometers ahead. He kept a nervous eye on the engine readouts as Skarleth pushed the hovercraft to the max. He was tossed up and down in his seat when they went over a bump.

An hour ago, Point Two had chosen a better pass through a line of hills, and did not have to turn around like Rafeny's Point. Rafeny had cursed his navigational chart's lack of detail. He also wished they had the usual VTOL among the Herd to help them fix that problem.

He was yanked to the left as Skarleth dodged rough ground, but he praised his driver's skill. The wrong debris could rip the hoverskirt open and bring their whole journey to a tragic end.

Ahead, Rafeny saw a thick line of trees. They grew taller as the minutes passed. Since the two competitors ahead were both hovercraft, he knew they could not plow into the trees. Unless there was a way in, they would have to turn. If they found a path, the choice of which turns were made could change which Point would be in the lead.

The two vehicles disappeared into the tree line. Rafeny urged Skarleth on. More painful minutes dragged by as the competition sped ahead, out of sight. It was almost a relief as Rafeny's Point passed the entrance to the woods and trees began whipping by at uncomfortable speeds. The engine throttled down as Skarleth slowed the Epona and swerved between the trees. Claustrophobia enveloped Rafeny as the forest flew by too quickly and years of training screamed that they should not be there.

He glanced at the radar to confirm their Hephaestus was still with them. "Palomino Nine to Ten. Can you jump and tell us about the road ahead?"

"*Aff*, Nine. Jumping."

Seconds later, Palomino Ten was back on the comm. "It is one big maze out there. Point Two appears to have split up."

"Acknowledged. We should slow and give the engines a little break."

They spent twenty minutes ducking in and out of dead ends and tight curves that seemed to go nowhere. Eventually, they had to stop as they came nose to nose with Point Two's Shamash. Its Pointmate, the Epona, pulled up behind it.

"Palomino Nine to Point Three," Rafeny radioed. "Does this mean you have not found a way through?"

"That sums things up nicely, Nine."

"Palomino Nine to Ten. Turn around. We are leaving the way we came." Rafeny turned to Skarleth, who nodded and spun the vehicle without needing an official order.

"We will lose the better part of an hour," Rafeny lamented. "That means we probably lost our advantage over the other Points."

"It is greener than I remembered it a few hours ago," Arismaily remarked.

Darkness obscured the plain as she tossed Rafeny a bag of rations that had been warming in the engine compartment. Both of the Point's vehicles were parked along a tree line on the edge of a plain, to help hide them from observation. The other competitors had agreed to stop for the night so everyone had a clear mind for the inevitable Jade Falcon confrontation that might happen tomorrow.

"That's the moonlight filtering through the balaoverde swarms." Propped up against the side of the tank, Rafeny ripped open the rations and grimaced as the engine smell mingled with food smell.

"Watch that language, freebirth," Arismaily poked him playfully.

Glancing up for a moment, Rafeny remembered her proportions were a little off. Her head seemed too big for a body that small. And her eyes seemed a little large for her face, but none of that was out of the ordinary for an aerospace-pilot phenotype. He had seen them his whole life. But a little voice in the back of his head still told him something was off.

He grunted and continued eating.

Arismaily sat down next to him with her own rations. "Are you all right? You are unusually quiet. You even ignored my freebirth-baiting."

He grunted again.

"A kerensky for your thoughts."

He sighed. "Palomino Five. It was a bad way to go."

"*Aff*." She frowned. "They were warriors. Few of us live to old age. That is the nature of things."

He watched waves form in the grass as the wind gusted. After a pause, he said, "Their lives came to nothing."

"Nothing? They were warriors. Like you, some rose from their birth caste to the pinnacle of Clan society. What more could they ask for, besides a mention in *The Remembrance* or *The Book of Barding*?"

He laid down the empty ration bag. "As things stand now, my life will amount to nothing more than a short literary reference in *The Book of Barding*, or if I'm really lucky, a line in *The Remembrance*."

She tried to lighten the mood. "Not if you continue using language like that."

"I apologize. I spent a great deal of time among the lower cases in my *sibko* days on unicorn-herd duties." He sighed. "If we do not have offspring, do our lives truly matter? As tankers, we cannot realistically expect our genes to be used to breed *sibkos*. *Aff*, we are warriors, but not *good enough* warriors. We are only useful as cannon fodder to help MechWarriors win the battles."

"I must disagree with you there. Such a notion may be true in all the other Clans, but in our Clan, even tankers can command MechWarriors."

"*Aff*, but normally the MechWarriors are in charge. And how often do we end up contributing to the gene pool?"

She paused. "I do not know."

"Indeed. This is why I pushed us to take part in this competition. If we win the race, the powers that be will take notice. We will still have a chance to be a part of the next generation of warriors. Our lives will have had meaning. But today, we lost three warriors, not even in combat. If we lose half, we will all be disgraced, and the gene pool will be forever closed to us."

Rafeny turned to her. "What happens when the Jade Falcons find us, and the shooting starts in earnest? Up to this point, our losses have been lighter than other Stampedes, but that is because the locals have been unable to track us. And find us they will, simply by following our tracks. How many of us will make it back to the DropShip?

"Whatever happens, we must do everything we can to bring our people back alive."

A huge flock of squeaking aerial creatures spent several minutes passing overhead and gradually disappeared into the night. Had it been daylight, the warriors below might have noticed disturbing numbers of balaoverdes dropping from the sky.

JADE FALCON COMMAND CENTER
DENIZLI
JADE FALCON OCCUPATION ZONE
3 FEBRUARY 3141

Galaxy Commander Pryde suppressed a yawn as he entered the command center. "Any new developments, Star Colonel?"

"The Horses' DropShip has moved twice since the initial landing," Robert said. "Both times in the region currently being obscured by balaoverdes."

"How long until we can get our VTOLs up?"

"Meteorology forecasts clear skies and warm temperatures. The balaoverdes should warm up enough to reach a safe altitude in just over an hour. The Nacons are following multiple sets of tracks, but some have been obscured by grune-herd activity. I have contacted the DropShip again, and they still insist they are having a race."

Pryde chuckled. "Why would they do something so asinine as to travel all this way to have a race for second-line warriors on a hostile world? What I do not understand is what they are looking for. There is absolutely nothing in the region they are operating in—no cities, settlements, mines, or even agriculture centers."

He began pacing. "This kind of operation has happened a few times before. There have been a few raids and trials afterward. Maybe the DropShip does reconnaissance imaging whenever it moves around. Do an analysis of what it could have seen when it moved."

"Galaxy Commander!" One of the staff practically jumped out of his seat. "A gap is forming in the balaoverde layer. I have moving thermal contacts!"

Both senior officers raced over and examined the screen. They turned to each other and smiled.

"Star Colonel," Pryde said, "it is time for that pony hunt."

DENDERA PLAINS
DENIZLI
JADE FALCON OCCUPATION ZONE
3 FEBRUARY 3141

"This is Palomino Four. I have contacts in the sky: a Point each of Donars and Skadis."

Rafeny expanded the map area to include the new information from the data feed. Ahead, the horizon was dotted with trees, some grouped in thick forests. Normally, they would have their own VTOLs in the air, feeding the ground units a complete picture of the tactical situation. The Horses were known for using Donars for that role in most operations. Now, the tables were turned, and he was liking none of it.

"This is Palomino Nine," Rafeny said. "They seem to be vectoring in, not just watching. I think they are the Falcon attack force. Can anyone see any other support?"

He was greeted by a chorus of negatives.

"This is Palomino Three. If they have support, they are not waiting for them. I am being targeted by a Skadi."

Three's Epona swerved as tracer rounds from the Skadi's autocannon chewed up the ground around them. The small, rectangular Shamash hovercraft on its right was getting the same treatment from the other Skadi. The Epona swiveled its turret and fired two racks of long-range missiles at the Skadi, forcing it to rapidly turn away. The flat rotor assemblies attached to each side of the VTOL wobbled as the pilot realized they had turned too fast and tried to bring it back under control. Just as it leveled out, the Epona fired a second salvo of forty LRMs. Smoke and missile exhaust blurred the Skadi as the swarm intersected it. The VTOL cleared the cloud, but dipped right and spun downward, then crashed into a light stand of trees.

The second Skadi was blasting up the ground as the Shamash dodged and swerved from the tracers, but the VTOL paused when its Pointmate hit the ground.

Trees were not normally a hovercraft's best friend, but the Shamash's pilot was desperate for cover and zoomed along a narrow path that cut through the forest.

"Norvin," Rafeny radioed, "get out of there and head for the clearing just to the east! If you get caught in a dead end—"

"I know that, but that Skadi is right on me!"

"All Palomino units, this is Palomino Nine. Forget *zellbrigen*. We fight for the honor of the Herd, and we leave no one to die. Norvin, get out of there. We have you covered."

Norvin turned his Shamash at speed just like Rafeny had seen him do a dozen times before, but this time he skidded into the trees. The hovertank stopped moving and its lift fans whined at an unnaturally high pitch that meant the air was escaping from his hoverskirt. The left side of the vehicle was sitting on top of a small tree it had knocked down, leaving a huge gap for air to escape.

"This is Palomino Four. I am immobilized. My vehicle is on a tree. If someone could attach a chain and pull me off, I can get it moving again."

"Negative," Rafeny replied. "Not with three VTOLs still up there. We just lost the Odin. Get out of your vehicle and be ready to run when we reach you. Palomino Six, can you pick up Palomino One and Two?"

"We will do our best."

"Palomino Nine to Ten. We need to cover Palomino Three."

Three's Epona weaved through the trees to get to its Pointmate, but lost speed each time it turned. The Skadi made a strafing pass from behind, and autocannon rounds rhythmically banged off the hull. The Epona returned fire with both LRM launchers but missed altogether, blasting limbs off trees in the process. Missiles and tracer rounds crossed paths several more times before the Epona stopped, pulled the diminutive Shamash pilot to safety, and spun back into motion.

As Palomino Three cleared the trees, the Skadi strafed it again. Bits and pieces of the Epona's hoverskirt blasted out along the side of the vehicle as it sank and slowed to a halt. Crew members slipped out of hatches as the turret swiveled to track its attacker. This time some of the missiles hit, but the Falcon's tracers tore into the armor, and the turret exploded.

The Skadi wobbled off beyond the horizon, followed by the Donars.

"Palomino Nine to Six," Rafeny radioed. "We have another pickup for you."

He watched the VTOLs disappear in the distance. Bitterly, he watched smoke pour out of the mutilated Epona. He counted four warriors and called to the Hephaestus from the second Point for a pickup. There should have been a total of six Horse warriors on foot. With regret, he noted two had met their ends.

Two who would not be represented in the next generation.

As the Hephaestus pulled up and popped its hatch, Rafeny opened the Star's communication frequency. "I doubt the Falcons bid that low. More will be coming."

"We should try to recover the Shamash, *quiaff*?"

"*Neg*, they know where we are. We know they have Nacons that can keep up with us. Their advanced tactical missiles could do a great deal of damage, and if we are immobilized, we do not have the rest of a Cluster to pick us up. We are on our own. We simply do not have the time to recover it, even if it is not torn up underneath. I abhor the waste, but if we linger, we could lose far more than we already have."

They left.

DENDERA HILLS
DENIZLI
JADE FALCON OCCUPATION ZONE
3 FEBRUARY 3141

MechWarrior Kerbit listened to the radio chatter from the rest of his improvised Star as he desperately ran his *Fire Moth* at full speed to intercept the Horses' vehicles. His fingers caressed the switch for his Myomer Accelerator Signal Circuitry system as he weighed the dangers of locking up his leg myomers.

His life was an unending frustration of inactivity. In his first postings, he came to know the sweet bliss of glorious battle on two occasions, though his commanding officers were incredulous at how he behaved in combat. At times, they looked at and talked to him like he was mentally defective. *But what do they know?*

The Star's Nacon scout cars and operational Donar VTOLs were nipping at the Horses' heels, which had forced them to turn and fight, giving him time to reach the battle. He shrugged when he heard of one of the Nacons was already out of the fight because its wheels had been blown off. He dismissed the fragility of the vehicle as a consequence of massing only 20 tons.

Then he remembered his 'Mech only massed 20 tons.

His eyebrows creased together at the dark thought, but that worry instantly melted away as he assured himself that a 'Mech was made of sterner stuff.

His eyes fixed on the dust and smoke rising in the distance. He knew time was running out. Either the Horses would be destroyed or would escape, and then there would be no glory left for him. He would be included in no more bids, and then he would be forgotten. He needed to get there fast.

He triggered his MASC and let it run for thirty seconds before disengaging it. He waited thirty seconds and triggered it again. He could feel the battle growing closer. He could almost taste the dust, the smoke, and the tang of ozone. He triggered the MASC again, then waited. He could see the enemy vehicles moving. *Must go faster!*

He triggered the MASC once more, but he did not stop. Seconds ticked away as he drew even closer. His MASC system warned him to disengage, but he kept it active. His heart beat in time with the stomping of his 'Mech's feet. His soul sang as he ignored the MASC alarm. His pulse throbbed in his ears, and he could hear nothing else. He lined up his crosshairs on a wheeled Zephyros.

There was a jarring, audible lurch as the myomers froze up. But at this speed, inertia was not prepared to release its hold on the speedy 'Mech. For two seconds, the *Fire Moth* was airborne. Kerbit felt his organs moving in opposition to gravity. The most ancient part of his brain had a few milliseconds to realize something was horribly wrong as it registered that the ground was moving very fast in front of him and not *below* him. He had just enough time to tell himself never to do that again.

The first part of his 'Mech to contact the ground was his jutting cockpit. The rest of the 'Mech obeyed the siren song of momentum and pushed it along and down into the planet's surface. Metal plates were thrown off as the legs flipped forward and the 'Mech tumbled and rolled several times, eventually coming to a stop.

The *Fire Moth* signaled its finale in the form of a fireworks display as its short-range-missile ammunition cooked off into the air.

JADE FALCON COMMAND CENTER
DENIZLI
JADE FALCON OCCUPATION ZONE
3 FEBRUARY 3141

Dumbfounded, Clarence Pryde stared at the holoimage. "Did I just see that right?"

"Clarence..." Star Colonel Robert said, "I have no words."

Both men slowly shook their heads as they watched footage of the *Fire Moth* belching smoke.

Robert opened a data window on the holotable next to the image of the downed 'Mech. "There is no telemetry coming from the cockpit recorder. I think it is a total loss."

Clarence Pryde shrugged.

"Galaxy Commander?" A commtech held out a data pad. "A courier JumpShip just arrived with a priority message for you. It is from the Chingis Khan."

He stared darkly at the device. What kind of malevolence was waiting to be unleashed from it? Every time Malvina Hazen issued an order, the universe seemed to break a little bit more.

Pryde gestured at the image of the destroyed *Fire Moth*. "I hope that is not an omen of what is to come."

"That MechWarrior stole our kill," Arismaily complained sarcastically.

Skarleth made a hard turn and lined up on a Nacon. "Must have been a cadet."

As the Jade Falcon vehicles turned off to the east as if to disengage, the orphaned Hephaestus finally caught up to the rest of the Herd after picking up the survivors of the two wheeled vehicles, crippled kilometers away.

"This is Palomino Six. Are the Falcons running?"

"Maybe. They can do damage, but they cannot stop all of us. Although a typical Jade Falcon warrior would not let that stop them from trying to achieve a kill."

"I say we let them go. That highway just west of us will take us through the hills. After that, it is just eighty-five kilometers to the finish line."

In pairs, the vehicles took to the road. As they passed through the forested hills, Rafeny grew uneasy. On both flanks, all he could see were the branches and trunks of the trees lining the road. It was a good place for an ambush.

"Palomino Nine to Palomino Ten. Give us a good jump to give us a lay of the land."

The jumping Hephaestus triggered its jets and took off. Rafeny watched the twin rear fins wag like a fish's tail as they balanced the vehicle in flight. The hovertank then arced back down and returned to the earth with a slight lurch.

"Nine, we have a problem. There is a *Piranha* four klicks ahead in the trees on the left."

"We have no room to maneuver here," Rafeny replied. "If it gets behind us with all those machine guns, it will shoot out all our hoverskirts."

As if by mutual agreement, they slowed to a halt.

Rafeny took a deep breath. The trees were waving vigorously. To the west, the skies were a clear blue. The balaoverde clusters were being pushed ahead of the cold front; the Horses would soon lose their cover. A detour could take many hours.

Time they did not have.

"This is Palomino Six. We have seismic returns. It knows that we know. It is coming."

"No choice here, Six," Rafeny said. "We go back the way we came. Hang a left at the plain, and hug the forest until we find an opening."

The Zephyros backed up and did a three-point turn as the hovercraft spun in place. They all took off down the road, and upon reaching the clearing, they detected the Falcon vehicles waiting for them in the distance.

"This is Nine," Rafeny radioed. "Point Five will challenge the *Piranha*. Palomino Six, handle the others.

His Epona and the jumping Hephaestus circled as they waited for the *Piranha* to approach. They split as it neared weapons range, and maneuvered to attack from each side. When they reached long range for their medium lasers, both vehicles opened fire on the 'Mech, which lashed out at the Epona with its lasers. All missed, and the combatants continued to dance around each other.

Skarleth drove the Epona at the *Piranha* to keep its least-vulnerable front armor pointed toward the 'Mech, but broke to the side before the dozen machine guns could come into range. The Hephaestus came up on the *Piranha*'s rear as it fired both medium lasers, and one hit the 'Mech's leg. Arismaily missed with the Epona's medium lasers and failed to lock with her Streak SRMs. In response, the *Piranha* burned off the Epona's armor with one of its medium lasers.

The three combatants continued to spin around each other as they jockeyed for good firing positions. The *Piranha* angled in toward the Epona, cutting the distance enough to strafe Rafeny's tank with its machine guns.

"The skirt is hit," Skarleth cried. "I am losing speed."

"Horscat!" Rafeny cursed as he watched the pressure readings and speedometer drop. He knew it would be easy for the *Piranha* to get behind them now.

Arismaily swiveled the turret to the rear as he heard a multitude of bullets *plink* off the rear armor. The tank's instruments and readouts screamed in pain.

Arismaily screamed too, but Rafeny soon realized she was screaming in victory. In the wraparound viewscreen, he saw the *Piranha* on the ground, one of its legs lying beyond it. It propped itself up, but Arismaily took careful aim and shot the arm off.

The high-pitched whine of the lift fan announced that their Epona would not be finishing the race. Rafeny smashed his hands on the instrument panel and then took a breath. He paused a few seconds, then stroked the instrument panel and apologized to the vehicle.

"That MechWarrior has left his cockpit." Arismaily stared into her targeting screen. "He has his sidearm."

Rafeny brought up the image on his monitor. He took note of the other Jade Falcons breaking off.

"I should kill him, *quiaff*? He ended the race for us."

Rafeny pondered. His brows furrowed together as he stared off into space. *"Neg... Neg."* He paused. "He is like us now. Skarleth, shut off the fans."

The Jade Falcon MechWarrior raised his sidearm at the Epona and pulled the trigger continuously. The bullets bounced harmlessly off the armor, and when they stopped, the Falcon lowered the weapon and stared at the hovercraft.

Rafeny activated the tank's exterior speaker. "MechWarrior, why did you do that?"

The warrior said simply: "I am Jade Falcon."

"So?"

"If my 'Mech goes down, I must continue the fight. If I can shoot my enemy, I shoot. If I cannot shoot, I stab. If I cannot stab, I punch."

"Does that not seem stupid to you?"

The Falcon threw his pistol, and it bounced off the Epona.

"How much did that accomplish? Were you expecting more?"

The MechWarrior closed his eyes. "*Neg.*"

"Why bother?"

"The Chingis Khan would be wrathful."

"She has no power here."

The Falcon looked around sharply, as if expecting Malvina Hazen to pop out of the ground.

Rafeny grinned. "It is that bad, *quiaff*?"

The MechWarrior stared off to the side awkwardly.

"All right, we are taking you as a bondsman. No more Mad Malvina for you."

Rafeny called for pickup, and they left the crippled hovercraft. As a pair of Hephaestuses pulled up, he placed his hand on his stricken Epona and whispered: "I am sorry. Someday, I will come back for you."

He patted the tank and departed.

DROPSHIP *LAUREN BOURJON*
DENIZLI
JADE FALCON OCCUPATION ZONE
3 FEBRUARY 3141

When the Hephaestus came to a stop, the rear hatch popped open. Rafeny stepped out with Arismaily and their bondsman, MechWarrior Serkan, onto the floor of the cavernous DropShip bay. A tech crew had already run over and was preparing to clamp the Hephaestus into its cubicle in preparation of their launch.

Several cubicles down, a crowd was gathered around the Asshur crew, celebrating their victory in the race. A few techs noticed smoke coming off the engine and gathered fire-fighting equipment.

Rafeny sighed at the scene. "*The Book of Barding* will not remember us as the victors of this Stampede. It seems I will have to try another strategy for securing my genetic legacy."

Arismaily distractedly ran fingers through her hair. "Do you have one yet?"

"I do. I just need to convince a lower-caste woman to have a child with me."

Arismaily stared at him with a grin. "Good luck with that."

SOLAHMA DEATH SONG

PHILLIP JOHNSTON

Howling wolves pierce
the silent night
while I look upon
the Strana Mechty sky
for the last time.

As the wolves howl,
my mind wanders,
filled with remembrances:
stalking prey with my *sibkin*,
tearing down the enemies
who dared stand against us.

Only I remain—
outpaced by the pups
who do the hunting now.
What is the wolf
without his pack?

Tonight, I wander
into the wild
for my final hunt.

*—A poem scrawled on a scrap of paper,
found alongside an abandoned Wolf warrior's
cloak and pistol belt, near the forest of Gunzberg.*

INFORMATION SOFTWARE AT WAR: THE AUTOMATED BATTLEMECH RECOGNITION FRAMEWORK

JAMES BIXBY

Presented by Broadie Wozniak, PhD
A lecture at the Republic Institute of Strategic Combat
1 April 3149

It was said, almost infamously, that "Information is ammunition." The modern MechWarrior has a bevy of information at their fingertips, whether it is topographical information downloaded from local weather satellites, ambient atmospheric conditions from onboard sensors, or internal diagnostic information of their own BattleMech's performance.

Still, none would argue that anything is more important than who or what is shooting at you. As 'Mech technology proliferated across the Inner Sphere, and various powers began developing more than mere clones of the MSK *Mackie* series to fit their own vision of warfare, simply calling out "BattleMech" on the battlefield was an inaccurate means of identification.

This often led to intelligence services analyzing 'Mechs and their capabilities from battlefield footage, and assigning them reporting names, like the NATO and Soviet alliances of pre-spaceflight Terra. Most famously, operatives from the Ministry of Information, Intelligence, and Operations called the original Mackie "Fat Man" after the first atomic bomb, as they were convinced of the power of this new weapon system. This designation survived as the Armed Forces of the Federated Suns developed its own *Mackie* clones as BattleMech technology proliferated.

Predictably, Draconis Combine troops returning from the Battle of Styx spoke of "Kaiju" despite commercial WorkMechs having existed for nearly a century.

The formation of the Star League, combined with numerous private entities creating BattleMechs and selling them to all comers, demanded a more standardized approach. The combined Star League Defense Force needed a unified reporting system, as well as a framework in which all newly spotted 'Mechs could be identified and given an army-wide provisional designation to be ratified by intelligence services later. This led to the computer program that most MechWarriors simply call the "warbook," though the technical designation is the Automated BattleMech Recognition Framework. As the buildup to the Reunification War continued and the industrial-intelligence vaults opened in the name of unity, the grand solution of reporting names was reached: BattleMechs would be called out by their final factory designations. In 2573, the Maltex Corporation's THG-11E *Thug* became the first BattleMech entered into the ABRF using its native designation.

The framework software is stored in the diagnostic interpretation computer, and tied to the protocols that directly affect the 'Mech's targeting and tracking system, as well as the bevy of external sensors and cameras that dot a 'Mech's body. When a MechWarrior actively selects a target, the system goes to work. Using a similar artificial-intelligence system as most facial-recognition programs used for personal-computer security, the ABRF software will analyze the profile of the target BattleMech and compare it in real time to the preloaded blueprint of the target. In less than a second, the target is identified with near certainty, and the information is displayed to the MechWarrior to provide at-a-glance target and tracking information.

Originally, the Star League wanted full target specifications to be uploaded and available, with the BattleMech's DI computer determining target condition based on percentages. However, the inherent chaos of a battlefield, combined with a MechWarrior needing to focus on piloting and fighting, made such a detailed system untenable. The debacle of the United Triumph exercises, which saw many MechWarriors overwhelmed with extraneous data, sealed the fate of the ARBF 1.0 system. The rapidly developed 2.0 provided a more limited amount of data in the form of the BattleMech's designation and a simple mugshot of the target, with no indication of its relative condition.

The later 3.1 update of the software simplified the use of photorealistic readouts and depictions to the more familiar wireframe or polygonal outlines on a tertiary display. This outline gave MechWarriors a relatively easy to digest readout of their target and its relative condition. Eventually the universal color coding of Blue-Green-Yellow-Red-Black was adopted to reflect the system's estimated appraisal of the target's condition.

ABRF 3.1 also utilized a more enhanced outline-recognition system, allowing it to identify factory-installed weaponry and equipment on BattleMechs, and to recognize them as damaged, altered, or even missing completely. This became handy for the SLDF Intelligence Directorate to identify many House-specific variations of BattleMechs, such as House Davion's TDR-5Sd *Thunderbolt*, with its distinctive autocannon in place of the missile launcher. As the final feature of note, armor and even aerospace programs were uploaded into the ABRF.

This advanced silhouette-recognition algorithm became infamous with the coming of the Clans, most notably, of course, with the confusion of the Clan *Timber Wolf* as a hybrid between a *Marauder* and *Catapult*. Other BattleMechs received half identifiers, such as the *Dire Wolf* being identified as part *Stalker*, part *Marauder*, or the *Mad Dog* as a combination of a *Catapult*, *Archer*, and *Rifleman*. Other Clan BattleMechs, such as the *Mist Lynx* and *Glass Spider*, returned long-dead Star League models (*Sling* and *Galahad*, respectively), and a few returned the dreaded "UKWN" designation. This forced the ComStar office responsible for updating the database to increase its typically meager workforce into a full-blown analysis department under ROM's Mu/Mu directorate. By 3055, the first major update to the ABRF in over 300 years, version 3.2, was completed and disseminated to every manufacturing and military supply depot.

These disseminations and updates happened in a rather ingenious way. Before the invention of hyperpulse generators, any ABRF updates were included in pre-mission intelligence packs provided by the SLDF, and were uploaded through the computer systems in BattleMech repair gantries. As permanent Star League bases were developed and the HPG network was established, these updates were sent via HPG in background packages in each base's daily-briefing package. Once the SLDF updated their systems, member-state militaries and territorial states received edited update packages, which typically omitted data about classified or Royal Division equipment. ComStar reinstituted this system after the Battle of Tukayyid, allowing Successor State militaries to update to the 3.2 system by the end of 3053, and receive regular updates afterward.

An odd footnote occurred during the Word of Blake's Inner Sphere-wide Jihad. In the months after the infamous Whiteout of 3068, scattered reports of errors in targeting and tracking systems occurred across all armies actively engaging the Word of Blake. From documents recovered in the Blakist archives, the Whiteout attack disseminated junk data as part of the standard ABRF update. The practical effect of this was minor, but persistent glitches occurred when Blakist assets were directly targeted. While this had little real impact on targeting accuracy, it did provide distractions that could prove deadly or disruptive. Fortunately for the armies of the Inner Sphere, this glitch was resolved by a simple downgrade of the system to its prior iteration and suspending further updates from the HPG-centered infrastructure. This led to the Houses and Clans of the Inner Sphere seriously reevaluating their reliance on a fairly open-source program. Even with the seeming demilitarization of ComStar, interstellar powers took great care since the end of the Jihad to vet updates for any other malware that could cause drastic effects to BattleMech targeting performance.

Still, for the last 500 years, the ABRF has permitted MechWarriors everywhere to maintain practical battlefield awareness in the heat of combat. And while the HPG-update system has been unavailable for the past two decades, individual intelligence services, and the use of open-source data systems like the famous *Technical Readout* series, has permitted a continued, albeit slower, updating of the ever-advancing pace of military hardware.

TABLE I: AN ABRIDGED LIST OF EARLY BATTLEMECH REPORTING NAMES

Armed Forces of the Federated Suns

House Davion chose to name other nations' BattleMechs after preexisting weapon systems. This would later cause some confusion among military historians, and led to the mass editing of history books and official documentation to update BattleMech designations using the ABRF.

Archer: Bombardier
Crossbow: Cestus
Firebee: Zip Gun
Gladiator: Little Boy
Mackie: Fat Man

Capellan Confederation Armed Forces

House Liao simplified designations with a two-letter code of the House that manufactured the 'Mech, followed by a numerical designation indicating the order in which the CCAF first encountered them.

Hector: FW Type 06
Hammerhands: FS Type-05
Icarus II: FW Type-02
Mackie: TH Type-01
Wolverine: FS Type-05

Draconis Combine Mustered Soldiery

All DCMS reporting names used various Japanese words or phrases that embodied the spirit of the 'Mech in question.

Battleaxe: Judoka
Commando: Kabutomushi
Crossbow: Fuyu no Kaze
Mackie: Kaiju
Swordsman: Kunai
Ymir: Kyojin

Free Worlds League Military

As is typical with the balkanized nature of the Free Worlds League, individual provinces developed their own reporting names. Reports from the National Intelligence Agency (the precursor to SAFE), however, used various nonsensical names starting with the letter B.

Commando: Bearing
Crossbow: Ballista
Firebee: Bootheel
Koschei: Blunderbuss
Mackie: Bouncer
Ymir: Breaker

Hegemony Armed Forces

The Terran Hegemony's BattleMech designations started with the letter of the 'Mech's weight class.

Commando: Leapfrog
Thunderbolt: Hooligan
Von Rohrs: Highwayman
Wolverine: Minx
Ymir: Arquebus

Lyran Commonwealth Armed Forces

After witnessing the seemingly indestructible nature of BattleMechs, the LCAF chose to name new BattleMechs after mythical undead creatures, though the *Mackie* was initially referred to as "Jotun" in intelligence documents. This tendency is also what gave the *Thunderbolt* its classic nickname "Zombie."

Hector: Draugr
Gladiator: Damphir
Griffin: Lich
Thunderbolt: Zombie

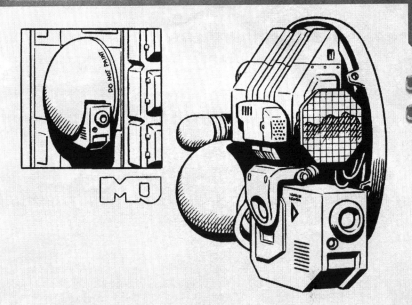

TABLE II: ABRF FALSE READS OF CLAN OMNIMECHS

Fire Moth: Stinger/Wasp/Spider/ERROR*
Mist Lynx: Sling
Kit Fox: Jenner/Locust
Adder: UKWN
Viper: UKWN
Ice Ferret****:** Ostscout/Panther/Assassin/Hermes II/Sentinel/Phoenix
    Hawk/Vulcan
Nova: UKWN
Stormcrow: Crab/Dervish/Talos
Mad Dog: Catapult/Archer/Rifleman or Galahad/Catapult†
Hellbringer: Warhammer
Summoner: Warhammer/Marauder/Victor
Timber Wolf: Marauder/Catapult
Gargoyle: Atlas/Warhammer/Blackjack
Warhawk: Annihilator/Nightstar
Executioner: Atlas/Charger/Victor
Dire Wolf: Stalker/Marauder/King Crab

  * Due to upswung arms
  ** Reading dependent on pod configuration
  † Configuration C only

THREE WAYS HOME

TOM LEVEEN

PART 3 (OF 4)

CHAPTER TEN

ALPHA CONTINENT
SOUTHERN HEMISPHERE
TIERAPOLVO
TRAUSSIN
TAURIAN CONCORDAT
11 JUNE 2581
0600 HOURS

Toma joins me by the stream. He peels off thickly woven socks and stuffs them into his boots before putting his feet in the water.

He looks at me, then away. "You were pretty amazing back there, against those 'Mechs."

"Yeah, well. It would've been even more amazing if we hadn't been found."

"Still. One against three. Not bad."

I snort a disagreement. Toma reaches out with one hand, which he pulls back quickly. I think he was going to put it on my shoulder.

"I won't punch you," I say.

"All the same, I don't want to pull back a stump," Toma replies.

I give him another snort—only, it has the vague shape of a laugh, too. "Is this water safe to drink?"

"Sure. This close to the mountain, no agriculture upstream. There might be a little leoray pee in it, though."

He grins as I roll my eyes. Leorays—massive meat-eating cats that roam the entire Besalis Desert—mostly come out at night.

I lie on my belly and take in a few handfuls of the stream. It's cool, not cold, but sweet with the flavor of melted ice from the mountaintops somewhere much farther to the south. Toma does the same.

We wipe our hands on our clothes to dry them. And that's when the world turns under me.

"Uh...Toma...?" It sounds like my voice is coming from very far away. Toma only stares at me.

Then the world upends. It's as if the planet is a toy ball, and some great creator has flicked it with celestial fingers. The flora around me spins in a circle, and I hear a deep *thud*. I can't breathe. Was I shot?

Breath claws back into my lungs, hot and dusty. I'm staring at the blue sky—so pretty, so warm—and can't make my eyes close.

Toma's face appears over me like an eclipse. He says something, maybe my name, but it's all dull. I still can't blink. My skin turns cold, very cold, and I think: *Yes—I'm hit, someone got me, maybe even one of our own operators. One good sniper shot, and this is how it ends.*

Something taps my cheeks. Toma's palms. Not hard, not soft.

"Ixy? Come on. Stay with me."

I don't know how long all this has been going on, but when I suck in another breath, it's like my lungs cry *Thank you*. But now I can't stop breathing. It's coming in and going out so fast, too fast...

Toma grabs my fingers. "Squeeze my hand, Ixy. Show me you're in there, squeeze my hand."

I do. Once. Then again. Barely.

"Good," he says. "That's good. Now breathe. You're fine. You're safe. Breathe. Slow down."

Somehow his words transform into those of my many drill instructors. Slowly, I piece together what's happened.

Shock. I remember this feeling, this helplessness my body is putting me through. It's like it has to do this to cleanse itself.

Eventually I get my breathing under control and can sit up.

"You all right?"

"Yeah. No. I will be. You're still bleeding, go get the IFAK."

Toma blinks and touches his cheek. His roughshod bandaging job isn't secure. He climbs into the *Griffin* and comes back with the first aid kit.

I douse the scratches on his face with liquid cleanser, making him suck in a sharp breath between his teeth. But he doesn't flinch, I'll give him that.

"You might have some scarring on those markings when it's healed," I say. "Sorry about that."

"They're called *neyora*."

"Oh, yeah?"

"The lines are based on the ancient language of our ancestors."

"I didn't know that." I press a nonstick pad to his face and keep it there to stanch the bleeding.

"There are thirteen families that descended from the people who first came from the Hegemony. According to tradition, anyway. It's probably not literally true. Each design is particular to the family you're from. A lot of Tierapolvos don't bother getting them anymore. We've sort of homogenized."

"Where the hell did you go to school, anyway?"

He smirks, then grunts—bad idea to make faces right now. "I like to read."

I tell him to keep the pad in place while I apply tape. "Do the marks... the *neyora*? Do they mean anything?"

"Each family has a—a motto, I guess you could call it. Or set of rules or ideas. It varies."

"What's yours mean?"

The bandage is in place, but Toma traces the lines with one finger from memory. "Faith. Fidelity. Family."

He drops his hand and meets my eyes. "I have to ask, Ixy...what would yours say?"

For some reason, even though I want to, I can't turn away from his gaze. "Mine would say..." I close the IFAK. "Mine would say, 'Take care of your 'Mech and it will take care of you.'"

Toma nods—and maybe looks disappointed.

"Go get our boots," I tell him, and it sounds more like an order than I'd intended. Toma confirms as much when he stands and gives me a sarcastic little salute. But he walks off to the stream, so, that's all that matters, I guess.

I do a once-over walkaround on the *Griffin*, examining its various wounds. It's bleeding green coolant out of one leg and the rear torso, as I feared. The left knee is mangled pretty bad, but the fact the great machine hasn't toppled over is a good sign.

I climb into the 'pit and fire up the 'Mech. The electronics seem to be running smoothly, so that's a good start. Ammo checks out. Gyroscope operational. Head-up display working across all spectra. Good.

Then I check our critical problem: the *Griffin*, even after time to cool off, is getting really warm really fast.

Cursing, I flick the life support's climate control a few times, thump it once, twice, and hold my breath, waiting for the oppressive heat to dissipate. It doesn't.

I climb back down just as Toma returns from the stream with our boots in hand, our canteens filled. "We have a problem."

Toma hands me a canteen. "Just the one? Things are looking up."

I take a drink. The sun is up over the mountains. Some primal urge makes me glance at the sky as I speak. "The 'Mech'll work. It'll get us where we need to go if we can avoid any more firefights. But the interior climate control is broken."

Toma really does know his 'Mechs, because I don't have to explain it. He shuts his eyes with a sigh. "In other words, it's a walking death trap."

"Copy that."

"Options?"

"None. We walk with the canopy open."

Toma mimics my look to the sky and blows out a sigh. "Toasty."

"Copy that, back at ya."

Toma and I get into the 'Mech. I let the canopy stay propped open on its hydraulics. It's not going to keep us cool, but it'll prevent us from suffocating in the heat that would build up in the cockpit if I closed it.

I get the 'Mech moving south. Between my own injuries and the *Griffin*'s, we have a noticeable limp.

"I'm not gonna say we *can't* finish this mission without repairs," I tell Toma, "but it'll make things a whole lot tougher if we don't get fixed up."

"I've been thinking about that. It's *broiling* back here."

"I'm open to suggestions." The heat gauge, even after having cooled off, is at 90 percent. "There's not a friendly 'Mech hangar anywhere out here, I'm guessing. At this rate of travel, when would we reach Tabin?"

"Sundown, maybe. If the heat doesn't kill us first."

"You and me would probably be all right. Adding another three people back there, I'm not so sure. And we're not fitting three in there, anyway. Someone would die before we got back to Erobern unless we only traveled at night, which just gives an angry *carcieta* more time to find us. This is a nonpermissive environment, and we've still got an Erobern special-operator team looking for us. Getting the radio fixed wouldn't be the worst idea, and if we can lower this temp even a little bit, I know I'd feel a lot better. What I don't know is the timing. We're already half a day into this thing, driving a busted 'Mech that can't go much faster than this. It's your call, Toma."

"Not my call to make, Ixy."

"Yeah. I know. Just had to say it."

We don't even make it a kilometer before my clothes are drenched in sweat. That's sort of a good sign—as long as you're sweating, you're not on the way to heat exhaustion. It's just as hot as it is back home, but there, I'm constantly going into air-conditioned buildings, or getting sprayed by hoses on the wash deck, and have access to liter after liter of clean water.

Here, now...riding in 55 tons of metal with only enough water to last the rest of the day...

Toma is right. It's a death trap.

We don't talk as I drive the *Griffin* north to avoid the upcoming small town. There's more than one moment I consider beelining for the border wall and jumping right back over into Erobern. Or, if the *Griffin* can't handle that, following the wall until we reach an official border crossing, surrendering, and demanding to talk to my father.

But I won't do that. I won't leave those women behind.

As we trudge through the desert, each jolt sending fresh pain into my hand, I even let myself daydream about not just Toma's family but every girl in his nation. About coming back and getting them out one by one if I have to.

I could be a superhero. Like something in a book. *One lone MechWarrior, out to disarm and disrupt her nation's great foe, and help those who suffer under their cruel domination...*

How did things get to be like this? Why am I out here, by myself, trying to help? The entire Fort Erobern detachment should be here, protecting the innocent Tierapolvos who can't make it over the wall. And what's the wall *for* in the first place? We—well, *we* being the people who founded Erobern—bled and died for how I get to live, so how can we just stand by and watch it happen next door?

Maybe if the damned Star League would leave us the hell alone, we could do something. Davion in particular, those shit-eaters, clearly have no issue giving Tierapolvo BattleMechs while turning a blind eye to what the citizens actually need...

If it was up to me...

If I was my father...

If I...

If—

"*Ixy!*"

I sit up straight. "What—"

"Hey, you all right? You were muttering something. We're drifting."

I rub my eyes, blink, and take a drink of warm water before correcting course. "I'm fine."

"Look, if you go down from heat exhaustion, *all* of us are done."

"I said I'm *fine!*" I take another drink. The problem here is, he's right. I wipe my forehead, but my hand comes back dry.

Confusion. Fatigue. No more sweating.

Classic heat exhaustion symptoms. Untreated, it will lead to heatstroke. Then it's just a matter of time before I'm dead.

I check the map. We still have kilometers to go to get past the first of the two towns on our way to Tabin.

"Keep talking."

From behind my seat, Toma says, "What?"

"Just, say things. I don't care, just talk."

"You sound worried."

"Dust *me*, would you just do what I say, Toma?"

He doesn't reply right away. It takes a minute, or maybe more. If not for the clock in my console, I'd have no idea what time it is. The sun is almost directly overhead now, burning relentlessly above us. It's so hot I can smell it. In the distance, transparent, false rivers run thick along the ground. I hear no birds, and no animal calls. Even they know better than to be out in this misery.

"I'm still not sure why you're doing this."

His voice startles me. That's good, though. I need the hit.

"But whatever happens, I want to say thank you, right now. Just so I know I've said it. You don't owe me anything. You don't even know my family. But you're risking your life with every step we take, and I won't forget that. I mean, if I live through this."

"Everyone lives through this," I say. "If I don't believe that, there's no point. Three ways home."

"I won't argue with you. But honestly, Ixy, you don't know much about this place. I don't think you'd be doing this if you did."

"I know enough."

"Oh. All right. Well, do you know that this is a place where hanging a body from a bridge is a sign of kindness from the *carcietas*? If they do that, the family gets a body to bury. *That's* kindness. That's the kind of hell we're talking about. I can't believe I let you go into it."

"You did not and never will 'let' me do anything. They want me, they'll have to hang my 'Mech with me."

Toma gives something like a laugh. "And maybe that right there is why I didn't try harder to stop you. You're pretty tough, you know that?"

"It's come up once or twice."

"Got it. So, just for my own little peace of mind...*do* you really have three ways for us to get home, or...?"

Something like homesickness suddenly clenches in my belly. "The special-ops teams in Erobern have this saying. It started as a tactical reminder, years ago. 'Always plan for three ways to get home.' It just means that when they're planning a mission, they have contingencies in place to exfil no matter what happens or what might go wrong. That's the default. It goes into every mission plan."

My fingertips drift across my console. "My father told me a story about one of his first missions as an operator. He was put in charge of planning this smash-and-grab operation—you know, go grab one of the big bad guys and bring him back for questioning. He got it all worked out, they trained for it, spent weeks preparing. Then on the day of the op, there was a really bad storm. They had to call it off. My father's boss said it was Pa's fault."

"*His* fault there was a storm?"

"That's what my father said. His boss told him, 'You should have planned for that, too. Plan for the things you can't control. Make sure you and your team have every possible option open to complete the mission, and always have at least three ways home.' So the expression is partly a reminder of that. Always have a plan. But over time, it started taking on this other meaning, that one of the ways you're allowed to come home is in a box. Meaning you never quit the mission unless you're dead."

As I say it, the weight of how much time we've lost sinks in. We should've been on our way back to Erobern by now.

I hadn't planned for anything. Not even a little bit. I'd just ran straight ahead without thinking about the results.

We should be dead already.

I turn to look toward Toma.

"You need to know *we* don't have three ways home. The fact is, jumping the wall and doing all this was impulsive and stupid, and it'll probably do nothing more than get all of us killed. Me, you. Your family. All of us. So listen: the border isn't far north. If you and me are going to try to get back home to Erobern in one piece, now is the time."

Toma slides his hand into mine—my left, the one without the bandages. Surprisingly, I let him take it.

He looks straight back at me. "I'll risk taking that box over the alternative for my mother and sisters."

He squeezes my hand.

I squeeze back. "All right then. Three ways home."

"Three ways home."

CHAPTER ELEVEN

TIERAPOLVO
TRAUSSIN
TAURIAN CONCORDAT
11 JUNE 2581
0856 HOURS

"How much farther do you think?"

"A couple hours, maybe," Toma says. His voice drags. The heat is relentless, and we shouldn't even waste the moisture to talk. "When the sun is highest. That might be a good thing, most people will be under cover then. Even *carcietamen* don't enjoy being under the sun."

A large boulder looms a little to one side. I veer for it, and tell Toma to hang on. I goose the jump jets a little to see if we can clear the rock—and we do. I don't want to try a full jump, but it's nice to know there's still some control there.

"I've been thinking about *that*, too," I say after we land and keep walking. "What kind of place is Tabin, what's the tactical situation there? I mean, am I supposed to just walk this 'Mech up to your front door and have your family jump in? Because that would be kind of nice."

"It would be. But no, I don't recommend it. Tabin's small, not many buildings over two stories. It's rural, mostly farmland. The main road through town has most of the businesses, with homes behind them on either side. Then the fields all around beyond that."

"Can I guess what crop they farm?"

"Yes. So, please don't."

"Copy that. Go on."

"There's going to be *carcieta* there, I assume you know that. Maybe some 'Mechs, maybe not. They don't need them as much in a place like Tabin. But there will be armed *carcietamen* there, for sure. It's just a question of how many, and whether they're going to pay attention to us."

I think about my sidearm. Ten rounds. No body armor. And no actual infantry-combat experience.

I release a breath as steadily as I can. "All right. From this point on, then, you're going to have to take point. What do we do? I'm not looking for a fight."

"There's a place just outside of town, by the river. Very green, lots of trees. I think we stash the 'Mech there, hide it as best we can, and walk into town. We go to my house, get everyone packed up to move fast... walk back to the 'Mech...and run back to Erobern as fast as possible."

"That's the plan?"

"That's the plan."

"Well, it's elegant. The key is going to be staying together. We never split up the team. Can you identify *carcieta* by sight?"

"They're the ones with rifles."

It's not remotely funny, but I laugh anyway, feeling like it might be the last time I ever get a chance to hear myself do it. "Copy that."

We go on another few minutes in silence before I speak, "Toma, listen—"

"No. You don't have to say it, I know. A lot of things have to go right, and a lot of things can go wrong. And I promise I won't say this again, but if you want out, I understand. You've already done more than I could ever repay you for. Any time you want me to jump out and go it alone so you can go home, I get it. I think you *should*, in fact."

"I don't leave people behind."

"I know. I just had to say it. And if you see a better plan once we get there, hey, you're the soldier, it's your call."

"Right," I say quietly. "I'm the soldier."

We keep driving.

The desert as we approach Tabin isn't much different from back home; we're not geographically that terribly far from Erobern, considering how long and narrow a country Tierapolvo is. I know from my studies that farther south, the desert gradually adds moisture and eventually becomes a tropical rainforest, then turns into jagged mountains. That's several hundred kilometers from here, though.

Running my 'Mech though Tierapolvo now, in relative calm, I wonder what a rainforest would really be like. I've seen pictures and videos, but that's not quite the same. I could climb tall trees with broad, wet leaves. I could play with the furry, four-legged critters that spend their entire lives in the branches overhead, never once touching the ground.

I shake my head to clear it. No sense in that kind of thinking. Even if we do somehow manage to survive all the way back to Erobern, I'll only be facing a court-martial.

But I don't like *that* line of thought, either, so I go back to observing the desert flora, trying to absorb its stark, pristine beauty.

Outside the *Griffin*, there is noticeably more greenery. It's the same type of trees and bushes, but there are more of them. There are even a few patches of low, scrubby grass, valiantly straining out of the dirt.

Two more hours pass before Toma sticks his head by the side of my seat. "We're getting close. Veer west, let's pick up the river."

I turn the limping *Griffin* that direction. "I'm going to try the radio again. If the Erobern team is still out there, it would be good to tell them who I am. Can the *carcietas* pick up my signal if I transmit?"

"I don't think so."

"Let's find out," I mutter, and hit the radio button. "This is Echo Zero-Zero-Two, Echo Zero-Zero-Two. Any friendlies nearby?"

I pause, and try again. No response. I try once more; nothing.

"Any chance they wouldn't respond?" Toma asks.

"No. They'd know my electronic sig, or figure it out pretty quick. Wherever they are, I don't think they're in range."

But that's not all. I'm reminded again that it's entirely possible the spec-ops team is on communications-blackout orders—dead radios except for among the three of them. It's not standard operating procedure to go dark while on a mission, but there are times—I've learned from both Pa and in my classes—that maintaining strict radio silence is ordered.

This may be one of those times, for all I know.

We find the river, and I turn left to follow it. It's a real river this time, or what passes for one in the Besalis Desert, about fifty meters across at the widest point. It flows north, toward Erobern, but I know from school that it cuts west before hitting the border and dumps into the ocean. The river is dark and blue, rolling fast over smooth stones. Its small crests twinkle white under the sun.

There's more vegetation here. Actual grass spreads out in wide swaths from the edge of the river. I hate to trample on it; we have nothing like this back home, apart from small patches of cultivated grass in some of the athletic parks on base. The trees, still very much desert varieties, are bigger here and offer shade to smaller bushes. I might be wrong, but I think I even see some rat-like animal scurrying around in the branches of one of them.

"Tabin is near the river," I hear myself say. I hadn't meant to.

"Yes," Toma says. "Why?"

"Nothing. It's...pretty, is all."

Toma doesn't reply, and I'm grateful.

The tranquil feeling in my body dissolves as the trees grow thicker and I see a light haze growing on the horizon.

Civilization.

Tabin.

"I think we're almost there."

Toma comes forward. "Yes. Not far now. Keep going until I tell you."

I sharpen my gaze out the cockpit canopy, looking for incoming BattleMechs or ambush spots. I also check all my gauges, relieved to see that everything appears normal—not counting our heat.

"All right," Toma says quietly, as if someone might be listening. "There's a grove of trees up ahead. That'll put us about a half kilometer from town. Let's park there."

By now I've slowed to a walk, and drive the *Griffin* into the grove. It takes a little maneuvering to find the right blend of camouflage and the ability to leave the canopy open and hike down, but it works.

Toma and I climb out of the *Griffin*. He carries his bag, and we have all the water we have canteens for. I spend a few minutes playing with my sidearm, trying to find the best way to hold it in my bandaged hand. It's awkward, but I can always tear the wrapping away if necessary.

After locking the *Griffin*'s canopy, I walk with Toma out of the grove and along the river. It's ridiculously hot, but here near the river, it's also noticeably cooler. I find myself stopping suddenly, right on the grassy riverbank, to close my eyes against the sun and take a deep breath of the cooler air. The scent is a curious mix of the acrid desert plants and smooth aroma of river water.

When I open my eyes, I see Toma beside me doing the same thing. When his eyes open, we look at each other.

"All right," he says.

"All right. We get to your house, we grab them, we run back here—"

"No running. That will only attract attention."

"Fine. We walk *very quickly* back here, get in, and run like hell for the border."

"I once heard someone say no plan survives the first shot fired."

I can't help a half grin. There's hope for him. "Basically, yeah. So let's not let any shots get fired."

We nod to one another, and Toma leads the way along the riverbank.

In the distance, I can make out vast, tall green fields. I recognize the plants from studying: it's pop. Or rather, it's the papaver plant that flowers and gets turned into the drug we call pop. It's similar to corn and sunflowers, stretching about two meters high, with thick stalks and broad, dark leaves. Eventually, giant, red-and-pink flowers will blossom at the top, and the seeds inside will be harvested to make the drug.

Looking at the fields as we get closer, I can imagine it must be a beautiful sight when the blossoms emerge. Even now, without them, the plants are impressive. They are strong and well-tended, not withered and desiccated the way my mother was when she died.

Seems unfair somehow.

"There," I say, pointing to a long-abandoned vehicle on the edge of a papaver field. It's little more than a shell, rusted out and stripped. "That's how we'll carry them."

"You think?" Toma says.

"Doors are all gone, but the structure looks sound enough. I've been carrying cargo for the last year. I can give them a smooth ride."

"Provided we don't get into any fights."

I look at him sharply. There's no need to reply.

After a short walk along the river, Toma cuts left, and not long after that, we reach a paved road. "This is the main strip through Tabin, Dalucia Street," he says, not looking at me when he speaks. "We can follow it for most of the way to my house."

"Where is your house? I mean, relatively speaking."

"Center of town." He licks his lips. His eyes seem to never blink.

"Toma—hey. You need to relax."

He spins his head fast toward me. "What? What?"

"*Relax.* Or at least fake it. Take some deep breaths. Anyone sees you like that, they're gonna ask questions."

He licks his lips one more time, but nods and forces a few breaths. Better.

Wheeled vehicles show up on the road, passing us at maybe 60 kph. Old ones, caked with dust and studded with dents and chipped paint. I try not to stare at the drivers as they go past, but I do make eye contact—let them know I see them. Step one in any self-defense scenario. And this entire gambit is one giant self-defense scenario.

"Anyone gonna recognize you?" I ask as the first small buildings appear on the horizon.

"I doubt it." He grunts. "Maybe not even Rasha. The next oldest. She was so young when I left."

"I'm sorry. But listen, she's not who I'm worried about recognizing you."

"Oh. No, I don't think so."

We walk into Tabin together, passing low-slung, one-story brick houses. They're packed closely together. Wire fences that look absolutely useless encircle the front yards, which consist of dust, dirt, and rocks. A few scraggly canines watch us go, their eyes half shut, then go back to their naps beneath the shade of sloping porch roofs.

Toma and I stick to the edge of Dalucia Street. There are no sidewalks like at Fort Erobern; the blacktop just bleeds into the dirt like it was poured there and left to harden where it fell.

We pass a house with two little boys playing in the shade of a big tree. I can't understand the words they chirp to each other, but I recognize the approximate sounds of bullets being fired and of explosions as they bang long rocks together.

I think they are pretending to be MechWarriors.

I take a quick drink of water to unstick my tongue, and hurry on.

Once past the homes, a little more life shows up. The streets are laid out in a simple grid fashion, with blocks about the same size as any in Erobern. People come in and out of small one-and two-story shops lining the streets: laundries, pharmacies, small grocers. Many wear enormous, wide-brimmed hats to shade themselves. We blend into the foot traffic readily enough; no one acknowledges us.

Erobern is cleaner than Tabin, but I don't see people lying in the street, starving to death. The citizens here wear bright, woven clothes, and many are even smiling. Some are missing teeth, but somehow, it doesn't detract from their grins. I hear quiet music coming from some of the shops, and the pace of the pedestrians is unhurried. I smell Tierapolvo bread baking nearby, savory and rich.

Then I spot my first rifle.

Outside a small electronics-repair shop, a young man in a red shirt sits on a stoop of stairs beneath a shade tree. He smokes something from a rolled-up brown leaf and glares at everyone within eyeshot.

"Just keep walking," Toma whispers before I can form a question. "He's with Diamos. They always wear red in this part of the country. Here, we're almost at my intersection."

I don't make eye contact with the *carcieta keyote*, but I feel his eyes on me. On *every* part of me, all the way until we reach a relatively busy intersection and turn right.

My heart is racing. Just walking in this town is a challenge.

The intersection has no traffic signals. Everyone just goes whenever they feel like, and it's everyone else's job to get out of the way. One vehicle barely misses us as it swerves around someone else not going fast enough for the driver's liking.

"Is it always like this?" I say, scowling.

Toma is walking us more quickly now. "Pretty much."

The street we turn onto—a green sign reads BRISTOY—runs west, toward the direction of the fields and the river. The homes here are no different from the ones at the edge of town—simple wood-and-brick constructions, sometimes painted, sometimes not. Many of

the small homes have places for vehicles, but not many vehicles are actually parked.

"Momai!" Toma shouts suddenly.

He breaks into a run, running west down Bristoy Street. I call his name to get him to stop, to slow down, but he's focused on a tiny house, its once-green paint now faded to a dismal gray.

I follow him.

Toma stops at the worthless wire gate set into a length of fence. He sucks in a breath as he stands and stares at two girls hanging laundry on a line in the front yard.

"Toma? Is this it?"

He doesn't answer.

CHAPTER TWELVE

TIERAPOLVO
TRAUSSIN
TAURIAN CONCORDAT
11 JUNE 2581
1218 HOURS

Toma stands perfectly still, gazing at the two girls.

They are wearing simple faded pink dresses, the older one with a belt cinching her narrow waist. They both look hungry; thin, but not frail. As they stare back at Toma, even from this distance I can see fire in their eyes.

I like to think of myself as fairly tough. For lots of reasons. Life things. Training. But these two have a toughness I couldn't hope to compete with.

"Rasha," Toma says, his hand on the flimsy gate. "It's me. It's Toma." But he doesn't go in.

The older girl, about twelve years old, throws a pile of clothing into the basket at their feet and spits something back in 'Polvo. The younger girl swivels her head between the two of them, mostly curious and uncaring.

Toma's jaw clenches. I can feel the tension in his body. "What is it?"

"She doesn't remember my face. She thinks I'm *carcieta*, pretending to be her brother."

"Toma..." I whisper, not meaning to.

I put a hand on his forearm. Toma doesn't notice.

Another voice sounds from inside the house. All four of us look toward the front door.

The door opens and a narrow woman hustles out, wearing a similar shapeless dress as the girls, but with a frayed, knit lace around the collar. She is tiny, almost as small as Rasha, but her shoulders are broad, and I swear I can see calluses on her hands even from here.

She barrels out of the house with a wooden roller for breadmaking, waving it over her head and spitting in 'Polvo. She makes it about halfway across the yard—and freezes.

"Momai," Toma says softly.

I don't know if the woman can hear him, but it doesn't matter. She says, "Toma?"

In the same instant, he unlatches the gate and throws it wide, and she drops the roller. They careen into each other and embrace tightly. He has to lean over to get his arms around her. I can hear Toma sobbing over her shoulder.

The two girls watch all this with confused expressions. Rasha still stands defiantly, unconvinced Toma is not an enemy. Quite suddenly, her expression is all too familiar, and hard for me to look at.

Toma and his mother part. He gestures at me, speaking quickly to her in their language. She eyes me with distaste at first. In the middle his speech, I hear Toma say, *"Ixchel, Ixy,"* and gesticulating. His mother's expression softens, and she waves me into the yard.

I go over to them. The woman reaches up and hugs me close. I have no idea what she's saying, but I do hear the word *momai*.

"She wants you to call her 'Mother,'" Toma says. "You don't have to, she—"

"It's fine," I say quickly, and pull away, choking on something. Dust, I'm sure. "We gotta move."

Toma nods, and speaks again. Momai listens intently, argues briefly...then shouts at the two girls. They immediately run inside, with the seriousness of children used to obeying not out of fear of their parent, but fear of what their parent is afraid of.

When she starts speaking again, I grab Toma's arm. "I'll stay here and keep an eye out. You get them moving."

He nods and ushers his mother back into the house.

I take a deep breath to center myself and go back to Bristoy Street. It's quiet; no one else is outside at the moment. I walk to the next cross street, Dalucia, which runs north–south the way we'd entered town, and glance up and down it.

North of us, the way we came, the guy in the red shirt is a block away, smoking, and looking right at me. As I watch, he lifts a radio to his mouth.

Trying in vain to pretend I didn't see him, I scan the street once more before turning and going back to Toma's yard.

The front door bangs open as I reach the gate. Toma leads their ragged procession: Momai with a black canvas satchel over one shoulder, Rasha and the younger girl, Bita, with woven bags over theirs.

"The *carcietaman* we walked past on the way in," I say quickly as they move toward me. "The one in the red shirt. He's down the street, on a radio."

Toma curses. Momai—still a mother, no matter the circumstance—slaps his arm.

"We'll go around the back," Toma says. "Maybe we can cut through the fields."

I pull the sidearm from my waistband and rack the slide. "I hope you're right."

No one appears surprised at the gun in my hand as Toma breaks into a jog away from Dalucia Street and to the west. The two girls hold hands behind him, and Momai follows. I bring up the rear, keeping a lookout behind us.

Toma is just turning the corner of Bristoy Street when the red-shirted *carcietaman* appears at the corner of Bristoy and Dalucia. He's trying to play it cool, but when he sees how quickly we are moving, he drops the pretense. His makeshift cigarette drops from his mouth as he lifts the radio in his left hand and the rifle in his right.

I raise my pistol in both hands the way I've been drilled, gripping as hard as I can. "Drop your weapon! Lemme see your hands! *Drop your weapon!*"

He shouts something back at me. I hear a whistle, then a *pop*, then realize he's got the rifle against his shoulder.

So this is what it's like to be shot at outside of a 'Mech.

The world melts and slows while simultaneously speeding up beyond the speed of thought. All I can hear is the sound of my own breathing as I get the red shirt in my sight picture and squeeze the trigger twice.

The *carcietaman* jumps high to avoid the shots, and lands on his back. Many years later—at least that's what it feels like—I realize he's not moving.

He didn't jump to dodge; even with a bad hand, my shots took him off his feet. He does not move.

In my head, a dozen-plus instructors' voices yell at me. Telling me what to do next. It's ingrained in me to obey, so I do. Weapon still raised, I run full speed to where the *carcietaman* is sprawled on the ground.

His eyes are open. He's staring right at the sun, but it has no power to make him blink anymore. Death is stronger than sunlight. Two small, black holes puncture his shirt, right in the middle of his chest. That's all.

I've killed another man.

His radio bursts to life, speaking 'Polvo. A male voice. It snaps me back to our tactical situation.

I shove my pistol back into my waistband and grab the rifle. I check it; nearly a full mag. I sling the weapon diagonally across my body and pick up the radio. As I stand to run back to Toma, a black, four-wheeled vehicle spins around a corner farther along Dalucia Street.

This is it. It's on now.

"Go!" I scream as Toma's family peers around a house.

Toma waves at his family, urging them along, running parallel to Dalucia.

I run past Toma's house to catch up. "Wheels coming!"

Toma knows what I mean. He pushes the family up the street.

My *Griffin* feels very, very far away.

Because of the grid layout of the residential streets, we have to cross the next east–west road as we head north. We're right in the middle of the street when the black vehicle roars past on Dalucia.

"Did they see us?" Toma shouts.

A squeal of brakes is all the answer we need.

I shove the radio into his hands. "Listen! Tell me what they're saying. Go!"

Toma and his family keep running north. I break to the side and take cover behind the engine block of an old vehicle parked in someone's yard, aiming the rifle down the east–west street.

The black vehicle squeals in reverse. Before the driver can crank the wheel our direction, I go semi-auto, firing five evenly spaced shots into the passenger side.

Instead of turning now, the driver hits the accelerator. The vehicle roars backward some more, out of my line of sight. Good that I've scared them; bad that they're now going north, the same direction we are.

I run for Toma's family. Despite moving at a good pace, they're not going nearly fast enough. I shout at them again, as if it will do any good.

Gunshots.

The family raises their shoulders in response to the sound, but they don't stop running. I dash to the next east–west street ahead of us and raise the rifle.

The black vehicle is parked at an angle on the blacktop, doors open. Three men point long guns this way. They fire in the untrained manner of civilians.

They're focused on the tight group of Toma and his family. In the time it takes them to notice me bringing up the rear, I've got the rifle seated against my shoulder. Switching to fully automatic, I empty the magazine in their direction.

The rifle kicks comfortably against me, but my bandaged hand makes it impossible for proper trigger control. The shots ping in a wide grouping off the vehicle. The men instinctively crouch for cover. I hit none of them.

With the mag empty, I drop the rifle and sprint toward Toma. More whistles and pops sound near my head. Then a booming, two-syllable explosion that's unlike any sound I'd expect from a rifle. The noise of it quakes my eardrums and makes me stumble in the road.

From the ground, I turn my head toward the three *carcietamen*. One is on the ground, not moving. The other two are spinning away from our direction to acquire new targets.

Another explosion. One of the *carcietamen* flies backward and lands in a tangle of limbs. Two more explosive shots, and the last of the men drops.

That's when I see two Tierapolvos walking toward the vehicle. An older man and a younger woman. They carry ancient shotguns, raised high, keeping the dead *carcietamen* covered in case their devastating shots haven't done the job.

They needn't worry. All three criminals are dead.

The pair of Tierapolvos look my way. The old man shouts something; the woman waves me away.

They're protecting us. Their guns aren't combat models; they're designed for hunting. Still, better than rocks and sticks...

I scramble to my feet and wave my gratitude as best I can. It feels shallow.

Toma and the women are crouched behind a short, thick bush at the next intersection. All of us breathe hard and fast as I hunker down with them.

"Three men," I gasp. "Dead."

Toma raises the radio. "More coming."

"What about police?"

"Hour or two. If at all."

"Dust me..." I squint north. We've got a long way to go to reach the *Griffin*.

Part of me wants to send them on ahead while I wait and distract whoever is coming. But that would be breaking up the team, and that's something an operator never does.

Several streets to the west, I see the tall, green pop fields. Going through them will slow us down, but grant some cover. Maybe buy us some time.

"We'll take the fields," I say. "Everyone on me!"

I head west, glancing back to make sure everyone is following. I wish they could run faster.

More gunshots echo in the neighborhood behind us. The shotguns, and rifles. A lot of rifles. The shotguns only echo three or four times before falling silent under a hail of rifle fire.

The two Tierapolvos never had a chance. They must have *known* they never had a chance, and they had helped us anyway.

Rocks and sticks...

We crash into the edge of the fields and turn north.

The old man and the young woman are dead. I know it in my gut. Sacrificed.

I will get Toma's family back to Erobern if it's the last thing I do.

The drug made from pop plants has no odor that I can recall, but the plants themselves smell like mint and pepper in nauseating proportions. As a plant, the flowers from which pop is made are inert. While we won't get high from the scent, the smell makes it uncomfortable to breathe.

But so would a chest full of rifle bullets. We'll deal.

Papaver has broad leaves and thick stalks. It grows in clusters, tightly packed like corn. Moving through them is akin to swimming—I have to use both hands in a sweeping-back motion to move through. The leaves rattle each time I touch them.

We're still close enough to the street that I can hear vehicles screeching to a halt.

"They're coming!" Toma says.

We've been in this field less than a minute, and already I can't tell for certain what direction we're headed. The sun is directly overhead, beating on us through the leaves, giving me no sense of east or west. We came straight in west, but then turned right—north. Moving so hastily through the field, it's impossible now to tell how straight a path we've been carving.

"They'll have to spread out," I call back to him. "Just keep going!"

With any luck, we won't accidentally double back and run into them. I don't say that part.

The heat is oppressive now, weighing me down. I'm getting dizzy from the odor of the plants. What direction are we going?

A man yells in the distance. It's behind us, anyway. Hopefully that's good. I plow ahead, ignoring the sweat stinging my eyes.

Then Toma is beside me, pushing faster. *"Run."*

"I'm *trying* to."

More shouts behind us. Not too close, but obviously close enough to hear.

Toma's face is panicked. So are the faces of his mother and sisters. They *pass* me through the thick stalks.

"What?" I bark at Toma.

"They lit it."

Just as I form the thought to ask him what he's talking about, a new smell hits me.

Smoke.

For some damned stupid reason, I actually stop and turn around to look behind us.

Gray smoke wafts high into the still air. First one plume, then another next to it, then another. Someone with some kind of fire-starter is just walking along the line of plants and lighting them up.

They'd rather flush us out and destroy this entire crop than let us escape.

"Ixy!" Toma's voice shakes my attention loose.

I bat stalks aside to catch up. "Is this the right way?"

"Don't know!"

I cough as we try to increase our pace. The plants make it impossible. Fire has no such barrier—I can already hear it crackling behind us.

Don't look, don't look, don't look...

The primal part of my brain kicks in. Panic squeezes my heart in an unforgiving fist. My breath shortens.

Ahead, I hear the little girl, Bita, starting to cry, Momai and Rasha urging her on. Toma is saving his breath, pushing them on with both hands. When he looks back at me, his eyes are watering from the smoke slithering through the stalks.

I can't help it. I look back.

The smoke cloud has tripled in size overhead. I catch a brief glimpse of orange and yellow fire flickering behind us. It *seems* several meters behind us yet. In this maze of a field, I can't tell.

My brain plays back the layout of Tabin as we'd walked in. The fields on this side abruptly stop, cut off by a dirt road. I remember that. If we are headed due north, we'll crash right out of the field and into the desert. Then it's just a long sprint to the *Griffin*.

A very long sprint.

The little girl stumbles. Everyone shouts. Toma tumbles too as he tries to catch her.

I'm closest to Bita by the time that happens, and reach for her while still moving forward. I've drilled this before—running across uneven fields in full combat gear and picking up a sandbag without stopping. It was meant to simulate picking up ammo boxes, radios, weapons— anything that might get dropped in a firefight. It was exhausting back then, and felt absurd.

Now I silently sing the praises of all my instructors over the years as I lift Bita into my arms without breaking stride. I don't respond when Toma shouts my name; he can see what I'm doing. In the next choking breath, he's back on his feet, bringing up the rear.

Bita clings to me, arms around my neck. I've never carried a child, only other cadets. Trained instinct takes over—I sling her across the back of my neck in a buddy carry, her right arm and right leg draped over my shoulders like a shawl. She weighs next to nothing compared to my fellow trainees.

Next to nothing isn't nothing, though, and within twenty meters I can feel her weight slowing me. Dragging me through the stalks. Smoke is now ahead of us, obscuring my vision; I can hear the fire snapping loudly behind us like miniature bullets, and just as deadly.

If we fall—if we stop—if we can't find the edge in time—we'll be surrounded by this conflagration. With luck, we'll die of smoke inhalation before the flames eat our bodies.

"Momai!" Bita cries, clutching my shirt.

I grit my teeth and pick up my pace. I *will not* let these girls down.

Momai suddenly disappears in front of me. I shout, fearing she's been shot.

Instead, one gasping breath later...we're through. We're on the dirt road.

I set Bita on the ground and spin, looking for Toma. He crashes through the edge of the field a moment later, his face black, the bandage over his wound hanging off his face by a strip of once-white adhesive.

The fire rages behind us. Tongues of flame are now visible above the tops of the plants, no more than twenty meters into the field...but we made it. We're not done, but we made it.

I look up and down the dirt road. The *carcieta* will be here soon; they'll know this is one of the places we could exit, and they'll come to cover this route.

Toma, thankfully, is already sidestepping away, pinwheeling his arms. He's no longer holding the *carcieta* radio. "This way!"

I cough, hard, and follow him. Momai, Rasha, and Bita stay close. The girls hold hands.

Ahead of us, to the north, the desert stretches interminably. It's as if there is no horizon. Cacti and bushes seem to go on and on. I can't see the river.

Behind me and to the right, some of Tabin's taller buildings are visible, but that's it. The only good thing is that the bushes, cacti, and trees in front of us are just thick enough to give any wheeled vehicle a hard time.

Coughing again, I spit to get the taste of smoke out of my mouth. It doesn't help. I push myself to run hard. "Where's the river?"

"That big tree!" Toma shouts, also coughing. "Go left!"

The five of us race for a low, broad tree with thick branches, then pivot and run to the west. I keep waiting to hear vehicles closing in. If that happens, if they find us out here, we're finished.

Magically, the dirt beneath our feet transitions to grass. I hear myself cry out in relief as the sounds of the bubbling river meet my ears. Bita also cries and races for the riverbank.

I grab her hand. "No, no. *Nentay*. This way. No time, no time."

The little girl, her face smeared with black ash, pouts at me. I squeeze her hand. "I know, I know. Me too. But we have to run, understand? We have to run."

Which is a shame, because Bita has the right idea: flinging myself into the cool water of the river would be heaven. But we can't afford even a drink right now. My *Griffin* is the only thing standing between us and a furious gang of armed outlaws. Water must wait.

Despite the encouragement of having found the river and knowing it's only a matter of distance to my BattleMech, our pace slows. We've been going full speed since the red-shirted man shot at us. The smoke in our lungs, the lack of training, the merciless sun overhead...we're only as fast as our weakest link, and the energy we've put out to get here has drained our resources. It's taking all I have to maintain anything more than a walk.

"There...!" Toma croaks, as if his voice itself has been barbecued.

I lift my head, not realizing I'd let my gaze drop to the ground. Ahead of us is the cluster of trees, and the *Griffin* hidden among the branches.

While we can't take the time to leap into the river, the relief flooding my body as I see the 'Mech feels very similar.

We reach the stand of trees. Bita collapses in a heap, gasping. Rasha and Momai kneel beside her, also trying to catch their breath. Toma and I reach for the branches we used to camouflage my *Griffin*, grinning manically at one another now that we've made it.

All I have to do is fire up the 'Mech, go grab the abandoned vehicle we saw earlier, and run out of here like hell was on our heels.

We freeze in tandem as the ground vibrates. It's slight, sending little tremors through my boots and into my ankles, but unmistakable.

Toma and I turn southward. Smoke from the field fire rises high into the still air.

I knew a wheeled vehicle would have had a tough time following us through the desert.

But not a BattleMech.

And right now there are three of the war machines running toward us in the distance, closing fast.

TO BE CONCLUDED IN SHRAPNEL #12!

THE FEW AND THE MANY: THE CANOPIAN MEDICAL INDUSTRY'S CULTURAL ISOLATION

WUNJI LAU

**INTERNAL REPORT
ARCSHIP *ATLANTEAN*, SKATE KHANATE, CLAN SEA FOX
17 MARCH 3152**

Though little talked about and generally taken for granted, the societal underpinnings of the Magistracy of Canopus' famed medical industry are worthy of some note. Despite its Periphery status and historically poor educational system (only slightly improved in recent decades), the Magistracy somehow produces the finest medical professionals and medical biotechnology researchers in known space, with its med/bio industry nearly as lucrative as the Magistracy's far more well-known entertainment industry. This relatively small portion of the nation's population is responsible for a huge percentage of the Magistracy's wealth. Of greater note (especially to Clan warriors) is that the Straios, a few thousand of the most highly trained and successful individuals, shoulder the most critical aspects of maintaining the bleeding-edge competitiveness that has stymied challenges from far wealthier realms for over a century.

    The fostering of peerless doctor-scientists is a deeply refined process controlled with a heavy hand (by Canopian standards) by the Magistracy's Human Health Administration. Despite its bureaucratically bland name, the HHA is functionally a guild. It originated as a loose collection of physicians, researchers, and academics during the late

Succession Wars, and gradually leveraged its educational value to gain government influence and eventually formal oversight over an entire segment of the Magistracy's economy. The HHA manages standards and rankings, polices ethical violations, quashes infighting between corporations and nobility, and has an internal control structure independent of a member's social rank. Its independence is also valuable in preserving its industry's reputation for impartiality and reliability, a perception that makes Canopian medical personnel trusted across the Inner Sphere, with few exceptions. Most importantly, the HHA operates its own schooling system, which is not merely the only avenue of advanced health and bioscience education to be had in the rimward Periphery, but arguably the best medical training to be had anywhere.

The Straios training programs are open only to Canopian citizens, and consist of decades of mentally and physically punishing study, research, and work rotations, a gauntlet that washes out the vast majority of aspirants (who would already be leaders in their fields anywhere else in the Inner Sphere). The expense is enormous, and the expectations are correspondingly high. High-value candidates are essentially prisoners to an industrial feeder system, and those who reach the rank of Straios are kept in secure (albeit luxurious) accommodations or deployed across the Inner Sphere in closely monitored self-isolation. This results in a tiny, semi-monastic upper class of Canopian citizens who are effectively viewed as aliens in their own land. This perception goes beyond the undereducated masses, encompassing traditionally high-tech industries (such as 'Mech design and spacecraft construction) and the military (perhaps in response to the Magistracy's unusual dismissiveness toward martial professions).

Such a system is at odds with the general outlook of the Magistracy, but it has become something of a self-sustaining beast. The only way for the small nation to maintain its dominance is for the quality of its human capital to provide the innovation, insights, and efficiencies that other nations acquire via cash and numbers. In their own words:

Private Memo: Ingieu Terguson, Y14 Straios Candidate
Precision Instruments of Luxen
2 September 3150

Fourth-millennium medical research isn't an industry for the poorly prepared. Top-end research necessitates a combination of cutting-edge chemistry, physics, biology, computer science, and other disciplines. While many natural diseases of historical importance have been dealt with, humanity itself is a never-ending source of insidious maladies. Many 32nd-century viruses would be nearly unrecognizable to an Old Terra microbiologist, having been repeatedly engineered to escape detection and treatment. Also, while the human genome and life processes are well understood, the addition of impacts from thousands of new and changing environments (including hyperspace travel) has exponentially increased the difficulty of classifying, elucidating, and diagnosing diseases, much less treating them.

A Canopian Straios is equal to an entire team of researchers or clinicians, able to adaptively think and act on personal, community, and planetary-policy levels. Their presence on a distant world can speed health care improvements by years, even decades. They can integrate vast amounts of disparate data to synthesize and execute R&D programs with efficiency even the Clans can't match.

I was pulled from a farmhouse school at age nine, put through the Evaluation, and shipped off-world a year later. I haven't been back since. I completed the Luxen MSRT honors curriculum early, and was invited into the Straios program along with 2,000 colleagues. There are 80 of us left.

Straios washouts go on to local medical practice, corporate research, and other careers. Washouts from the earlier stages are still far better educated than 95 percent of the population, and seldom want for work. Those who go into education are especially important, since they take on the responsibility for flagging children with high potential for Evaluation; every Straios started out being noticed by a former candidate.

The training has been difficult, but understandably so. I've studied and worked on seven vastly different worlds. I am subject to immovable structure and regimen, and yet must also demonstrate the independence and will to explore and innovate on my own. I am perfectly aware of the HHA's indoctrination process, but I am not immune from its effects, as is proper; rogue or criminal Straios are nearly unheard of, a vital statistic in ensuring the level of trust and revenue we command throughout the human Sphere.

I have already become wealthy. In time, I may be a noble. There are shackles, but I wear them willingly. There is, however, also the matter of how we are seen by our fellow citizens. As an example, this post I noted:

**VANMURGES INDUSTRIPLEX
CANDIEAR
10 MAY 3149**

Even with decades of Pax Republica and neighbor alliances, local funding for education is still miserable. If you don't get picked for Eval, you might go to tech school, the Magistracy Armed Forces, or uni if you're real lucky, but the real odds are you're done with schooling. I hear about the cost of running HHA Evals on every world, how they lose so much money by washing out 95 percent of those who actually pass the Eval. I guess it all comes back in profit later, but hell if we ever seem to see any of it.

It's all mostly for the nobility and the rich. Fact is, being born into the right family gets you the kind of tutors and care that give you a leg up. Sure, there are plenty of farm kids out here in the boonies who get flagged, but they're pretty much guaranteed to wash out long before they get to Luxen, much less Straios training. Yeah, they can come back home and make a half-decent living running a rehab center or town clinic, but that's basically still down here in the dirt with the rest of us. Most of the Straios and top-ranked medbios come from families with generational wealth and nobility. Oh, you say the kids in those families have an abnormally high rate of mental deterioration and suicide? Cry me a river.

We don't talk about it much to outsiders. Not really the kind of fun topic tourists come here for, right? It's not any kind of secret either, though. It's just that most people who see Canopian doctors are happy with the results and aren't inclined to ask too many questions.

Look, I don't care that the Straios are rich shut-ins. They're just weird.

They're fine most of the time, but then out of nowhere, they'll say something bizarre. One time, our temple congregation was at a district picnic, and Denbia, this Straios visiting her family, suddenly cocks her head, stares into space, and mutters, "The warblers are quieter, but it's mating season... An early shipment of grain from Wildwood three months ago... Bio-Edge updated antifungal recs for swim competitions... Fourteen people have switched from the mild salsa to spicy... Your kids are going to need an updated mycodyne tab." And then she goes right back to munching chips and arguing about the baseball finals.

I hear that the ones sent to other nations get special training to be super personable, but we don't ever see those around here. Either they retire to some mansion somewhere, or they never come home at all. And not to sound harsh, but that's probably better for the rest of us. Sounds a little too fake, you know?

But yeah, okay, they're not bad folk, either. You'd think they'd act like they're smarter and better than us, but mostly, they just seem to be super stressed and unhealthy all the time.

Well, empirically speaking, we are smarter than everyone else. There's simply no need to highlight it. On a more sobering note, the poster is correct about mental-health issues. Indeed, they vastly understate the problem, which we also try not to highlight: most Straios and other high-ranking Canopian med/ bio personnel suffer from mental health issues and coping mechanisms that manifest as other disorders.

Addictions are common, but also stringently controlled; our profession's importance to the Canopian nation affords no error or leeway. Other resultant behaviors described as "off-putting" are of lesser concern, and we generally make no effort to constrain them. Even though most of us must effectively cut ties to our families simply due to the demands on our time and the need to remain free of any perceived biases, there's an underlying truth: most of our families don't really want us around anymore, either. We're not particularly fun at holiday dinners.

I should note that while people often compare our training and professional erudition to ComStar's old mystical trappings, our "secrets" are available to anyone who has the intellect and drive to understand them. Also, while our commitment to our roles isn't as individuality-subsuming as the Capellan caste system, we do find a loose kinship there in our perception of lifelong service to our nation. At the same time, the sink-or- swim aspect of the Canopian biotech industry finds broad acceptance in the Federated Suns, Free Worlds League, and Lyran Commonwealth, all of which culturally prize initiative and drive.

For Clan Sea Fox, of course, the most useful comparison here is to our culture's own handling of doctors and medical research. With all merited respect to our warriors, it is becoming clear that, in the context of expanding our Clan's permanent influence in the Inner Sphere, we should look to the scientist- and technician-caste traditions that produced advanced medical technology from limited resources during the Golden Century. The Canopian system's unremittingly competitive, perform-or-perish outlook is not unfamiliar to our scientists, but the greater rewards and administrative latitude, especially with an eye toward the same long-term returns and prestige we merchants pursue, show the benefits of emphasizing the carrot rather than the stick.

Initial overtures are promising. We have discussed installing permanent Canopian-run medical and training facilities in Sea Fox fleets, as well as partnering to establish branded mobile hospitals and micro-manufactories on roving trading flotillas. In exchange, the Canopians likely desire access to our data archives, hoping to research stasis technology and enhance their databases.

Regardless of the ongoing concerns on Terra, a shared transfer of skills and technology—and yes, even culture—will surely benefit us, with or without an ilClan.

MERRYMAKERS

ALAYNA M. WEATHERS

Blue flames lick up from the
center of a campfire,
guns laid to rest at boots,
and with the visors,
guards are also down.

A star twinkles overhead,
glowing against a
blanket of black
while comrades drink
and laughter, like smoke,
drifts up to the sky.

A song rises up to the gods,
to the ancestors,
and to the many who have fallen,
bouncing off armor
and ricocheting around like
a crossfire of survivors' voices.

There is no battle, tonight.
Arms are slung across shoulders
and fingers jabbed into chests until
each, in their own time,
turn from loosened tongues
and lowered inhibitions
to the drunken sleep of merrymakers,
glad to be alive.

THE SPACE COWBOYS
FROM QUATRE BELLE

R. J. THOMAS

TRESSPASS SYSTEM
SPINWARD PERIPHERY
22 NOVEMBER 3063

Weapon lock warnings blared in Section Leader Clayton Reese's ears as he snap-skidded his wedge-shaped *Slayer* fighter to the right and rolled it ninety degrees to attack a pirate *Shologar*, grunting as g-forces played havoc with his body. A nanosecond before the circular-winged aerofighter slipped through his firing arc, Clayton raked four fire-linked medium lasers across its canopy, blowing it apart and vaporizing the pilot.

Gunning the *Slayer*'s throttle, Clayton was slammed into his seat as the fighter surged forward. A slim-bodied *Transit* slipped in on his six o'clock, lining up a kill shot with its massive autocannon. Instead, a second *Slayer* piloted by his twin brother, Supervisor Clinton Reese, dove in and blasted the would-be assassin with concentrated fire from his fighter's own autocannon.

But there was no time for thanks or celebration.

"Bolo Six, got eyes on Bandit Three?" Clayton called out as he scanned the area.

"I'm looking!" Clinton replied. "I'm—split NOW!"

Warnings blared as both pilots snap-rolled their fighters. Clayton barely avoided a salvo of long-range missiles, but Clinton wasn't as lucky. "Son of a—" he shouted, static interrupting him as a scarred *Rogue* banked and sped away from the two Outworlds Alliance aerofighters.

"Bolo Six, status!" Clayton called out, turning toward the bandit.

"Lucky hits on my starboard side, autocannon is out," Clinton snarled. "Otherwise, just paint."

"Copy that," Clayton replied as he switched weapon presets. "I got 'em."

Under normal circumstances, the *Rogue* had made the right play, using the superior range of its LRMs to engage at distance while using its high acceleration to stay out of range of the *Slayer*'s return fire. *But these* aren't *normal circumstances*, Clayton reminded himself.

The *Rogue* didn't bother to maneuver; it kept on a straight course at max thrust. Even at extreme range, it took no effort for Clayton to line up a shot, his targeting reticle going green. A second later, a nickel-iron slug from the modified *Slayer*'s Gauss rifle gutted the *Rogue*. Clayton watched with grim satisfaction as the patchwork fighter's engine flamed out...then blew apart, just as the pilot ejected into the cold void of space.

"Never get cocky, friend, because you never know what your opponent's packing," Clayton said to himself as he circled the extravehicular pilot. Didn't matter that they'd been trying to kill each other less than a minute ago: no one was left behind in the cold darkness to die, not even pirates.

VENGEANCE-CLASS DROPSHIP OAS ACCEPTANCE
NADIR JUMP POINT
TRESSPASS SYSTEM
SPINWARD PERIPHERY
23 NOVEMBER 3063

The thing about DropShips, even large ones like the *Vengeance*-class OAS *Acceptance*, was that internal space was at a premium. This meant members of the Fifth Alliance Air Wing had to be creative when finding places to relax. During off-hours, that was Bay Three.

Clayton sat—as much as anyone could in zero-g—on one of the stacks of cargo containers. His mag-booted feet anchored him to a bulkhead as he tapped on his data pad, finishing a letter to send back home to Quatre Belle.

Three containers across and two down, Clinton was in the middle of a game of poker with Marcus Griffin and Tommy Connor also, of Second Regiment, Second Squadron. Malika Fayed was watching everyone, not playing, but quietly observing as usual, fingers playing with her hijab. Clayton tipped up the brim of his charcoal-gray Stetson and listened in on the game.

"I raise, all in," Clinton said, putting a magnetic chip down on the cargo container.

Marcus ran fingers over his dark, bald head and pondered. "Something's not right here. And I know I'm gonna kick myself for this, but...I fold."

Clinton then looked at Tommy with a predatory grin as the rookie pilot rubbed his chin, a worried look on his face.

But then Tommy looked him dead in the eyes, all presence of distress gone. "You know what, I call."

Clinton's grin disappeared. Frowning, he revealed his cards, jack-high. Tommy smiled triumphantly as he revealed his trio of threes, then plucked all the chips from the table. Bemoaning his misfortune, Clinton pulled back and kicked off from the table, floating over to join his brother.

"Thanks for the game, Clint!" Tommy playfully called out as he high-fived Marcus and Malika.

"Rookie finally got you?" Clayton asked.

Clinton stomped his mag-booted foot against the bulkhead. "Never you mind," he grumbled, adjusting his own gray Stetson before crossing his arms. "Last week he didn't know anything about poker, now suddenly he's a damn card shark! Almost like someone told him my tells."

Clayton couldn't hide the devilish smile on his face.

"Youuuuu..." Clinton said, irritated.

Clayton pulled his own Stetson down. "You were stomping on him for *weeks*. The kid deserved some payback. Besides, not like you lost any money."

"Not. The. Point. It's the principle of the—"

"Reesh!" a slightly slurred voice interrupted. "We needa have a talk!"

Clayton sighed as Supervisor Karl Owens from Third Regiment, First Squadron, floated up, three darts clenched in his fist. "You been duckin' me long enough. You owe me a rematch!" he said shoving the darts in *Clinton's* direction.

"Wrong Reese, *friend*," Clinton growled.

"Wha?" Owens said as Clayton tipped his Stetson back up. With mouth agape, it took Owens about thirty seconds to realize he was looking at the exact same faces on both men.

"Now, I understand your confusion," Clinton began in a mocking tone. "It's not often you see the likes of such handsome, rugged individuals, let alone two. I mean, twins; what're the odds? The strong jawline, the wavy brown hair with just a *touch* of red, and don't get me started on our abs. All prime packaging straight from the mountains of Quatre Belle. But then, rank insignia and nametags *are* a thing."

Everyone in Bay Three was now looking in their direction as Owens' face reddened.

Clayton sighed. "Owens, I honestly don't know what this is. We played a friendly game of darts last week and I won. No big."

Owens fumed. "I'm shick of hearing from ever'one that *yer* the best shot, at...well, ever'thing! I'm gonna prove that wrong."

"Look, Owens, this ain't worth it," Clayton said, trying to defuse things.

"Shounds like fear to me. I knew yer really a cowa—"

Clayton snatched one of the darts and sent it flying fifteen meters, past *and* between several people, and bull's-eyed a dartboard with a *thud* almost dead center, at a downward, forty-five-degree angle.

He looked Owens in the eye with icy calm. "Okay, I took my shot. Take yours or leave."

Owens floated for a few moments, face bright red and jaw clinched. He started to turn, but Clayton said, "And *Supervisor*, I'll forget this little display *if* you lose the hip flask that's printing against your breast pocket. You know the regs about alcohol on board."

Swallowing hard, Owens kicked off and made for the exit.

"There goes a problem for another day," Clinton said. "Nice shot, though. But don't think I'll forget your betrayal."

Clayton grunted in agreement, then went back to his letter as everyone else returned to their own business. Normally Bay Three was livelier, with games, socializing, cavorting, and people coming up with creative ways to combat boredom. But tonight, there were maybe a dozen souls present.

In his letter, Clayton wrote to his father about how unusually tedious the last six weeks had been, that their pirate sweep of the Tresspass system had found mostly abandoned pirate bases or caches. In fact, the only enemy contact over the last three weeks was the trio of fighters he and Clinton had engaged the day before. He hoped the intel officers would get something from the recovered pirate pilot, because the strain of inactivity among the squadrons was starting to show.

As he finished, Clayton heard a familiar voice call out: "Heads up, cowboys!"

Neither Reese brother looked up as the projectiles came straight at their heads. Clayton's left hand deftly caught the object centimeters from his Stetson's brim. By contrast, Clinton's hand shot out like a tiger's paw, snatching the object in mid-flight.

"The hell?" Clinton said as he looked at the drink pack. "Vacu-sealed *decaf* coffee? This is an affront to nature, you know."

"That's 'an affront to nature, *sir*,'" retorted Section Leader Rena Carmichael. "Or I'll accept *ma'am* because of your folksy upbringings, Clint." The CO of Two-Two Squadron floated up and expertly hooked her foot into some convenient cargo netting to stop her momentum and tossed additional packs to the rest of Bay Three's occupants.

"Despite my brother's insubordinate tone, he's got a point, *sir*," Clayton said. He took a swig of coffee and instantly regretted it. "You sure this isn't heat-sink coolant?"

Rena shrugged. "Quartermaster's out of the good stuff. Seems we went through it faster than normal. Guess when you're pirate hunting and barely find anything, people need to stay awake somehow. Oh, and before either of you ask, official kill count came back. Clint's at nine. Clay, you're officially at eleven. Congratulations on becoming a double ace."

Clayton smiled slyly at his brother, who begrudgingly grunted.

"Only 'cause you got that fancy Gauss rifle," Clinton said.

"For which I'm eternally grateful. Thank you for making that happen, Section Leader," Clayton said to Rena in a faux-official tone.

Rena shook her dreadlocked head. "What are squadron COs for? Besides, the Alliance Grenadiers' supply chief owed me. Just keep making *me* look good and remember *my* six gets priority if it needs saving out there, okay?"

Clayton raised his drink pack in salute as Clinton slurped down and crushed his.

Rena then turned serious. "Speaking of success, word's come down that the First AAW has an open spot. Command wants recommendations, and I know your name's already on the short list. You want me to take it off *again*, Clay?"

Clayton blankly looked at her. The First Alliance Air Wing was the career pinnacle of any pilot in the Alliance Military Corps. They were the best of the best in the AMC and likely, the galaxy. The only way to join was to be recommended *then* invited; you had to prove yourself elsewhere first.

But just because a door opens, doesn't mean you should walk through, Clayton thought.

"Fine," Rena said. "But you're not going to keep getting this opportunity. And you can't stay my XO forever."

"Maybe," he replied, glancing at his brother, whose Stetson was now covering his face.

"Well, I'm gonna to get some shuteye," Clinton said, putting hands behind his head. "Wake me up when something needs shooting."

Almost on cue, klaxons started blaring and the lighting changed to red.

"Action stations, action stations!" the PA blared. "This is not a drill, repeat this is NOT a drill! All hands to action stations!"

Clayton and Rena looked at Clinton, who popped his Stetson up, a hungry grin on his face.

"Well now, how 'bout that..."

Two hours later, Clayton was back in his *Slayer*, waiting with the rest of his squadron to sortie. Off his nose, a crew chief checked her data pad, then gave a thumbs-up just as Clayton's flight systems indicated all green. He gave her a thumbs-up in return.

As the support crews evacuated the launch bay, the words of the Fifth's CO, Chairman Jeff Pemrick, replayed in his mind.

"Earlier today, long-range sensors detected the drive signature of a Clan Titan-*class DropShip. Thirty minutes after detection, they changed course to intercept, and their CO, Star Colonel Hudson Shu of Clan Snow Raven, issued a...batchall to initiate a Trial of Possession for the* True North *with their own ship,* Wings of Midnight, *as collateral. Given our limited options, we accepted their challenge. Per rules of engagement, One-One, One-Three, and Two-Two squadrons will face fifteen Snow Raven fighters. The rest of our forces will be on standby...just in case.*

"I don't have to remind anyone of the consequences if we fail. This engagement isn't about a prize, it's about going home.

"You all have your assignments. Go show these intruders how the Fifth Alliance Air Wing does business. Good hunting!"

"Everyone ready for this?" Rena asked over the Two-Two Squadron channel.

"Damn right," Clinton replied. "I've heard about Clanners. Think they can show up and just take whatever. I don't suffer *those* types."

Marcus, Malika, and Tommy echoed his sentiment.

"Be smart though," Clayton interjected. "We're playing their game, so they've got the edge."

"Exactly," Rena said as the yellow warning lights above the launch bay doors activated. "But let's show 'em Two-Two Squadron doesn't back down."

Flight Ops then came in over the tac-channel. "Overwatch to Bolo Group, stand by for doors, stand by for launch."

Atmosphere vented as the doors opened and lights changed from yellow to red and a twenty-second countdown initiated. The six fighters of Two-Two Squadron throttled up, engines roaring as the launch rails held them fast.

Clayton looked to his left and saw Malika and Marcus' *Lightning*s—Bolo Three and Four—ready to go. Farther down was Bolo One and Two, Rena and Tommy's *Shilone*s.

As the countdown reached zero, the lights turned green, and Clayton and the rest of Two-Two shot forward as the rails released. The squadron then quickly formed up with One-One and One-Three Squadrons—Bone Group and Trap Group, respectively—with their mix of vintage *Ironsides*es and *Spad*s, along with newer *Hellcat*s and *Seydlitz*es.

Ahead, Clayton saw *Wings of Midnight* deploy its fighters...which expertly formed up and came right at the Alliance pilots. "Not wasting any time," he said to himself as five Clanners broke formation. "Bolo Five to Bone actual. Fast-moving bandits breaking wide. Looks like they're going for our six."

"I see them, Bolo Five," Pemrick replied. "Bone Group, break by squads and engage at will! Tallyho!"

Bandit IFF data flashed in the corner of Clayton's vision as he throttled up and saw that the fast movers were now vectoring toward One-Three, but would pass briefly into Two-Two's weapons range. "Bolo Five to One, you see what I'm seeing?"

"Oh yeah. Bolo Two, Bolo Five, select targets. Let's make life easier for Trap Group. The rest of you, watch our backs."

Breaking to starboard, Clayton targeted a Clan *Issus*. At this distance and speed, he'd only get one chance. Leading his Gauss rifle, Clayton waited a half second before the wide-winged *Issus* entered his sights. A nickel-iron slug slammed into the Clanner's port wing, sending the fighter into a spin and spoiling the Clanner's attack on Trap Three. But the Clanner recovered and pressed on.

"Damn," Clayton muttered to himself as Bolo One and Two both called out "Splash one!" Their targets, two *Chaeronea*s, were destroyed by LRM fire.

But Clayton didn't linger; warnings blared in his ear as he pitched over and gunned his throttle. Twin pulse lasers from a *Batu* barely missed him, but two more struck underneath his port side, burning away armor plating. The *Slayer* shuddered, but Clayton kept control as the *Batu* surged past, with Clinton in pursuit, peppering it with autocannon rounds.

"Die already!" Clinton bellowed.

But the *Batu* throttled up and rocketed away. Clayton then noticed another *Batu* diving on his brother.

"Bolo Six, *break*!" he called out, already lining up a shot on the second *Batu* as Clinton maneuvered.

Clayton worked an attack angle as his brother evaded four pulse lasers, but the *Batu*'s large laser cut deep into Clinton's port wing. Angling his nose down, Clayton drilled the second *Batu* with his medium lasers. One pair blew something off the Clanner's starboard wing while the other two vaporized armor.

In a mocking gesture, the Clanner did a victory roll as the two throttled up and pulled away. Clayton slammed the side of his canopy with his fist, then turned back toward his brother. Coming up on his starboard side, he inspected Clinton's mangled wing. "Bolo Six, status."

"Starboard medium lasers are gone," Clinton replied. "Wing armor's all but stripped. Landing gear compromised. Other than that, I'm *really* pissed off!"

Clayton's sensors indicated the *Batu*s were vectoring back. Over the comm channel, wingmates called out victories, others for help, while a few called out for the last time, their words punctuated by sounds of harsh static.

"Bolo Six, I'm sick of playing with these guys," Clayton said as cold resolve replaced his frustration. "Let's wax these suckers and help the group. On my wing!"

"Tallyho!" Clinton replied.

They yawed hard and nosed down as the enemy *Batu*s sniped with their large lasers, but the two *Slayer*s jinked and evaded. With the Clanners' speed and firepower advantage, Clayton knew the enemy would eventually pick them apart unless they did something quick.

"Bolo Six, let's see if they know the Thatch Weave!" Clayton called out, referencing a maneuver used during the Terran Second World War to defeat superior-performing craft.

"Copy *that*," Clinton replied.

Both *Slayer*s went full throttle and vectored toward *Acceptance*, attempting to look like they were fleeing. Which, Clayton hoped, would sucker the Clanners in.

It did.

The *Batu*s charged in, weapons blazing.

"Don't get cocky," Clayton, said to himself as they closed, waiting for just the right moment... "BREAK!"

Clayton and Clinton rolled their *Slayer*s ninety degrees, then split in opposite directions. The *Batu*s mirrored, each targeting a different *Slayer*. Clayton watched the *Batu* on his six, mentally urging him closer. "And...MERGE!" he called out.

Clayton cut throttle and fired maneuvering thrusters, spinning his fighter 180 degrees to starboard; g-forces grayed his vision and pushed his G-suit to its limits. Two seconds later, he rammed the throttle to full. Snap-rolling forty-five degrees, he surged beneath Clinton—who'd performed the same maneuver to port—with only a meter to spare between them.

Despite the g-forces, Clinton let out a war howl as he unloaded on Clayton's *Batu* with his remaining weapons. Laser and autocannon fire blew the Clan fighter apart.

Clinton's *Batu* tried to nose up and evade, but despite graying vision, Clayton put a Gauss rifle slug right into its fuel tank.

"YEAH! Splash one!" Clinton howled in triumph.

"Copy that, also splash one," Clayton added. He checked his sensors and comm channel, and immediately heard Bolo Four.

"—on me tight, engine failing, I need help!"

Before Clayton could reply, Bolo Four suddenly disappeared from sensors. Clayton came about with Clinton tight on his wing. It didn't take long to find Four's assassin. IDed as a *Turk*, the Snow Raven fighter continued to blast at Bolo Four's obvious wreckage, but didn't seem to detect the *Slayers*. Clayton decided to teach the Clanner a lesson in spatial awareness.

Coming in flat at the *Turk*'s seven o'clock, he lined his targeting brackets just behind the fighter's wing and fired. The nickel-iron Gauss rifle slug slammed into the Clanner, and an instant later, a massive secondary explosion ripped the wing free, sending both halves of the fighter spiraling. The Clan pilot ejected, and for a moment Clayton considered ending them, finger quivering on the trigger. But instead, he banked away, searching for another target.

Before him, the engagement continued. On his sensors, Clayton saw two *Spad*s gang up on a Clan *Avar*. Meanwhile, a *Scytha* heavy fighter obliterated a *Hellcat*. At his two o'clock, he saw an *Ironsides* and a Clan *Sulla* engage in mutually assured destruction via particle projection cannons.

Looking around for a target, Clayton was about to key up the comm channel when a familiar voice burst through: "Bolo Five, Six—LOOK OUT!"

The two *Slayers* split apart just as Rena's damaged *Shilone* shot past them, a Clan *Chaeronea* hot on her tail, its wingtip-mounted large lasers blasting away with alternating fire.

"Bolo One to Bolo Five, remember what I said about ass saving? Now's a good time!"

"Copy, One. On it!" Clayton replied, banking hard to pursue.

"Bolo Six to Five, bandit vectoring one-four-four-five!" Clinton interjected.

IFF tagged the bandit as a *Visigoth* coming in hot, its LRMs launching. Clayton felt several impacts on his hull, but managed to maintain control. Red indicators flashed in his vision; his aft-firing medium laser was gone, armor integrity was down 40 percent on his starboard wing and aft, and he ignored the rest.

"Damn! Bolo Five to Six, keep that bandit off my tail. I'm helping One."

"Copy, but hurry up!" Clinton bellowed as he broke to engage the *Visigoth*, barely avoiding a PPC beam.

Clayton fired his thrusters, spiral-spinning to get the angle as the *Chaeronea* landed a solid large-laser hit on Rena's primary engine, causing it to sputter. Over the comms, he heard Clinton swear as he traded shots with the *Visigoth* amid the sounds of metal rending and instruments popping in his cockpit. Clayton wanted to engage the *Visigoth*, but he couldn't abandon Rena.

Just a few more seconds, Clint... Clayton finished his spin. His targeting brackets went green, and he pulled the trigger, coring the *Chaeronea*.

He spun his fighter 180 degrees and gunned his throttle, just in time to see the *Visigoth*'s PPC blow Clint's starboard wing clean off, sending him into a spiral. There was no ejection. On pure instinct, Clayton flipped his weapon presets and triggered an alpha strike at the Clanner. The T-shaped fighter tried to evade, but took the full brunt just behind the cockpit. The dead craft kept going as flames licked and smoke billowed, armor and equipment spewing as Clayton streaked past.

But he didn't verify the kill. Instead, he yawed hard and keyed up their personal channel, desperately searching for a rescue beacon.

"Bolo Five to Bolo Six, do you copy? Bolo Five to Six, *do you copy*?! Dammit, Clint, *do you copy?!*" Tears formed in his eyes.

Before he could continue the search, a message broke through on his comm channel.

"I am Star Colonel Hudson Shu of Clan Snow Raven, piloting the lone *Scytha* in this battle. I hereby invoke *zellbrigen* and challenge the gray-and-black *Slayer*, ID number 225, to a duel of warriors. This is a solemn matter, let none interfere."

"What the hell...?" Clayton said to himself, suddenly raging because there were people were dying for what? Because *they* wanted a damn ship? And now this egomaniac wanted an *honor duel*?!

He took a couple breaths, quickly reasserting his resolve. "Fine. Sooner I splash you, sooner I find my brother," he replied coldly.

"Bargained well and done."

Shu instantly fired on Clayton, a large laser lancing out from extreme range, raking across his *Slayer*'s port wing. Glowing armor shards blew into space, and system warnings blared as Clayton rolled with the hit and turned into the Clanner, gunning the throttle as he returned fire. His laser shots went wide, but his Gauss rifle blew a pair of large lasers off the *Scytha*'s port wing.

As the two fighters passed each other, the *Scytha*'s rearward medium lasers fired. One missed, but the other grazed Clayton's canopy, leaving a long black scar just above his head.

Shu then spun around, his heavy Ultra-class autocannon spitting hot death. Clayton spun on his axis and swore he could *feel* the shells' kinetic force as they passed by. In response, he triggered a snapshot from his Gauss rifle, but missed by mere centimeters. Breaking hard to port, he quickly reversed his turn to avoid a duo of laser beams.

Clayton realized that while they were dead even for speed and maneuverability, he was grossly outgunned. But while his *Slayer* was also a heavy aerofighter, its wedge shape was more compact, which meant a smaller target profile. The two fighters danced around each other, neither able to land solid hits. But the damage was adding up, and Clayton's instruments began to flicker.

He needed to end this.

As he scored a laser hit on the *Scytha*, disabling another wing laser, an insane plan formed in Clayton's mind. *Okay, Shu, you want a gunfight? You picked the right cowboy.*

He throttled up and rocketed directly toward *Wings of Midnight.*

"Running away will not save you, cowardly freebirth!" Shu taunted. "I will take great pleasure in blowing you out of—"

Clayton simply flicked off the comm.

Weapon alerts from the Clan DropShip blared in his ears, but nothing fired. Closer and closer he got, with Shu hot on his tail. His control panel flickered, and engine power began to fall, but Clayton urged his fighter to hold on just a bit longer.

Wings of Midnight now loomed large in his view, but still held its fire. And just as he'd hoped, Shu held *his* fire too, to avoid damaging his DropShip.

"Come on, Clanner... Let's see how bad you want to splash me!" Clayton said.

Sure enough, Shu was burning hard and fast for him.

Mentally calculating because he didn't quite trust his instruments, Clayton continued forward until he got within approximately seventy meters of the Clan DropShip. Cutting thrust, he flipped his *Slayer's* nose up, let momentum do its work for three seconds, then gunned the throttle. The starboard engine groaned and almost flamed out, but he surged up along *Wings of Midnight's* hull. Just as he cleared the top, Clayton fired now-straining maneuvering thrusters, flip-spinning his fighter.

Clayton and Shu now faced each other, in a space version of a quick-draw gunfight.

For a heartbeat, both pilots stared each other in the eyes. Then, they suddenly fired; heavy Ultra autocannon versus Gauss rifle. But Clayton was faster on the metaphoric draw, his aim deadly accurate.

His iron-nickel slug blasted into the *Scytha's* nose just above the autocannon, causing its last salvo to go wide. A heartbeat later, a secondary explosion took the nose clean off, causing the Clan fighter's remains to bounce off *Wings of Midnight's* hull and into the dark, cold void of space.

There was no ejection.

As the adrenaline in his body faded, Clayton realized a myriad of alarms and warnings were screaming for his attention. And one by one, every instrument and control on his fighter failed. Even the ejection system was malfunctioning. Worse, he realized his flight suit's emergency oxygen system was compromised, the reserves depleting rapidly.

Leaning back, Clayton chuckled as a dark ring crept into his vision and frost formed on the scored canopy.

"Clint..." he said, hoping his flight recorder was still working. "If you're alive, thanks for always having my back as I tried to have yours. It was a joy to fly with you, fight with you. Sorry I couldn't come back for you. And if you're already dead, I'll see you soon and we'll raise hell together in the afterlife..."

And then darkness took him.

Clayton awoke, the sounds of beeping medical equipment lancing into his brain. He groaned in pain as his senses slowly returned, and eventually recognized the med bay on the *Acceptance*. He tried to turn his head to look around, but his body was completely secured to the zero-g bed. Panic crept in, and Clayton started to fight his restraints, his head pounding with the effort.

"Whoa, *whoa* there, cowboy! Easy!" said a familiar voice. "You're all right, Clay. Calm down."

Tears filled Clayton's eyes as he saw Clinton's face, despite almost the entire left side being covered in heavy trauma dressing.

"Wha...what happened?" he asked through his oxygen mask.

"We won," Clinton said, clasping his brother's hand. "After you blasted that lead Clanner, his second-in-command, named McCorkell, I think, called the fight. Afterward, both sides quickly recovered those who went EVA. Didn't matter who they were, each side picked up whoever was closest. Seems even these Clanners buy into the idea of no one being left to die in space. After that, they asked for something called, uh, *hi-gra, hee-gra, hydra,* or *hee-haw*—whatever. But anyway, never mind. You did it. *You did it*!"

"*We* did it," Clayton said weakly, tightening his grip on his brother's hand.

The Reese brothers sat there for a few moments in silence, but it wasn't long before the medicos came in and assured Clayton that he'd be fine, and all he needed was some rest.

"Well then," Clayton said. "With all due respect, I'm gonna get some sleep. Let me know when something needs shooting..."

THE RALLY POINT BAR
ARHEIMA
DNEIPER III
OUTWORLDS ALLIANCE
30 NOVEMBER 3063

Clayton raised his half-full glass of bourbon as Chairman Pemrick, now sporting a patch over his right eye, finished his toast.

"—to the victory of the Fifth Alliance Air Wing, and to those who remain forever on-mission, watching our sixes from the great beyond."

Clayton emptied his glass and winced a bit when he tapped it on the bar, his body still stiff and sore. Looking around, he watched the assembled members of the Fifth, and those of the hosting Second Alliance Air Wing, enjoy this "officially unofficial" victory celebration.

He saw Malika on crutches, her lower leg in a cast, touching pictures of Marcus and Tommy on a nearby table with other photos for a makeshift memorial. Her head bowed slightly as she said farewell to her friends.

Meanwhile, Clinton was sitting at the other end of the bar, his face covered in a less bulky dressing, regaling an extremely attractive brunette pilot from the Second with his recent exploits in battle. Clayton smiled as the two got up, Clinton giving his brother a knowing wink over his shoulder as they departed.

As he pulled a cigar from his flight-jacket's pocket, Rena walked up with a full bourbon in her left hand and a shot of something dark in her right, despite the sling that arm was currently occupying.

"Looks like you could use a reload," she said, handing Clayton the drink.

"Always, thank you," he said as Chairman Pemrick walked up. "Sir, to what do we owe the honor?"

"Honor's mine," Pemrick said. "I wanted to talk to you and Rena personally. One-One, One-Three, and Two-Two Squadrons are standing down for the next few months. We've been tasked with escorting our prize ship back to Alpheratz, and after that's done...we'll be awarded Pitcairn Stars by President Avellar himself. Seems someone considers our handiwork something of a big deal." He grinned.

For a few moments, neither Clayton nor Rena could speak. Rena smiled from ear to ear, but Clayton quickly got back to business. "What about the Clanners that came with us, sir?"

"Well, per our post-battle agreement, most of them are currently in a safehouse here planetside, waiting for their JumpShip to arrive and take them back to wherever. A few will be coming with us to Alpheratz, mostly techs to train our people on the new systems, so we don't blow ourselves up apparently." Pemrick sipped his beer. "But scuttlebutt says the Clanners have requested, and been granted, a meeting with some of our government officials. Everything else is above my pay grade."

Clayton stoically took Pemrick's words in, not sure how to feel. Rena simply nodded.

"Well, I'll let you both get back to it," Pemrick said, clinking his glass with Clayton's and Rena's. "Oh, one more thing, Clayton. Congratulations on becoming the youngest triple ace on active duty in the AMC."

"T-Thank you, sir," Clayton stuttered as Pemrick dismissed himself. Finally smiling, he lit a match for his cigar.

"Hey, you know you've had someone locked on you for a while now, right?" Rena said, nodding at a corner of the bar.

Clayton stopped mid-motion and flicked the match out as he casually looked over. A younger woman was sitting alone. She was a bit on the short side, with a very athletic frame. But what caught his attention was the paleness of her skin, her cool blue eyes, and the stark whiteness of her hair, which had black streaks running up the right side.

"Nice to know even a triple ace can lose situational awareness on occasion." Rena chuckled. "I'll leave you to whatever comes next. I have some things of my own to take care of. But honestly, thanks again for saving my six out there." She gently thumped her fist on his shoulder before heading off.

Glancing back toward the woman in the corner, Clayton walked out to the outdoor seating area. A cool breeze blew as he finally lit his cigar. He managed only a single drag before she joined him.

"So, at the risk of sounding cliché," he said, "what's a nice girl like you doing in a place like this?"

"I was looking for a place to rest. I did not realize there was to be a celebration here," she said. "I hope I am not intruding."

"Nah, it's a free planet. And this wasn't exactly planned, so no worries. But pardon me for asking... The way you talk, you're not exactly from around here, are you?"

She blinked for a moment, as if searching for an appropriate answer. "You are correct. I am not. I do not wish to be rude, but I would prefer not to discuss it. I am a...refugee of sorts. I was recently forced from my home, and now I am here."

Clayton nodded. "Sorry to hear that. So, what was it about me that got your attention? I gather you've been eyeballing me for a while now."

"You seemed...interesting," she replied.

Clayton chuckled. "You're not some kind of groupie—or worse, some kind of serial killer—are you?" he jokingly asked.

But she took the question seriously. "I do not wish you any harm."

Clayton smiled and took another drag from his cigar. "That's good. You don't seem like the type, but one must never become complacent, or underestimate any possible danger."

"I agree," she said. "But I am now curious: What if I did pose a threat?"

Clayton blew smoke from his mouth. "Let's just say a true cowboy is never far from his shootin' iron," he said, taking another drag. "That and I personally don't go down without a fight."

The white-haired woman nodded and was about to respond when two uniformed military police came out onto the back porch.

"I'm sorry, officers," Clayton said. "I didn't realize my squadmates and I were causing an iss—"

"No, sir, you're all fine," one of the MPs replied. "We're here to retrieve *her.*"

Clayton raised an eyebrow. "She do something wrong?"

"Not at liberty to say, sir. We're taking her back into protective custody. Ma'am, if you would please come with us?"

The white-haired woman acquiesced. "Thank you for your time," she said to Clayton before being escorted away.

Clayton downed a gulp of bourbon and took another pull from his cigar, wondering exactly what had just happened.

The door to the cabin closed, and the lock engaged with an audible *click.*

"Well, Star Commander Eris, your mission was successful, *quiaff?*" asked a thin man with a slightly large head and wide, brown eyes. He put down one of the quaint, old-style paper books provided by their Outworlder hosts.

Eris ran a hand through her white hair as she removed the garments she had borrowed from one of the city's residents. "*Aff*, Star Colonel. Thank you for trusting me with this task. And for allowing me to indulge my own personal curiosity in the process. I trust my departure did not cause an issue?"

Aaron McCorkell waved his hand dismissively. "I have been assured the *hegira* we were granted is still in effect. We simply await the arrival of our ship to complete the necessary transfer of personnel and materiel. Although, if our hosts had wanted us to remain in our assigned quarters, they should have specifically expressed that. Or assigned a more competent guard detail."

Eris nodded and began putting her field uniform back on. "I met the Outworlds Alliance pilot who defeated Star Colonel Hudson Shu... and myself. He appears to be a...unique individual. Also, I believe my impromptu reconnaissance mission has provided valuable insights about those who won the Trial of Possession."

"Good. In the coming months, as we travel to their homeworld, I know the Outworld Alliance leaders will no doubt put, as they say, their best face forward for us. But our new mission is not about carefully crafted masks, it is about truth. It is about what the Alliance's warriors, and people, are truly like. I have successfully impressed this on our superiors. It seems this minor defeat may, in fact, present a greater opportunity for our Clan."

Eris nodded. "Then we will not waste such an opportunity."

AFTER-ACTION REPORT: LONGBOW MOUNTAIN

ERIC SALZMAN

EXHIBIT: THE BATTLE OF LONGBOW MOUNTAIN
MYSTERIES OF THE PERIPHERY WING
THE SNORD MUSEUM
GALATEA

In 3151, Snord's Irregulars recovered data from the ruins of Santander-Valasek Ltd.'s offices in Santander's Jewel, which shed new light on an escapade that has long puzzled military analysts.

Helmar Valasek, the bandit king of Santander V, dispatched vessels carrying mercenaries on a mission to raid a Taurian Concordat fortress on the world of Sterope, more than 900 light-years away—a one-way journey of more than eight months. For decades, scholars of mercenary actions have speculated what Valasek could have intended, losing the use of scarce space assets for nearly two years only to send a ground force incapable of completing the assigned mission.

CORPORATE POLITICS

Records show dozens of minor nobles jointly ruled Sterope, each raising and maintaining a Noble regiment of infantry. In 3022, Baron Sebastian Agenor leveraged his new directorship of Taurus Territorial Industries' Sterope facility to dominate planetary affairs. A canny politician unafraid to play dirty, he disrupted several attempts to undercut his ascent and viciously retaliated against any competitors, initiating new mining and industrial projects that befouled his rivals' landholds.

Most damaged by such measures was Baroness Sophia Euryte, who had lost the TTI directorship to Baron Agenor, then saw her entire extended family killed in suspicious "accidents." With Agenor untouchable in his aerie atop Longbow Mountain, she turned to the criminal underworld, pledging House Euryte's remaining assets for Agenor's death.

Guilds operating near Taurian space took the contract, but failed in their efforts. The House of the Setting Sun's operatives attempted to scale the mountain's exterior, but were discovered between the first and second defensive rings, and artillery reduced them to a bloody smear on the slope. The Paladins acknowledged Agenor's vile deeds and also undertook the contract, but their operatives proved unable to breach the mountain's defenses, and an ambush of his convoy annihilated his Noble regiment outriders. Other guilds considered the site too distant to be worth their attention.

MAKING A NAME

While Valasek had already established a fearsome reputation as a pirate lord at the head of his Death's-Head Raiders, his newly assembled murder-for-hire force—Santander's Killers—lacked the reputation of established assassin guilds such as the Nekakami, Dofheicthe, Paladins, or Kageyoru. To establish himself as a serious competitor, Valasek took the contract once his agents relayed the details to him. The death of Baron Agenor at the heart of his stronghold would earn Valasek the respect of the other guilds, and the distance involved made Taurian retaliation unlikely.

To breach the mountain's defenses, Valasek planned a two-pronged attack. Ground forces would launch a conventional assault on the fortifications, drawing the full attention of the garrison, while a team of Santander's Killers took advantage of the distraction to penetrate Agenor's sanctum and claim the bounty. Unwilling to risk his own Death's-Head Raiders, Helmar chose Wilson's Hussars, a hard-luck mercenary unit hired in 3022, as his sacrificial lambs.

THE DEEPEST RAID

Valasek's bandits had previously ranged as far rimward as the Draconis March, and the captain of the JumpShip *Ranger* was skilled in evading both Kurita and Davion customs patrols. Resupply en route was facilitated by Valasek's vast network of spies and informants.

Setting out on 29 July 3023, the *Ranger* carried two *Union* DropShips bearing the Hussars' 'Mech companies and a platoon of Santander's Killers—veteran commandos representing the best of Valasek's fighting forces. As the months drew on and the vessel transited the Crucis March, Wilson's Hussars, who had not been briefed on their destination, began expressing reservations about the mission. These doubts were swiftly silenced when the Killers brutally murdered a Hussars MechWarrior as a cautionary example of questioning their blood oath to Valasek.

On 19 April 3024, the *Ranger* arrived at the Sterope system. Its DropShips made planetfall, using false transponders identifying them as a merchant delegation from Earthwerks, Inc. While the 'Mechs remained aboard the DropShips at the Taurus City port, the Killers made contact with Taurus Territorial Industries representatives on 26 April, presenting credentials as buyers seeking to acquire TTI's line of fixed gun emplacements.

THREE RINGS OF DOOM

Longbow Mountain's fortifications dated from the Reunification War, and were similar in design to the Taurian fortress on Ridgebrook that had held off a Star League assault regiment for four months. Sterope's remoteness meant it had never been successfully attacked, leaving the three concentric rings of fortifications encircling the mountain intact, bristling with heavy artillery and missile batteries manned by Baron Agenor's Noble regiment. The TTI plant in Taurus City, below, had long made use of Longbow Mountain as a functional showroom for their product lines, and readily offered tours of the outer ring to prospective buyers.

Once inside, the Killers overwhelmed their TTI security escorts. Using stolen uniforms and codes supplied by Baroness Euryte, they penetrated to the second ring of defenses. The Killers signaled the Hussars to begin their assault, then took advantage of the distraction to further ascend the mountain. No bandit had been so foolhardy to attack the fort in living memory, and the chaotic scramble to action stations enabled Valasek's commandos to reach the command center buried beneath the mountain's peak unquestioned.

With weapons seized from an armory, the Killers slaughtered Baron Agenor and his command staff, then set explosives to cover their extraction. Emerging on the windswept high slopes as Noble regiment's infantry struggled to reach the ruined command center, the assassins deployed wingsuits and glided down to the rendezvous point where the DropShips had relocated.

Meanwhile, massed fire poured down from the defensive rings had shattered Wilson's Hussars. The mercenaries lost two lances before Captain Wilson's "strategic withdrawal" turned into a panicked rout. The barely functional remnants arrived at the extraction rendezvous ahead of the Killers, and both groups returned to the *Ranger* to begin the circuitous, year-long journey back to Santander V. However, the Killers had always intended to leave the Hussars behind; only the mercenaries' cowardice and quick retreat saved them from being abandoned in the Concordat. The Killers rectified this by marooning the Hussars on Lushann during a supply stop in the Outworlds Alliance.

With incontrovertible evidence of his team making the hit, Helmar Valasek's "Murder, Inc." operation brought the reputation he'd sought in the interstellar underworld. He subsequently folded the Death's-Head Raiders into Santander's Killers and had the veterans of Longbow Mountain train them as assassins, ensuring a bloody and profitable future for the bandit king over the next quarter century.

BATTLEFORCE SCENARIO: OUR TWO WEEKS' NOTICE

TOM STANLEY

This scenario is for use with *Interstellar Operations: BattleForce*.

In April 3150, the Rasalhague Dominion sent invasion forces into the Draconis Combine. Three Clusters hit Lambrecht, but encountered militia forces and mercenaries instead of Combine troops. Omega Galaxy clashed with these forces for three weeks, but eventually the mercenaries departed; their aerospace forces sacrificing themselves to clear enough space for their DropShips to head deeper into Combine territory.

Blue Leader: *Gold One, say again: How many forces inbound? Are the Ghost Bears just here for a trial?*

Gold One: *Negative, Blue Leader, no trials. There's at least one Trinary barreling down on us, maybe more. Not "Jihad Bear" mad, but...they seem pretty pissed.*

Blue Leader: *It's fine if they're just regular mad. Go ahead and return to base.*

Gold One: *Roger. ETA, thirt—[loud static]*

Blue Leader: *Gold One?*

Gold One: *[static]*

Blue Leader: *Gold One, please come in. [Pause] Blue Leader to Base. Gold One might be KIA. Bears inbound, minimum one Trinary. Start hauling people into the ships. We're leaving.*

Base: *Understood, Blue. We're sorry for your loss.*

SITUATION

**LAMBRECHT
DRACONIS COMBINE
APRIL 3150**

The Dominion's Omega Galaxy began assaulting Lambrecht after the Draconis Combine Mustered Soldiery was distracted by a raid on Shionoha. Omega encountered a battalion of mercenary units, a joint force of Darrell's Double Barrels and the newly formed Harriet's Vengeance. The latter—inexperienced against Clan forces—was swept away while the Double Barrels attempted to recover survivors and fought a tactical retreat to the spaceport, where civilians and key planetary leaders were awaiting liftoff. The mercenaries had to ensure as many civilians could be collected as possible. Turning their 'Mechs toward the Bears, the Double Barrels bought some time before eventually retreating.

GAME SETUP

The Defender picks two mapsheets, preferably from sets such as *MapPack: CityTech Map* or *MapPack: City Ruins*. If such mapsheets are not available, substitute with any maps, and arrange both maps so their long sides are touching. Place 4–10 building tokens (mediums to heavy) on the eastern half of the map. Players may place building tokens up to 12 hexes from their edge.

The Defender's forces may be deployed up to twice their running speed from the eastern edge before play starts. The Defender's HQ must be adjacent to or on a heavy or hardened building; this HQ represents the spaceport, where the Defender's forces will lift off. The Attacker may place the HQ no closer than 12 hexes from the western edge.

The Attacker's units start on the western map, and may be deployed from that edge up to a number of hexes equal to the MP of their slowest 'Mech Element. The Attacker's HQ may be deployed up to twice this distance; the Defender will place the Attacker's HQ, but it must be no farther than 10 hexes from the Defender's HQ. This HQ represents the facilities used to coordinate the Attacker's front-line forces.

Both players each have two Objectives, which can be placed on the map no more than 6 hexes from either of the two HQs. The Attacker and Defender each place their own Objectives.

Attacker

A Trinary from Omega Galaxy has been tasked to swiftly overrun any opposition and secure the spaceport for the Dominion. They are

also tasked with testing this world's defenders. They were originally expecting DCMS regulars, but were surprised to encounter only a planetary militia and some mercenary forces.

Defender

Two mercenary companies, Darrell's Double Barrels and Harriet's Vengeance, pooled their forces to split the "quiet" contract on this system. Originally anticipating the occasional Trial of Possession for supplies or a raid from the former Republic borders, the mercs did not anticipate a full Rasalhague Dominion invasion. After holding out for weeks, buying time for civilians and planetary leaders, they have begun their retreat from the system.

VICTORY POINT CONDITIONS/OPTIONS

Along with the following victory-point options, please consult the *Victory Points Table* on p. 53 of *Interstellar Operations: BattleForce*.

"Mercs. WE. ARE. LEAVING!" (Defender Only)

The Defender is holding the line for six turns. After that, any surviving friendly Element that makes it to the Defender's HQ will be taken off the table at end of turn. The Defender earns Element PV x 1.5 Victory Points.

Attacking Forces

Alpha Star
Ursus II, Skill Rating 4
Ursus II, Skill Rating 4
Black Hawk (Standard), Skill Rating 4
Black Hawk (Standard), Skill Rating 4
Black Hawk (Standard), Skill Rating 4

Bravo Star
SHD-12C *Shadow Hawk*, Skill Rating 4
Solitaire, Skill Rating 4
Bear Cub, Skill Rating 4
Bear Cub, Skill Rating 4
Bear Cub, Skill Rating 4

Charlie Star
10x Skanda Light Tank, Skill Rating 5

Defending Forces

Blue Lance
WVR-9M *Wolverine*, Skill Rating 4
HCT-7S *Hatchetman*, Skill Rating 4
TR-1 *Wraith*, Skill Rating 4
CLN-7V *Chameleon*, Skill Rating 4

Green Lance
WSP-8T *Wasp*, Skill Rating 4
WLF-5 *Wolfhound*, Skill Rating 4
BLD-XL *Blade*, Skill Rating 4
NX-80 *Nyx*, Skill Rating 4

Red Lance
GRF-1N *Griffin*, Skill Rating 4
GRF-1N *Griffin*, Skill Rating 4
CN9-Ar *Centurion*, Skill Rating 4
GST-10 *Ghost*, Skill Rating 4

AFTERMATH

The mercenaries retreated to their DropShips with heavy casualties, and their aerospace wing sacrificed itself to clear a path free from Dominion opposition. After their escape, they spread news of the Dominion's advance. The few survivors of Harriet's Vengeance were offered positions in the Double Barrels to shore up their own losses.

The Third An Ting Legion on Ascella collected forces to strike back at Lambrecht, and later succumbed to the firepower of the Dominion's defensive measures. Some of the Third Legion's forces might be hiding in the southern continents, but the rumors have not yet been confirmed.

SEAL THE DEAL

RUSSELL ZIMMERMAN

**NORTH WHITMAN
HESPERUS II
LYRAN COMMONWEALTH
16 AUGUST 2990**

"Papa, when can we go home?!" Brandon O'Leary hopped up and down on the very tippy end of the *Ceridwen*'s loading ramp, skipping over greeting his father to instead ask his question before it slipped through his fingers, like his thoughts so often did.

Bran was slight and short, and strangers placed him at about six or eight years old. The rising whine in his voice didn't do him any favors in that regard.

His father, Michael, didn't miss a step as he started up the ramp. "I told you not to leave the ship," he said, impatiently grabbing Bran by the forearm and hauling him back up the ramp.

Young Brandon hadn't quite left; he'd just gone down to the very bottom edge of the ramp to wait there for his father to return. He'd thought if he didn't set foot on the planet, he'd count as staying aboard.

Apparently, his father disagreed.

"And we *are* home," he growled as they entered the cool darkness of the DropShip's loading bay.

He was righter than the boy liked to admit. It was all still confusing to someone so young. "Home" was supposed to be a safe place where you lived forever, wasn't it? He didn't want to live on the *Ceridwen* forever!

Brandon tucked himself into his father's shadow as the elder O'Leary watched the final preparations get underway, the *Ceridwen*'s crew scrambling about and doing all the work that needed doing before they could take off.

Brandon, meanwhile, mulled over his father's brusque answer.

The *Ceridwen* was a DropShip, not a home! A *Leopard*-class, it was 1,900 tons of weapon-bristling, armor-plated curves, a sleek machine of war with a cavernous cargo hold. All the furniture in the *Ceridwen* had once been novel and exciting to the boy: tables that folded up into the wall to stay out of the way; some chairs that were bolted in place so the roughest planetary entry wouldn't disturb them; mugs and cups and bowls, all looking fine and fancy, but with magnets in their bases so they'd stay in place atop cool metal tables.

It had all been exciting at first, but now...tedious. Cold. Mechanical. The first time he'd thought about how his room—his "quarters"—was where an aerospace fighter once slept and now was where *he* slept, it was fun. The first time he'd seen BattleMechs stomping down the ramps to go to work or stomping up the ramps to return, it was all really neat. The first time he'd tumbled out of bed from being rocked as the DropShip hit atmosphere and struggled to penetrate it, it was exciting. But the tenth time or hundredth time or billionth time, it wasn't.

Brandon was in awe of the *Ceridwen*, sure. He was a little afraid of it, with its lasers, particle projection cannons, and missile racks all bristling and stuff. He assumed anyone out to hurt him was afraid of it, too, so everyone would leave them alone, and that kind of made it safe...

But that didn't make it a *home*.

He remembered having a home! The memories weren't as sharp as they used to be, but they were comforting. He remembered wind and shiver-cold outside, but warmth and light inside; mountains that loomed taller than anything he'd ever seen since then; hands tingly cold from playing in the snow and taking a drink of tea that warmed him from the inside out like one of the fusion engines Papa always went on about. He *remembered* home. He forgot the name of it, sometimes, but he knew he'd been there, back when Mama had been alive.

He could ask Papa again, maybe...?

"Hey there, Peter!"

Oh. No. No talking to Papa. He was on his perscomm again. Already.

"What's that? Yeah, we're just now taking off. I wanted to call you real quick and just thank you again for that meeting yesterday. I think it went well."

Follow through, Papa always told him.

"I'm confident you'll come over to my side of things after you've had a chance to read over those projections. I think you'll see this proposal has some real potential! When people hear '*Sling*' they think 'Coventry,' right? The best damned launchers on the best damned 'Mech to ever carry them? Well, let's play our cards right and make it so when they hear '*Night Hawk*,' they think 'Defiance,' hmm? What do you say? A little factory access, let us get our engineers together with yours, and we can get something going, can't we? What's that? All right, yeah, sure, I'll talk to you later."

Bran wanted to ask his father about home again—*just what it's called?!*— after they settled in for takeoff, but it was no use. He was already back on his perscomm after that *last* call, talking to someone else. It never took him long. Father was *always* talking to someone else.

Stay busy, that was one of the other rules of business he had seared into the boy's memory.

Michael O'Leary was a busy man.

"Thanks again for meeting with me, Simon. I think we made some really good progress today, and I hope you'll reach out if you find you have any further questions after giving those reports a full read-through. I appreciate you taking the time to sit down, and I'm sure we'll meet somewhere in the middle on this. When people think '*Sling*' they think 'Coventry,' am I right? Well let's get everyone thinking 'Kincaid' alongside 'Mountain Wolf,' and vice versa. Two peas in a pod, name recognition all around, you know? With just a little factory access, I'm sure we could work something out! What's that? Uh-huh. Sure, sure. Next time."

Michael had just flown into Hesperus II three days earlier, and despite having multiple business meetings each day—he insisted on handling real negotiations face to face—their stay had only taken as long as the refueling and regular upkeep on the *Ceridwen*. That wasn't a coincidence, it was by design. There was always someplace else to be, and he wasn't a patient man who wanted to idly sit around. He flew someplace, did what he had to do, and then they were gone.

Always think a step ahead. That was another thing Brandon had learned from his father. That, and *Do two things at once*.

Brandon had trouble doing even just one thing! Especially left alone on the ship—not *alone* alone, of course, Captain Jessup and Chief Technician Kol and everyone else was always around, they were just always busy—it was sometimes hard for Brandon to concentrate. There was always something easier to think about than what he was supposed to be thinking about. Chief Kol said Brandon was bright, but he had to be like a laser, and focus perfectly. Sometimes when Brandon tried to think, he felt more like a missile rack, and a *big* one like the *Ceridwen* had, not little ones like *Sling*s carried. Thoughts, like missiles, exploding everywhere!

It was easier to sit and look out a porthole at stuff than to study, especially when the stuff out the porthole was the really cool-looking Kincaid Defiance Industries compound. It was easier to daydream about getting to see more of a planet instead of being "safe" and "where I know where you are" and "ready to go" than it was to read dull, old books. It was easier to go down to the cargo bay and watch Kol and the rest work on the 'Mechs than it was to memorize stupid charts and tables and stuff.

Papa was always a little upset with Brandon's schoolwork progress, even when he did his best to work on just one thing. If he could barely do one thing, how could he always try to do two?

"Hurry up, Captain. Get this bucket moving." His father was off the perscomm now, holding up a wire-mounted headset to grouch into the microphone, not even wearing it, disinterested in hearing anything back. Brandon pictured Captain Jessup rolling her eyes and making faces on the other end. She never ever ever would, but Brandon liked to imagine it. He fought a giggle at the mental image as Papa kept grouching. He held up the little headset in one hand and had his ancient, polished wooden pipe in the other. He never smoked it, just held it; he sometimes used it to accentuate his talking, waving it like a small hammer or holding the head in his hand to poke the bit out at people to accentuate a point. It was an old, old pipe.

"Burn harder if you have to. Just get us to the damned *Olympus* station and strap us to a JumpShip. Let's get the hell away from Marik space, huh? Does that sound okay with you, do you think?!"

Papa didn't like trips to Hesperus, no matter how much he got done, and he was always even more eager to leave than normal. The world was "too damned close" to the Free Worlds League, he said, and "too damned important." That was why he made Brandon stay on the ship. He always thought something bad was going to happen. Brandon didn't know much about the Mariks, but he knew they did bad things to factories. Every place Papa visited had factories, always trying to get them to let Papa and Chief Kol in, so Brandon was secretly always kind of worried for him.

Once the engine was done roaring and the *Ceridwen* was done with the worst of her shuddering, Brandon—after one last look at his father, confirming he was engrossed in a stack of papers now, still too busy for Bran—unbuckled himself, hopped from his seat, and glumly headed to his quarters. His room had been the aft aerofighter bay a long time ago. They didn't have an aerofighter anymore, so Brandon got to use it.

He knew a JumpShip was coming up eventually, and then a jump to another star system. He didn't know anything more than that, didn't try to guess where they were going. There was always somewhere to go. Somewhere that wasn't home. Papa always had more meetings. Papa always had things he was trying to buy or sell or lease—which was like buying, right?—so he always had perscomm calls to make and dinners to go to and people to talk with who weren't Brandon.

Always, always, *always*.

Always be moving, Michael had told his son over and over again. *Sharks never stop swimming.*

Brandon didn't really like sharks, but he was pretty sure the shark wasn't the point of that saying.

He sighed and sat on the floor in his quarters with some of his toy 'Mechs. The good guys today were his usual good guys, a *Sling* and a *Night Hawk.* He had more—lots more—but these were his favorites. On the rare occasion he had another kid to play with—who wasn't Chief Kol's boy, Rowan—they didn't even know what a *Sling* or a *Night Hawk* were, but that just made Brandon like them more.

As always, the enemy machines were, in his head, agents of the sinister House Marik, even though Bran had to move them around and make noises and stuff himself. Rowan hadn't come with them on this trip, so Bran didn't have anyone to play against but himself.

He'd gotten used to that.

"Always be moving," he said, scooting his tiny *Sling* around and making pitter-pat fast-footstep *toom-toom-toom* noises as it sprinted a wide circle. An assortment of *shhhhhew shhhhhew* noises followed as the lean 'Mech loosed a volley of fifteen missiles, and a scattering of *pakow*s as the imaginary munitions cratered armor on an unlucky Marik *Wasp.*

Take that!

"Stay busy," he said, sliding his little *Night Hawk* along, rushing it in a tighter spiral than the circling *Sling* toy so it closed on its opponent. When the eyeballed range looked about right, he gave it a few *pchew pchew* laser noises for good measure. The MechWarrior of a broad-shouldered *Griffin* let out a high-pitched cry of frustration as his machine was scored and savaged.

And that!

"Do two things at once." A return volley came as he stomped the *Griffin* and *Wasp* together in lockstep, chasing after the pair of skirmishers. The *Sling* was cornered against Brandon's dirty laundry. The looming *Griffin* pressed the *Night Hawk* until the smaller, laser-armed 'Mech was backed against the cabin wall. The *Wasp* began to lash out with flashing beams of laser fire and pairs of terribly destructive short-range missiles, battering the *Sling*, and the *Night Hawk* knew he was up next.

Cornered!

"Always think a step ahead," he said triumphantly as his *Night Hawk*—secretly his absolute favorite—turned the tables and advanced against the larger *Griffin*, lashing out with imagined beams of light from laser after laser. The *Griffin* staggered under the onslaught, and then things took a turn for the worse. The *Sling* selflessly ignored the brutal hammering it was taking and pivoted to launch a wave of long-range missiles at the *Griffin*, rescuing its hard-pressed friend, laying it on heavy.

The *Griffin* MechWarrior was pummeled from both sides. He knew he was beaten. Or was he?!

"Follow through!"

The *Griffin*'s pilot made a final, madcap leap, jump jets hurling it bodily against the elusive *Night Hawk* in a startlingly accurate and powerful flight that turned the *Griffin* entirely sideways, somehow rocketing the burly 'Mech unerringly, horizontally, in what would truly be a headbutt for the ages. How could our hero in the *Night Hawk* possibly avoid this devastating attack?! Only the most perfect-est laser shot ever, right to the cockpit of the oncoming *Griffin*, could possibl—

"What the hell are you doing?!"

Brandon started so hard he dropped his toys, and, wide-eyed, stared up at Papa standing in the hatchway to his quarters.

"I w-was just...um..." he stammered, shooting a sideways look to where his long-ignored stack of homework was sprawled out. "I did *some* of my reading, Papa, I'll finish it, I promise!"

No, wait. He was worried about the wrong thing.

"You *know* that's not how jump jets work." Scorn leaked from his father's voice. No, poured from it. He clutched his old pipe—Great-Grandpa Eli's old pipe—and stabbed the air with it, used it like a pointer, jabbed it right at Brandon.

"Blake's Blood, boy, a *Griffin* would never get in close against a *Night Hawk*. It should be trying to stay at range and just use its damned Fusigon and Delta to outgun our Maxell. It should be the *'Hawk* that's pressing the attack, not the damned *Griffin*, using its speed to get inside the *Griffin*'s range, stupid. And how the hell did a *Wasp* get a *Sling* up against a wall like that, huh? We can run circles around those little..."

Michael O'Leary turned to leave, almost spitting, then doubled back for more scorn.

"You're as dumb as your damn mother, do you know that? I could have lived with that in a daughter—Blake knows if you were a girl, nobody would care what was in your damned head—but you're my *son*. You're *my* son! And you sit here and act like you don't even know what our 'Mechs are capable of, or how any other goddamned 'Mech even works, or..."

He stood in the hatchway, shaking his head. All Brandon could do was stammer and fight tears.

"Sometimes I don't even know why I'm bothering to do all this. What are *you* going to do with whatever the hell I leave you, huh?"

Bran held it together until the angry stomping receded far enough, and then let the tears come. Hot tears, stinging against blushing, shame-hot, cheeks. His slender frame was wracked by one good sob, then he snatched up his toys—*Why'd you get me into trouble?!*—and threw them against the cramped wall of his quarters. The tiny magnets in the 'Mechs' bases wobbled them upright and snapped them against the deck of the ship after they landed; they didn't even have the good grace to fall messily like he'd wanted.

A *Sling* and a *Night Hawk*. His toys, but they were more than that. They were Papa's 'Mechs, his job, his whole life. The real versions of those looming war-titans slept nearby, in the belly of the *Ceridwen*, a precious single *Sling* and a pair of meticulously maintained *Night Hawk*s, all of them constantly upkept and tinkered with by Chief Kol and his technicians. Papa said they were the last ones, but he always said they wouldn't be the last ones forever. They were always being shown off, being licensed, being talked up, being sold. Desperately.

They were the past and present Mountain Wolf BattleMechs. They were *Brandon's* future—and Brandon was theirs.

ALPHERATZ IV
OUTWORLDS ALLIANCE
4 JUNE 2997

"Don't you worry, Madam President," Michael O'Leary's voice crackled in Brandon's earpiece. His father was using his salesman tone, his pleasant tone, the reassuring, warm, confident tone Brandon only got to hear when his father was talking to someone else. "My *Night Hawk* will make short work of this course, just you wait! It's a machine so perfect, even a child can pilot it!"

Child. Brandon snorted. *I'm fourteen, not a child! And you know as well as I do I'm only here because Scarlet's touring the facility site with Chief Kol!*

Bran tried to control his breathing, tried to keep his hands from shaking. He tried to tell himself it was from impatience, not nerves or anger. He tried to remind himself he knew this *Night Hawk* better than almost anyone else alive. He'd spent his whole childhood learning *Night Hawk*s and *Sling*s inside and out—literally—with Chief Kol, and more recently with Scarlet.

Bran's cheeks flushed as he thought of her.

Cassandra Fox, callsign "Scarlet," was a MechWarrior who'd been a leutnant in the Lyran Regulars, but was also a talented engineer. A Vendrellian, she'd signed on with Mountain Wolf BattleMechs during their last visit. Bran thought it was the last great deal Michael O'Leary had made, a two-for-one, getting them an imaginative new 'Mech technician alongside a combat veteran pilot. Brandon was pretty sure he had a crush on her, too. She'd shown him a few piloting tricks, and he was eager to impress her.

But Scarlet and Kol were busy examining the ruins of Mountain Wolf's Alpheratz facility, so today's pitch was just Bran and his father. They had to, of course, do two things at once. While the engineers were trying to figure out how to make the once-proud factory do *something* productive, the O'Leary men were trying to make sales for the 'Mechs they might someday build there. Selling another slice of the future.

Brandon's *Night Hawk* stood amid wreckage and rubble, a rough-hewn obstacle and target course made up of 'Mechs too badly savaged to be repaired, even by the desperate MechWarriors of the Outworlds Alliance. That took a *lot* of damage. Their scattered husks reminded him of a child's toys, carelessly dropped and far more broken than not. *Wasp*s and *Stinger*s to a one, the light BattleMechs were propped up here and there, skeletons and partial skeletons with limbs sometimes locked in raised positions; about a third of a *Stinger* was on the ground in front of him, and that one in particular looked for all the world like a zombie clawing out of a grave.

Like Mountain Wolf BattleMechs, trying to show the Sphere it's not truly dead.

Brandon's father did what Brandon's father did, and kept on talking. "—You'll see, Madam President, you'll see. Once you watch it at work with your own two eyes, well, you'll want a dozen just for the Alpheratz Guard! We'll find some way to get them made if you can just offer a reasonable down payment like we discussed. Guaranteed factory access and a little up-front money, and you'll be in love with the things! It was specifically designed for raids, did you know that? And for *counter*raids? Why, some of these Periphery pirates, they'd probably up and quit if they heard you had a lance or two of *Night Hawk*s...or maybe they'd just change sides!"

Waiting in the *Night Hawk* cockpit, Bran fidgeted in his MechWarrior vest, listened to his father's voice ringing inside his neurohelmet, and felt his pulse roaring in his temples. The crush he had on Cassandra Fox wasn't the only thing changing about Brandon as he hit his teens: he was getting more and more frustrated with—and infuriated by—his father. The blowhard. Not least because he'd learned more about the state of the family's finances.

What might've been the last working *Sling* in existence had been majority-owned for years by Chief Kol, as it turned out, and Scarlet was co-owner of the *Night Hawk* Brandon sat in as he waited to start the weapons display. He had recently learned that even the *Ceridwen* itself, their *Leopard*-class DropShip, was partially owned by Captain Jessup, and a few shares were owned by the rest of the crew, too, who'd either pooled their money over the years, or been offered shares in lieu of C-bill payment from his father.

Michael O'Leary had been making money for years, but spending as little of it as possible. Every trip they took, every licensor and distributor that waved him off, he was hauling goods for, purchasing replacement parts as cheaply as possible, selling them halfway across the Sphere, wheeling and dealing, making a profit off their vagabond lifestyle. They were selling precious few 'Mechs and leasing factory access to construct even fewer, but the company had been making money of a sort all along. Tramp-freighter money. Michael was hoarding C-bills, scraping together all the money he could, even if it meant selling off shares of the company, shares of the DropShip and the BattleMechs that made up the company's holdings.

Selling bits and pieces of Brandon's future.

Why are you like this, Father? Did you grow up so desperate for wealth? Did you forget it's the company that matters, not just C-bills? Do you think money's going to kick-start this dead company if you don't do anything with it?!

"—ha ha, you'll see, Madam President! The *Night Hawk* will take your breath away! Whenever you're ready...*MechWarrior*!"

His father's voice turned a little hard and impatient there, with the last word. There was always that shift in tone, that subtle, or not-so-subtle, change. That shift to barking an order, summoning a servant. That change in tone that showed when he was done talking to a prospective customer and was talking to Brandon, instead.

That was his cue.

Get your head in the game, Bran.

Bran started running the *Night Hawk* through its paces, its powerful engine pushing the 'Mech to a sprint in no time. A specialized, all-energy machine, the *Night Hawk* was equipped with nothing but lasers, and in Mountain Wolf's glory days, they had been nothing but impressive ones: a Maxwell extended-range large laser had once been the 'Mech's devastating right arm; its left arm had been a stunningly accurate Defiance P5M medium pulse laser; and secure in the machine's belly, just below the angular cockpit where Brandon now sat and sweated, remained a sturdy, reliable Defiance B3L large laser for tremendous punch.

These days, though, the flashier laser models were long gone, *lostech*, and Brandon was driving what Mountain Wolf called an NTK-2P, their "temporarily" downgraded model. It now bristled with lasers salvaged from whatever deals Michael O'Leary could make, whatever weapons he could buy the most of, the cheapest, from whatever world he could get them.

Even with more basic tech, though, the *Night Hawk* packed a lot of firepower on a fast frame. Bran danced through the course just like Scarlet had taught him, the 'Mech light and fast, feet churning up the earth as he cornered, skidded to a halt, twisted to strafe this way and that.

Again and again his lasers reached out fingers of pure energy, dazzlingly bright, to scour and slash at the dead Outworlds machines. Bran timed his shots just like Scarlet and Chief Kol had coached, cycling from his ventral large laser to his left-arm medium, to the pair of guns—a medium and a small laser, for good measure—that now made up the 'Mech's right arm. The machine could move at an almost three-digit lope, still fire...*some*...of the weapons at the same time, all while staying within comfortable temperature specs. If he timed the shots right and kept a steady stream of some sort of fire going, it looked plenty impressive.

The weak targets helped with that. The thin armor of even pristine *Wasp*s and *Stinger*s wouldn't hold up long against the kilojoules of light and heat the *Night Hawk* poured out, so the wrecked, barely-there corpses of the lighter 'Mechs stood no chance whatsoever. Feeling confident, Bran even flipped the arms once—the weapon pods, not arms, technically, as the 'Mech didn't have hand actuators or elbows at all—and fired straight behind him while at a run. He smiled like a wolf as the arms reoriented themselves after scoring a good hit.

"Ha-*ha*, see that one, Madam President? Right through the cockpit! Let some pirate chase you and get a face full of *that*, huh? And did you mark the range on that shot? Did you see just how far away that target was?"

Brandon grimaced in the heat of the cockpit as his father almost, accidentally, sounded proud of him. He knew it was the machine, not the MechWarrior, his father was crowing about. So did the President of the Outworlds Alliance.

"Not much ca—well, no, President Avellar, not *every* one of the *Night Hawk*s we could assemble and deliver for you with my proposed schedule would have every laser the product specs describe, no. Yes, Madam President, you're correct, it *is* just an assortment of regular models on our showcase model here, yes. I'm sure you know how hard those are to source, but these more conventional lasers are plenty of firepower...but I'm...I'm sure with the right facility access and a proper team of engineers we could—"

Brandon gritted his teeth and leaned the 'Mech into a hard turn, engine thrumming beneath him, as though the machine responded to his anger, his impatience, and his growing frustration and disgust with his father.

The way Brandon saw it, his father had two problems: he was proud of the wrong things, and he didn't know how to shut up about them.

He snarled as he worked the controls. Bran felt the heat in the cockpit surge as he triggered every weapon at once, superimposing his father's red face and portly body over the targeting data for a downed *Stinger* in front of him. The foursome of energy beams blasted out, converged, and savaged the helpless 'Mech.

"—well, no, no, Madam President, please—Ronaine, come on now, you know full well that...of course it's *hard* to track down those extralight engines, so they wouldn't all have the full—and, no, the heat sinks, also, are...but you have to understand, on a specialized machine like this, something with absolutely no ammunition requirements whatsoever, there are *some* trade-offs, and heat is...is just...a part of... again, perhaps with full facility access, we could..."

Brandon blasted with every laser again, snarling inside his helmet. And again. He felt his body cover itself in a layer of sweat, then felt the sweat get flashed dry. The engine growled, pushing the 'Mech as fast as it would go, heat rising, and all three lasers lashed out again even on the run.

No matter how hard he pushed the engine, though, how desperately he wanted the voice in his head to go away, no matter how hard the shutdown warnings blared and rang out, the voice of Bran's father followed him in his headset.

"—not what you're interested in, fine, fine, but I understand the Outworlds Alliance *needs* more 'Mechs, of course! Perhaps some *Sling*s then, Madam President? If you could give us a writ offering access to Alliance Defenders Limited's factories, I'm sure we could arrange something to your liking! The...the *Night Hawk* isn't for everybody, it's a specialized machine, but, well, I imagine these pirates wouldn't... know how to deal with a...well, no, of course we don't have Thunder munitions anymore, or the *exact* engines a *Sling* used, of course, but— Madam President, no, yes, of course, I understand you need 'Mechs, not promises, but...Ronaine, come on, now..."

Damn it!

Bran panted in the heat of the cockpit as the 'Mech came to a stop. He knew when a demonstration was over. He knew when no sale was being made. He knew when a whole world was a bust. Brandon had learned, through the years, just what it sounded like when his father failed to sell someone a gleaming yesterday.

Again.

Brandon walked the *Night Hawk* back toward the ship. Another wasted display, another time when the blowhard bragged about all the wrong things, all the things Mountain Wolf couldn't do any more, and hadn't been able to do in generations. Another lost sale. Another trip halfway across the Inner Sphere, doing nothing but ferrying around parts, selling spares, making sales for everyone *but* Mountain Wolf BattleMechs. Another failure in a long string of them.

Michael O'Leary, though, tore into his son as soon as Brandon climbed down out of the *Night Hawk* and into the main bay of the *Ceridwen*. His old pipe— Eli O'Leary's pipe—was in his hand, and he used it to stab the air as he started in on his son.

"What the hell was that? Those heat spikes?! Did you think nobody was watching any of the linked-up screens?"

"You said to showcase the firepow—"

"We don't *have* double heat sinks, Bran, and you know it! We don't *have* them, so we can't *install* them, so we can't *sell* them, so why would you push the heat so high? Why run and gun that hard and get them thinking about heat at all? You idiot! I put you in the cockpit of one of the finest weapons of war ever created, and you *still* can't make the best-looking 'Mech look good, you ca—"

Brandon sighed and tried to tune him out to a background roar. He was tired. Sick and tired. Tired of hearing how specialized *Sling*s were as fast-moving, long-range fire support (because no one had wanted that since the Star League fell, and Mountain Wolf couldn't make them if someone *did* call their bluff). Tired of hearing how specialized *Night Hawk*s were for long-term operations (because it couldn't do any of that any longer, since the specs had been so bastardized due to lost technology). Tired of hearing how *damned great* both 'Mechs were, when the *Ceridwen* might hold the only examples of either model that were still in any kind of condition, maybe the only Mountain Wolf machines that were even close to being assembled as designed.

"—could probably mess up a *Sling* demonstration, too, couldn't you? Useless. Just like your damn mother. Well, we're showing it off tomorrow, anyway, so try not to crap the bed like you did with the *Night Hawk*, huh, Brandon? Are you even listening to me? Do you think you can just run around a little and shoot some missiles without making us look bad? Do you think you can do *anything*, *ever*, to help me run this company and sell some 'Mechs? Huh? Some of the finest 'Mechs ever designed, some of the greatest-looking machines to ever exist, and you can't make 'em look goo—"

Enough!

"Then why doesn't anyone *want* them?" Brandon snarled, fourteen years old and feeling it.

His father gawked at him like he'd grown a fresh head or spoken in tongues.

"Honestly, *Michael*, if they're so good looking, *why don't they look good*?" He'd never called his father by his first name before. Saying it felt like an insult. Just like Brandon had wanted it to.

"When you hear '*Sling*,' you think 'Coventry'?" he mocked his father with a deep, gruff voice. "Really? News flash, *Michael*, nobody anywhere thinks '*Sling*'! No one has ever *heard* of a goddamned *Sling*!

They know *Night Hawk*s, maybe, by reputation, but so what?! It's not like we can *make* them! If they're so great, why is it so damned hard for us to find partners who want to make them for us? Why doesn't anyone trust us *to* make and sell them? Huh? What's wrong with *you*, that you can't sell th—"

Michael O'Leary's backhand sent Brandon reeling two steps back, tripping, and falling on his butt in the middle of the cargo bay. Chief Kol wasn't there, neither was Scarlet, nor Captain Jessup. No one who might maybe, maybe, stand up for him. The handful of astechs who remained didn't miss a beat. None of them gave any sign of noticing anything. The senior O'Leary lifted a foot like he was going to start stomping, and maybe never stop.

Brandon, defiant, glared up at him. His father balked, then turned and stormed away, ranting. The same tired old rant, only the slap had been new.

Ranting about how they'd never get anything done without a proper title, about how nobody appreciated the O'Leary name or the Mountain Wolf legacy, how nobody appreciated fine craftsmanship, about how nobody appreciated *him*, not even any of the ingrates on his own ship, or the biggest ingrate, his own son. On and on and on, raving about how they'd lost their factories, lost Snowgarden on Vendrell, lost Stonehold Estate here on Alpheratz, lost respect, lost everything.

Lost, lost, lost. All Michael O'Leary could think about was what he'd *heard* Mountain Wolf had been at its heyday. All he thought about was the myth of what the company had been generations earlier, at the height of the Star League. All that kept him going were handed-down memories and whole-cloth lies about the glory days of Mountain Wolf, things he'd been told from *his* father, and his grandfather, Eli.

Brandon refused to carry that weight. He refused to hold onto the old dreams and the new lies that propped them up.

He forced himself to stand without help, giving a dirty look to every junior technician that *now* dared to meet his gaze, and shook his head. He hated his father's bitterness and rage, and right then, he hated himself for not standing up to him more.

And he hated himself for knowing he *would* show off the damned *Sling* tomorrow. He'd trot around in the skinny thing, shoot a few anemic missile volleys, and try to sell it. What they had wasn't even a proper *Sling*, not really, but nobody cared enough to call them on their bluff. The O'Learys would do everything they could to impress President Ronaine Avellar. They'd beg, grovel, promise, half lie. They'd do everything they could to close the deal, to establish good relations with Alpheratz. They'd do anything to get a facility up and running again.

Anything except admit how badly they needed it.

Michael had made it clear, and more than once, that if Brandon had been a girl instead of a boy, he'd have "gotten rid of him" by now, married him off to someone, if only any of his potential business partners had wanted to. If only their name was worth a damn. If only Brandon was worth trading for anything.

But he wasn't. All they had to trade were half-imaginary 'Mechs, promises, and a cargo bay full of stray parts.

DUCAL ESTATE
KASPAR
VENDRELL I
LYRAN COMMONWEALTH
27 DECEMBER 2999

The Winter Holiday was a new-enough affair to feel novel, but a universally celebrated enough one to still feel communal. It was an eleven-night phenomenon, a conglomerate holiday commemorating the universal themes of a year's bittersweet end, a new year's joyous beginning, celebrating human warmth and light, surviving lean winters, and being thankful for bounties and generous gifts.

Here on Vendrell, hosted by the noble family Hart, the usual horns-of-plenty were playfully replaced by silver hunting horns, enameled artfully in white, a play on the heraldry of House Hart. Duke John-Michael Hart, lord of Vendrell, had passed away short weeks earlier, and the holiday's sentiments of rebirth and starting over rang out hard as the planet's young duchess prepared to take the reins. The heiress to House Hart was announced to be wed to the scion of House Rippon, their near-equals here. The Winter Holiday celebrations, then, were more powerful than most years' because of that change in rulership, the joyous recent announcement of betrothal, *and* the looming new millennium.

Michael O'Leary didn't celebrate, though: he worked. Holiday or not, he was busy, here—*especially* here—shaking hands, making promises, and sucking up to the noble and influential people of Vendrell. Amid garland-draped trees, silver-tinsel decorations, and the finest gowns and most gallant uniforms the Lyran Commonwealth had to offer, he was a tired old man in an expensive but old business suit. Working. Always working.

"—but that's just it, General," he said, smiling his best smile to the medal-adorned, stern-faced man whose hair was as white as the winter decorations throughout the banquet hall. "That's just it, you see?

The *Sling*, well, sure, it needs to stay at range, but it *can*, is what I'm telling you! There aren't many things that can catch a *Sling* on the run, much less on the jump, so it just peppers away with those missiles all damned day long while it dances away and—"

Brandon tugged at his collar, uncomfortable as always. He was no MechWarrior, not really, but he felt better in his cooling vest and neurohelmet than he did a suit. But maybe he just needed better suits. His father wasn't exactly a generous man, not when it came to Bran's comfort. He dressed his son up, but the way others might put sweaters on a dog: to show off as a novelty, never asking the dog if it wanted a sweater or not, much less if it was comfortable or liked the color.

Or...maybe this wine is just stronger than I think, Brandon smiled ruefully at himself, swirling his glass. He knew it was hitting him harder than he was used to. His father wasn't a generous man when it came to food and drink, either. Not unless he was trying to wine and dine a client, and Brandon wasn't there for most of those meals. Brandon was used to cheap, weak wine.

The Harts of Vendrell were determined not to look cheap *or* weak. Not right now. Rumors swirled about the actual finances of the noble house, but they had spared no expense when it came to the food and decorations for the Winter Holiday celebrations. Furthermore, though they paid at least lip service to the Muslim faith some long dead Hart had found on Dar-es-Salaam and brought home, the Harts hadn't spared any expense when it came to their *wine*, either. It was delicious, and Bran could tell it was hitting him like a PPC blast. Left alone as Scarlet—positively dashing in a dress uniform—had vanished to visit with old friends and family, Brandon was left to stand at a distance and listen to his father's bloviations. The alcohol just made it all the more exasperating.

"Well, yes, General, yes, of course my grandfather had a few *Sling*s on-duty when those Mariks attacked back in '45. *Sling*s and *Night Hawk*s, both! Eli O'Leary was a proud man who commanded proud 'Mechs, standing on this proud planet, ready to defen—well, no, see, some of the Marik assault force hot-dropped right onto Monte Lupus, so we didn't have the chance to outmaneu—well, yes, I know—no, General, I know the enemy doesn't always go where you want..."

Brandon looked around the pavilion, lingering near the edges, enjoying the free-moving air. He hadn't seen it in decades, but he remembered that Snowgarden, their long-abandoned estate here on Vendrell, had been a place of cold air and beautiful mountains. Back on Vendrell for the first time in years, some part of Brandon's soul wanted that cold, and was pleased that this Winter Holiday party was up here, near Monte Lupus, instead of down in muggy, humid Zanzibar.

The cool mountain air enticed him, made the ill-fitting suit feel less stuffy. He avoided the center of the party, the warmer press of bodies, the dancing, the small braziers scattered artfully around the room to mimic and echo the traditional Winter Holiday bonfire merrily blazing a short distance away.

He liked it on the edges of the party instead, where it was quiet and cold.

Like a Sling, he snorted at himself, *skirting the edges of the battlefield. Doing nothing. Missed by no one.*

"—And, well, no, I mean, yes, General, the *Sling* and *Night Hawk* are both on the lighter end of things, but they're no less Lyran for all that, eh? They can more than hold their own, I assure you! What's that, sir? Well, no, nothing on hand. We've got a few test models, but we have contracts, you see, and friends elsewhere in the industry, and in due time, and with some additional shipping costs covered, we'd be able to fulfill any reasonable...contract...can I..."

Michael O'Leary deflated and ran his fingers through his thinning hair as the commander of the Vendrellian planetary militia simply *harrumphed* and walked away. Vendrell's economy had been in a slump for long enough that everyone knew the ruling house was circling the wagons, more interested in maintaining their handful of heavy, family-owned 'Mechs than they were in branching out to buy lighter fare.

Or maybe Slings *just suck*, Brandon thought, *Not that we can make them anymore anyway.*

He shook his head and gulped down his wine, knowing what was coming. Sure enough, Michael stalked over to his son, face splotchy, out of breath, and taking out his anger on the only person on the planet—the only person in the galaxy—he could.

"Fat lot of help you were! You couldn't have my back? Hanging out over here, doing nothing while I try to make us a living?" Michael grabbed Brandon by the elbow, hard, and turned him half away from the rest of the party, voice low and angry. "I suppose you're just too damned busy looking at the pretty girls—or maybe the boys?—to help your own father put food on the table. Heaven forbid I make a sale!"

Brandon tried to tune him out and let him grouch. He didn't try to defend himself—*What, I was supposed to "back you up" by reminding the general the* Sling *is an over-teched, impossible-to-source BattleMech that's more specialized than a* Valkyrie, *not much better at its only job, dies in a stiff breeze, costs half again as much, and that we couldn't make even if he asked us to? Ringing endorsement, the truth!*—he just let his father ramble on. If he was used to anything, he was used to taking fire from Michael O'Leary. He knew better than to argue back, knew the trick was to weather the storm until his father ran out of breath like a MechWarrior whose ammunition bins had run dry.

His father running out of breath was coming quicker these days, luckily.

Eventually, the senior O'Leary ran out of steam, and petered off to his usual low-key mutterings and grumblings. Any time a potential customer wasn't in earshot, Michael complained—and often about the last customer that had been in earshot. These days, the long-running grumbling about nobles and Mariks and how unfair the galaxy was to hard-working businessmen was mixed in with a new target for his ire. "Classism" was a strange thing to complain about for a man with millions upon millions of C-bills hoarded away, but as time went on, Michael O'Leary had become certain that the aristocracy of the Inner Sphere, not his business rivals, was to blame for Mountain Wolf's woes. He increasingly lashed out in private about how Brandon's lack of high-blood—as though that was Bran's fault, not his own?—was why the future of the company looked so dim, why no one took them seriously, why no one cared enough to give them a shot.

"And another thing—!" Michael O'Leary began, but Brandon decided he was done being a punching bag for the night.

It was time to eject.

"Might I have this dance?" he said suddenly, reaching out and grabbing the white-gloved hand of the nearest person he saw and just continuing with them onto the dance floor.

The stranger whirled gracefully into his arms with just a pleasantly surprised "Oh!" before falling into step with him. Her skin was a rich sepia and stood in stark contrast to her snow-white gown, her tightly curled hair was in an updo, making her look even taller than she was, which was saying something, given her impressive height and athletic build. Brandon had absolutely no doubt she could have pulled away if she'd wanted, could very likely have picked him up and thrown him, bodily. Instead, she took his daring, desperate offer with aplomb and good humor.

"It's lovely to meet you," she said, casting a glance over his shoulder several seconds into their dance, appraising the clear threat he'd just as clearly been avoiding. Her brown eyes sparkled with mischief. "Ah, that explains it. Was Old Man O'Leary trying to sell you something?"

Oh.

Brandon fought a grin. "Not exactly."

"He's a talker, that one. A hungry one, too, living up to the 'Wolf' in the company name," she continued, dancing and warning him all at the same time. "He's always out to chew someone's ear off about ancient 'Mechs, from what I hear."

"I'm afraid it's too late for that," Brandon said, smirking a little. "'*Sling*' this, '*Night Hawk*' that..."

"Right? As though proper Lyrans wouldn't rather hear '*Archer*' or '*BattleMaster*' instead, and as though he could even still make either one!" She laughed and made a face. "All the officers warned me to avoid him! Oh, and be careful, he's got a son running around somewhere, too. They might try to corner you. You know how wolves are!"

"A son, hmm?" Bran lifted his eyebrows and fought a smile. "Did the officers tell you what he looks like?"

"I'm told he...ah..." She didn't miss a beat in their dance, even as her features twisted in chagrin and she scrunched up her nose. "I'm talking to him, aren't I?"

"The one and only Brandon O'Leary, I'm afraid," he said, feeling mildly smug for the first time in ages. At least he could pull one over on *somebody* at a fancy shindig like this. Miracle of miracles, he'd found someone even more embarrassed to be here than he was, even if only for a few moments!

"Please, truly. I am very sorry." Her tone took on an air of formality and sincerity all at once. The music faded away, and the pair of them stopped moving as the song ended. "I didn't mean to offen—"

"Who the hell do you think you are?"

The angry snarl reminded Brandon of his father, but it wasn't. The rough hand on his shoulder did, too. He got half spun around and found himself face-to-face with a young man even taller and stronger than Bran's lovely dance partner. Decked out in the formal dress of the Vendrellian militia, he was lantern jawed, blond haired, and blue eyed, and as he jabbed an angry finger into Brandon's chest, he looked just like a Lyran recruitment poster come to life. Hell, knowing the Lyrans, he might *be* on a recruitment poster.

"Laying hands on my fiancée? You presumptuous little shit!"

"Sebastian, please, there was no 'laying hands.' It was just an invitation to dance. And it went splendidly. He was quite the gentleman, even when my own manners were lacking." The young woman in question interposed herself between the two, putting one hand on her betrothed's medallion-covered chest—*lots of medals for that age*, Brandon internally rolled his eyes—and holding him at arm's length with it. "Mr. O'Leary didn't mean anything by it. There is no need for—"

"*O'Leary?!*" The swaggering MechWarrior, Sebastian Something-or-Other, sidestepped to get past her and sneer down at Brandon. He stood a full head taller than Bran, and he seemed the sort who was used to looking down on people literally *and* figuratively. The man was furious, looking at the crowd to try and whip them up, too. "The salesman's boy? The beggar? A bloody *commoner* put hands on you?!"

Brandon looked to his dance partner and wondered just how deeply he'd stepped in it.

She gave her fiancé a half-exasperated look, lips pursed, then turned to face Brandon and curtsied formally.

"I am Olivia Hart," she said, somewhere between an apology and an introduction. "But truly, your behavior has been beyond reproach, and I took no offense. The O'Leary family and Mountain Wolf BattleMechs are always welcome here on Vendrell, and we hope that—"

The duchess. Oh—oh no. I grabbed the Duchess of Vendrell. I grabbed her and dragged her to the dance floor.

Brandon had just enough time for it to sink in how big a blunder he'd committed, when Sebastian—Sebastian *Rippon*, he now realized, scion of the Vendrell Rippons, the *other* most powerful family on the planet, and the man who would shortly be the duke-consort of the entire world—shouldered his way past Olivia and, after a melodramatic windup, laid Bran out with a single punch.

LEOPARD-CLASS DROPSHIP *CERIDWEN*
HIGH ORBIT
NEW SAMARKAND
DRACONIS COMBINE
8 JANUARY 3010

Brandon sat in what had once been the *Ceridwen*'s starboard aerofighter bay. For decades it had been an office, *the* office of Mountain Wolf BattleMechs, and the quarters of the man who called himself president and CEO.

His now. His office, his ship, his company, his problems. His name. His time.

He stared hard down at the comms gear resting before him, taking in a deep breath, letting it out slowly, and composing himself. He only wanted to do this once. He needed to focus. He needed to get it right.

He had three crucial messages that needed to be sent today.

These recordings would be delivered through slower, cheaper, more conventional means than ComStar and their exorbitant prices. They would travel slowly, but they would need to be perfect. These messages would require...finesse. Certainty. A smoothness Brandon didn't know was in him. A confidence he feared was bordering on being a lie.

For them to believe it, I have to believe it. Do I? Do I believe in Scarlet? In Chief Kol? Do I trust them, when they say this is possible? Do I believe in myself, enough to tell other people to do the same?

There was only one way to find out. He hit the RECORD button and began the first message.

"Thank you all for your kind words recently. We here at Mountain Wolf BattleMechs, and me personally, Brandon O'Leary, have had an outpouring of support from so many familiar faces that, frankly, my head is spinning. From the Lyran Commonwealth, Draconis Combine, and Federated Suns, from the Outworlds Alliance to the Magistracy of Canopus, my father made friends, not just partners, every place he went, and now those friends are reaching out to comfort me after his passing. I have received condolences from every corner of the Inner Sphere and the Periphery, and I am grateful for all of them."

Except the Free Worlds League. We never made a single sale to the Mariks after '45.

Another breath.

Focus. Look the situation right in the eye. Say it.

"But I don't need your condolences."

Damn, that felt good. But fix it. Smooth it over. Walk it back.

Brandon glanced down at the old wooden pipe that rested on his desk. His father's, and his father's, his father's. Now his.

"I don't need your condolences, because my father isn't dead. Not truly. So long as a single Mountain Wolf BattleMech is standing at the ready and helping you defend your worlds, Mountain Wolf BattleMechs is alive, and so long as Mountain Wolf BattleMechs is alive, every O'Leary is still with us in spirit."

There. That was good. Sounded sincere. Now do it. Take the leap.

"I'm not only sorry that I lost my father, though. Mountain Wolf BattleMechs lost its CEO. I'm crushed that my father passed before he could show you a presentation I've taken the liberty of attaching to this message. I hope it isn't crass to combine business with a personal communication like this, but you all knew Michael. 'Business waits for no one.'"

Living or dead.

"Please look over the attached documents, and consider Mountain Wolf, especially for your militia clientele. We've partnered with all of you over the years to maintain an exclusive, limited production and distribution of *Night Hawk*s and *Sling*s, and I know my father appreciated every one of those partnerships, and was proud to work with all of you."

"Exclusive, limited production" sure is a nice way of saying "an anemic trickle of failing life support." No one had produced or distributed a *Sling* in centuries, but now was the time to be polite, not honest.

"But now you'll see the specs for something new."

Do it. Take the leap. Say the words. Shock them all.

"And by 'new,' I mean not just new to Mountain Wolf BattleMechs, but all new. Entirely new. For centuries, Mountain Wolf has been synonymous with specialized machines, some say *over*specialized, and while nothing fills the niche of a *Night Hawk* quite like a *Night Hawk*, and nothing does what a *Sling* does exactly like a *Sling*...if there's one thing I've learned in all my travels, it's that overspecialization isn't always needed or wanted, especially by rural militia units."

Overspecialization is for bugs, Brandon had wanted to say. But talking down your theoretically current designs wasn't the best way to talk up your new one. The work Chief Kol and Scarlet had put in deserved praise, not just backhanded compliments thrown at Mountain Wolf's other machines. *We're too hungry to overspecialize.*

"Sometimes you need a 'Mech that can do it all and, ladies and gentlemen, I believe we've designed one. A brand-new BattleMech. Every one of you will recognize components as you look over Mountain Wolf's new design proposal. There, you'll see that I'd like to keep sourcing parts from all of you. Hesperus II, Dunianshire, Canopus IV, Quentin, Kirchbach, Luthien, Twycross, Tharkad, and of course, Vendrell and Alpheratz. I grew up on your homeworlds as you and my father did business. Mountain Wolf BattleMechs wouldn't be what it is without each and every one of you."

I grew up on the Ceridwen, he thought, half-angry still. Half-angry, half-sad. He hadn't had time to untangle all of his feelings since his father's heart attack. He hadn't had time to untangle the overcomplicated network of factories, distributors, and business contacts either. Untangling could wait. Right now he just had to work *through* the knots. Like a Lyran merchant flying through Kurita space, sometimes you had to Gordian Knot the problems and just keep going.

"And I want each and every one of you to continue this partnership, to make this new 'Mech—a *new 'Mech!*—a reality. Ladies and gentlemen, let me introduce you to the *Merlin*. If you want the energy-based long-ranged punch and endurance of the *Night Hawk*, he can do it, and then some. If you want to reach out and say hello with reliable long-range-missile volleys like a *Sling*, he can do that, too. If you want solid, reliable laser fire at moderate ranges, he has that covered. He also carries as much armor as those two *combined*, though, and brings a Zippo and a Sperry Browning along, to dissuade infantry and for additional in-close protection."

Brandon allowed himself a smile as he looked down at some of the many scribbled notes and sketches he, Kol, and Scarlet had drawn up. The *Merlin* was an ugly, effective beast.

"He's beautiful. The *Merlin* runs at the standard expected strategic speed for his weight class, he *jumps* when so many of his fellow heavies don't, he shoots like nobody's business, and he shoots at any range, against any target. He's been designed from the ground up for compatibility of parts, ruggedness, and simplicity. He's a dream to work on, with generous specs and input from our 'Mech techs every step of the way to make him easy to retrofit, maintain, and repair. He

can do it all. And, as I'm sure you've noticed, he does it for about five million C-bills."

He let that figure hang in the air just long enough that they'd all double-check it, they'd all do calculations, they'd all marvel. What Brandon O'Leary was proposing wasn't just bold, or breathtaking. It was considered impossible.

So sell the impossibility.

"The *Merlin* does everything you want a 'Mech to do, like magic."

Lie. Lie to them. Lie to them, here, at the end, but just at the end.

"My father loved the *Merlin*. And he knew you'd love him, too."

My father spat at me when I tried to show him Kol and Scarlet's work. My father said he'd rather the Alpheratz facility keep rotting than be hijacked for anything but Night Hawks.

Brandon swallowed.

My father is dead. The company is mine. So is its future.

"There is no more-versatile 'Mech in the galaxy, and certainly none newer than the *Merlin*. I'm taking preorders now, just like we all know Michael would have wanted. Ladies and gentlemen, thank you again for reaching out to me about my father's tragic passing. But I look forward to hearing from all of you again, very soon, to discuss the *Merlin*, not just my family's loss. As you raise a glass to my father's memory, please take a second drink, and toast to the *Merlin*'s future, and to yours. Good day, and best regards, from Mountain Wolf BattleMechs."

Brandon hit the button to stop recording and slumped, deflated, into his chair. He stared long and hard at the control panel as the *Ceridwen* shuddered beneath him, docking with a JumpShip, readying to depart. They had paid good money and called in good favors for safe passage through Draconis Combine space toward the Outworlds Alliance, and the trip had to continue whether his father had died or not.

Business didn't wait. The future didn't hold still. There was no savoring this momentous occasion because there was more work to be done. The *Merlin* needed to become a reality for business to continue, the *Merlin* needed to match the specs Bran and Cassandra and the Kols had been looking over if Mountain Wolf was going to have a future. The old Alpheratz factory needed minimal modifications, but it *needed* those modifications. He had work to do.

He sat there and listened to the *Ceridwen*, eyes closed, and willed the future he imagined into being.

That future didn't hinge only on the shake-up a CEO's death invariably caused, no, or on the cobbled-together 'Mech they had designed from every disparate business contact he'd inherited. There were other headlines, almost as recent, that were waves Brandon knew he'd need to surf. More nobility making the news. Another death. Another company changing hands that had gotten gears turning.

Another message he *had* to send, and that had to be well received, for any of this to work.

He cleared his throat and began.

"To the Duchess Olivia Rippon-Hart, allow me to extend my deepest sympathies for the recent loss of Duke-Consort Sebastian."

Even if he was an ass, I wouldn't wish someone dead at his—at our—age. Especially not a death like his.

"As you may have heard, my family has also suffered a recent loss. I apologize if my father's passing and the needs of the company have since caused any undue delays in my being able to get this message to you. I am certain all of Vendrell shares your sense of loss, though, and I am glad that means you and your children are surely not alone with your grief."

Children. Plural. I know you and Sebastian had one of each. Your line is secure, Olivia. Vendrell has birthed new rulers, as highborn as any Lyran could hope for. Your future is safe. I won't jeopardize it. Please hear me saying that.

"As my father would have said, though, we have obligations. You to your people, and me to mine. I am hoping, as we both struggle with our recent losses, that we might be able to help one another through them."

You didn't just lose a husband. I saw the news before that, too, and heard the rumors. You lost your fortunes before that. I know why he did what he did. I know what desperation drove him to it. Your economy hasn't been strong in a generation or more. He let that shame get the better of him. You won't.

Brandon steeled himself. This wasn't just a longshot, it was lunacy. He felt half-mad for even trying it—with a woman he'd shared one dance with, even if she *had* punched her own fiancé back after he'd coldcocked Bran—but the problem wasn't just that he felt bold, he felt something worse. He couldn't help but feel cruel. Opportunistic.

But a shark never stops swimming.

"Mountain Wolf BattleMechs would—*I* would—be honored to assist you in whatever way possible. Whatever way. As we once did. For many long years, my family called Vendrell home. Now I would like to do so again...if Vendrell would have us."

Brandon knew just what assistance she, and the planet, needed. Longer-term economic support could come in the future, reestablishing an industrial base, maybe even rebuilding on the scorched earth the Mariks had left. But, for now, she just needed C-bills, and Brandon had them in spades.

If Houses Steiner and Wellby could play at industry by purchasing TharHes Industries—giving Brandon this idea—couldn't he, an industrialist, play at nobility? Couldn't he earn nobility through marriage every bit as much as TharHes would earn kroner through business?

Couldn't Brandon finally do something *else* his father never had, not only innovate, but excel? Put some respect on the family name and open the doors that came with it?

Do it. Coward, do it. Ask her.

"And...if...*you* would have *me*."

That was as close as Brandon could come. No other words came, for an awkward few seconds. Nothing about love, no getting down on one knee, no poems or proclamations. Olivia was brilliant, though. Not just a MechWarrior, not just a duchess, but *good* at both of those things. She would understand. She must be doing her own research, just like he was. She must have some idea how much Michael O'Leary's desperate C-bill hoarding had accrued. She had to know how absurdly and abruptly wealthy Brandon was...and how she needed that, right now. She had to know how empty the Rippon-Hart vaults were, and how fat the O'Leary accounts were.

"In the meantime, though, my father will haunt me if I don't see to some business affairs. I have one stop to make, on Alpheratz, before I can bring the *Ceridwen* around and fly me...home...to Vendrell. There's a reconstruction I need to oversee in the Outworlds, but then I will make all haste on my flight back to Lyran space. I hope to make Snowgarden presentable well before year's end, and would be honored to host this year's Winter Holiday celebrations there. But only..."

He smiled, softly, mildly in awe at the fact he was having this conversation, mildly surprised at how sincerely he felt what he was saying.

"...only if you will be playing hostess there, alongside me. Celebrating a betrothal."

Enough. He stopped the recording, not saying any farewell. His hand was shaking as he reached for that old O'Leary pipe. He hadn't lied to her about pining away and needing a soulmate. He hadn't sent an attachment detailing his bank records or sharing headlines that showed the media's concern for House Rippon-Hart's finances, either. She would get the message. She would listen between the lines. She would understand.

And he hoped—he needed—her to accept, and for her acceptance message to beat him to Alpheratz.

Brandon hit RECORD a third time.

"Good day, Madam President, and thank you for reaching out about my father's death." He swallowed, mouth gone dry from all the talking. He had to keep going. "I was sorry to hear of your own recent health concerns, and it is my sincerest hope that this message finds both you and the Outworlds Alliance well."

It wouldn't, and he knew it. President Ronaine Avellar hadn't been "well" in quite some time. And neither—in a roundabout way *luckily* for Brandon—had the economy of the Outworlds Alliance. He had seen recent headlines about food riots. He had seen *too many* recent headlines about food riots. She and his father had decided to hate each other, then had dickered about the Alpheratz facility for so long one of them had died, accomplishing nothing, refusing to budge. A factory that had once turned out Star-League-quality *Night Hawk*s was now little more than a triage center for the Outworlds Alliance, filled with half-trained astechs. That was a slap in the face of history, and Brandon was tired of the stalemate.

He didn't want *her* to pass on, too...but if she did, he was prepared to take his offer to her successor, whether it be Neil or some other Avellar. He hoped it wouldn't come to that, so he'd decided to make the offer a generous one.

"I know my father had long been speaking with you about continuing repairs on Mountain Wolf's Alpheratz facility. With his passing, I've finally been able to look at some of the contracts he sent you, including his most recent. Those offers are no longer on the table, and I've destroyed the hardcopies."

Brandon allowed himself a small smile.

"Those deals weren't fair to you, or to the people of the Alliance."

That's it. Give her a second to sputter, then soften. Imagine that amused gleam in her eyes. Let her feel you trying to jerk against the leash, just a little. She'll respect it.

"Attached, you'll find Mountain Wolf BattleMechs' *new* proposal. My proposal. It's got nothing to do with *Night Hawk*s, and precious little to do with my father's old offers. It repairs only the most necessary parts of the facility, and, crucially, only the parts we *can* repair. And as you'll soon see, it turns the facility into a *Merlin* one. Look for that attachment, too, Madam President, to see just what a *Merlin* is. The first ever *Merlin* factory. A brand new 'Mech, coming from Outworlds Alliance space. My people have sourced the parts we need, including some already made right there on Alpheratz, and we're prepared to move forward."

Beyond the prestige the struggling Periphery state would get from that, beyond the economic shot in the arm, beyond even the impossibility of sourcing the parts needed for proper *Night Hawk*s to be made, the decision had been easy. The ailing President didn't need *Night Hawk*s to protect her from raiding pirates. She needed militia 'Mechs to protect her from her own people...*and* raiding pirates. She needed a show of force. She didn't need more light 'Mechs, not even the *Wasp*s and *Stinger*s whose Martell Model 5s and Sperry Brownings Mountain Wolf would be sourcing, no. She needed bulk. She needed the projection of strength. She needed heavy machines.

She needed *Merlin*s.

"Furthermore, I take issue with the salary offers my father repeatedly put on the table. I've taken the liberty of looking into the average household income—*household*, not individual—on Alpheratz, and I've based my proposed pay structure on that. I'm planning to start individual salary offers at one hundred and fifty percent of that figure, but between you, me, and ComStar, I'm willing to go to two hundred percent for up to one-fourth of our work force, as suggested by you."

ComStar wasn't handling the recordings' hard-tape delivery, couriers were, but Bran thought the joke would land, regardless. The more important part was the salary offer, even if the joke sputtered. President Avellar's people needed money, and she needed to look like the one giving it to them. She could handpick the dissenters and fence-sitters herself, and personally offer them the largesse of the most generous Mountain Wolf job offers, only to later reabsorb some fraction of all this new wealth via taxes and a strengthened economy. Brandon, meanwhile, could use the charismatic organizers of the Outworlds Alliance's most disgruntled, and let them channel their frustration and leadership skills into something constructive. Everyone would win.

Brandon didn't want to take advantage of Alpheratz's economic woes. He didn't want the almost-slave-labor so many business leaders scoured the Periphery for. He wanted to pay a fair wage for fair work. He wanted his people to be happy, and for that to translate to loyalty and production. He wanted to treat his people like *people*.

He would build this company back up, his way, or he would burn it down entirely by pissing away every last C-bill in the trying. No middle ground.

"Not included in the proposal documentation," he said, letting his eyes drift closed, as he—now, desperately—needed to decide on just how to finish this offer. The proposal itself was *fine*, the jobs were generous, the work needed to repair *and* refit the facility was manageable. It would all be good for everybody. He needed the kill shot, though. He needed the finisher. He needed the bribe that would push the offer past her wounded pride.

"I'm prepared to offer you one *Merlin* in ten that leaves the Alpheratz production line, until you have a company of them. Free of charge." He nodded. About sixty million C-bills worth of 60-ton BattleMechs, free. His father would have hated the almost-poetic symmetry, the generosity of it. "*And* the ongoing discount mentioned in the proposal itself, of course, for any additional purchases moving forward."

There. That was more than fair.

"I thank you for your time, Madam President, and I look forward to our next meeting. This recording will beat me there, and I hope by the time I arrive, you'll be prepared to shake hands on this."

He paused before stopping the recording. He thought long and hard about how best to sign off. He remembered the light in Duchess Olivia's eyes, remembered the grimace she'd given her own fiancée over his bullying, remembered the kindness and wit she'd displayed in just that one brief meeting. He remembered every kind thing he'd ever heard the native Vendrellian, Scarlet, say about Olivia and her reputation.

Olivia will say yes. And if she says yes, they both will.

Do it, Bran. Put the exclamation point on to end the sentence. Believe.

"Good day, and best regards from Graf-Consort Brandon O'Leary, of Vendrell," he finished.

Let President Avellar think on that*, alongside the rest of the proposal.* The prestige of doing business with a proper noble, just like Michael O'Leary had always wished he could offer. The implications of improved trade relations with the famously wealthy Lyran Commonwealth as a whole. The subtler, almost threatening, implication that Vendrell was back on the table, that Alpheratz might not be the only facility the hungry young wolf was looking at rebuilding.

Let the cunning old president put the pieces together. And if she put them together right—and if Duchess Olivia agreed with Bran's assessment of both their situations, so that his signature was a confident prediction, not a false claim of nobility—then Mountain Wolf BattleMechs would have a future, after all.

And Brandon O'Leary might just have found himself a way home.

SUBMISSION GUIDELINES

Shrapnel is the market for official short fiction set in the *BattleTech* universe.

WHAT WE WANT

We are looking for stories of **3,000–5,000 words** that are character-oriented, meaning the characters, rather than the technology, provide the main focus of the action. Stories can be set in any established *BattleTech* era, and although we prefer stories where BattleMechs are featured, this is by no means a mandatory element.

WHAT WE DON'T WANT

The following items are generally grounds for immediate disqualification:

- Stories not set in the *BattleTech* universe. There are other markets for these stories.

- Stories centering solely on romance, supernatural, fantasy, or horror elements. If your story isn't primarily military sci-fi, then it's probably not for us.

- Stories containing gratuitous sex, gore, or profanity. Keep it PG-13, and you should be fine.

- Stories under 3,000 words or over 5,000 words. We don't publish flash fiction, and although we do publish works longer than 5,000 words, these are reserved for established *BattleTech* authors.

- Vanity stories, which include personal units, author-as-character inserts, or tabletop game sessions retold in narrative form.

- Publicly available *BattleTech* fan-fiction. If your story has been posted in a forum or other public venue, then we will not accept it.

MANUSCRIPT FORMAT
- .rtf, .doc, .docx formats ONLY
- 12-point Times New Roman, Cambria, or Palatino fonts ONLY
- 1" (2.54 cm) margins all around
- Double-spaced lines
- DO NOT put an extra space between each paragraph
- Filename: "Submission Title by Jane Q. Writer"

PAYMENT & RIGHTS

We pay $0.06 per word after publication. By submitting to *Shrapnel*, you acknowledge that your work is set in an owned universe and that you retain no rights to any of the characters, settings, or "ideas" detailed in your story. We purchase **all rights** to every published story; those rights are automatically transferred to The Topps Company, Inc.

SUBMISSIONS PORTAL

To send us a submission, visit our submissions portal here:
https://pulsepublishingsubmissions.moksha.io/publication/shrapnel-the-battletech-magazine-fiction

BATTLETECH ERAS

The *BattleTech* universe is a living, vibrant entity that grows each year as more sourcebooks and fiction are published. A dynamic universe, its setting and characters evolve over time within a highly detailed continuity framework, bringing everything to life in a way a static game universe cannot match.

To help quickly and easily convey the timeline of the universe—and to allow a player to easily "plug in" a given novel or sourcebook—we've divided *BattleTech* into eight major eras.

STAR LEAGUE
(Present–2780)

Ian Cameron, ruler of the Terran Hegemony, concludes decades of tireless effort with the creation of the Star League, a political and military alliance between all Great Houses and the Hegemony. Star League armed forces immediately launch the Reunification War, forcing the Periphery realms to join. For the next two centuries, humanity experiences a golden age across the thousand light-years of human-occupied space known as the Inner Sphere. It also sees the creation of the most powerful military in human history.

(This era also covers the centuries before the founding of the Star League in 2571, most notably the Age of War.)

SUCCESSION WARS
(2781–3049)

Every last member of First Lord Richard Cameron's family is killed during a coup launched by Stefan Amaris. Following the thirteen-year war to unseat him, the rulers of each of the five Great Houses disband the Star League. General Aleksandr Kerensky departs with eighty percent of the Star League Defense Force beyond known space and the Inner Sphere collapses into centuries of warfare known as the Succession Wars that will eventually result in a massive loss of technology across most worlds.

CLAN INVASION
(3050–3061)

A mysterious invading force strikes the coreward region of the Inner Sphere. The invaders, called the Clans, are descendants of Kerensky's SLDF troops, forged into a society dedicated to becoming the greatest fighting force in history. With vastly superior technology and warriors, the Clans conquer world after world. Eventually this outside threat will forge a new Star League, something hundreds of years of warfare failed to accomplish. In addition, the Clans will act as a catalyst for a technological renaissance.

CIVIL WAR
(3062–3067)

The Clan threat is eventually lessened with the complete destruction of a Clan. With that massive external threat apparently neutralized, internal conflicts explode around the Inner Sphere. House Liao conquers its former Commonality, the St. Ives Compact; a rebellion of military units belonging to House Kurita sparks a war with their powerful border enemy, Clan Ghost Bear; the fabulously powerful Federated Commonwealth of House Steiner and House Davion collapses into five long years of bitter civil war.

JIHAD
(3067–3080)
Following the Federated Commonwealth Civil War, the leaders of the Great Houses meet and disband the new Star League, declaring it a sham. The pseudo-religious Word of Blake—a splinter group of ComStar, the protectors and controllers of interstellar communication—launch the Jihad: an interstellar war that pits every faction against each other and even against themselves, as weapons of mass destruction are used for the first time in centuries while new and frightening technologies are also unleashed.

DARK AGE
(3081-3150)
Under the guidance of Devlin Stone, the Republic of the Sphere is born at the heart of the Inner Sphere following the Jihad. One of the more extensive periods of peace begins to break out as the 32nd century dawns. The factions, to one degree or another, embrace disarmament, and the massive armies of the Succession Wars begin to fade. However, in 3132 eighty percent of interstellar communications collapses, throwing the universe into chaos. Wars erupt almost immediately, and the factions begin rebuilding their armies.

ILCLAN
(3151-present)
The once-invulnerable Republic of the Sphere lies in ruins, torn apart by the Great Houses and the Clans as they wage war against each other on a scale not seen in nearly a century. Mercenaries flourish once more, selling their might to the highest bidder. As Fortress Republic collapses, the Clans race toward Terra to claim their long-denied birthright and create a supreme authority that will fulfill the dream of Aleksandr Kerensky and rule the Inner Sphere by any means necessary: The ilClan.

CLAN HOMEWORLDS
(2786-present)
In 2784, General Aleksandr Kerensky launched Operation Exodus, and led most of the Star League Defense Force out of the Inner Sphere in a search for a new world, far away from the strife of the Great Houses. After more than two years and thousands of light years, they arrived at the Pentagon Worlds. Over the next two-and-a-half centuries, internal dissent and civil war led to the creation of a brutal new society—the Clans. And in 3049, they returned to the Inner Sphere with one goal—the complete conquest of the Great Houses.

The march of technology across BattleTech's eras is relentless...

Some BattleMech designs never die. Each installment of *Recognition Guide: IlClan*, currently a PDF-only series, not only includes a brand new BattleMech or OmniMech, but also details Classic 'Mech designs from both the Inner Sphere and the Clans, now fully rebuilt with Dark Age technology (3085 and beyond).

STORE.CATALYSTGAMELABS.COM

Made in the USA
Middletown, DE
21 March 2023

27345488R00124